• ROBBI

Golden Crown Literary Award Winner

Two on the Aisle

Bella BOOKS

2011

Copyright © 2011 by Robbi McCoy

Bella Books, Inc.
P.O. Box 10543
Tallahassee, FL 32302

All rights reserved. No part of this book may be reproduced or transmitted in any form or by any means, electronic or mechanical, including photocopying, without permission in writing from the publisher.

Printed in the United States of America on acid-free paper
First published 2011

Editor: Katherine V. Forrest
Cover Designer: Sandy Knowles

ISBN 13: 978-1-59493-259-5

Other Bella Books by Robbi McCoy

For Me and My Gal

Not Every River

Something to Believe

Songs Without Words

Waltzing at Midnight

Dedication

To all the stage actors and theater companies who have entertained me so often and so thoroughly over the decades. You have given much and inspired many.

Acknowledgments

First of all, this story would be meaningless without the great body of work left us by William Shakespeare. I've used him liberally and cheekily, as he used his literary predecessors. I hope I've been able to capture a little of his comedic spirit and remind readers why, after centuries, his romantic comedies remain popular and relevant with theater audiences the world over.

I am delighted with the contributions of Kaysi Peister and Sue Edmonds who won my contest and gave me character names so full of potential that they've engendered more than just characters, but also situations and plot twists. Before they suggested "Wren Landry" and "Eno Threlkeld," this book was a mere glimmer in my mind. I never suspected that the two winning names would be used for a single character. Thank you, ladies, for the inspiration. It's been great fun.

A special thank you goes to Kirsty for her brilliant cover ideas and to Lori for her cupcake expertise.

As always, much gratitude to my editor Katherine V. Forrest whose insights and instincts are remarkably precise. No, you cannot slip something by her.

Finally, to my sweetheart and collaborator, Dot, I say, *I love thee; none but thee; and thou deservest it.*

DRAMATIS PERSONAE

Wren Landry, a critic

Sophie Ward, a goatherd

Raven Landry, an actor

Kyle Somerset, an artist

Olivia Ward, a farmer

Ellie Marcus, a shopkeeper

John Bâtarde, a villain

Katrina Olafssen, a baker

Klaus Olafssen, a baker

Cassandra Marcus, a soothsayer

Dr. Warren Connor, a physician

Dena Ward, a saucy wench

Max, a "boy"

Cleo Keggermeister, a drama queen

Tallulah, Rose, Maribelle, Twopenny, Tater, Niblets and Poppy, the goats

About the Author

Robbi McCoy is a native Californian who lives in the Central Valley between the mountains and the sea. She is an avid hiker with a particular fondness for the deserts of the American Southwest. She also enjoys gardening, culinary adventures, travel and the theater. She works full-time as a software specialist and web designer for a major West Coast distribution company.

CHAPTER ONE

*If this were played upon a stage now,
I could condemn it as an improbable fiction.*

—*Twelfth Night*, Act III, Scene 4

Other than the fact that Maia had pushed several succulent ingredients aside—capers, Sicilian olives, roasted red peppers—and had picked out as much of the fresh basil as she could manage before she'd been willing to take a bite of her panzanella, their date, their *second* date, was going well. Better than many second dates, in Wren's experience. A year or so ago, picking inoffensive ingredients out of one's food would have been an immediate and permanent deal breaker for Wren. Tonight she would let it slide. She realized with some misgivings that she was lowering her standards.

Wren sighed. She wasn't ready to give up on Maia. She was lovely to look at. She was incredibly smart. She seemed to genuinely like Wren and that was a huge plus. The food thing—maybe she could be taught. Wren's life, both personal and professional, revolved around food and this was Josephine, a truly exceptional restaurant, one of San Francisco's best. Wren shuddered, imagining the chef watching Maia's fork weed out the offensive components of the dish, her mouth curled into a look of revulsion as if she were picking out mouse turds.

"I've got a feeling about us," Maia said, smiling warmly with her puckery, kissable mouth. "I really like you."

She reached a hand across the table and Wren took it, twining their fingers together. Maia was a few years younger, twenty-seven, with long dark brown hair and widely-spaced brown eyes. Their first date had been last weekend, a hike down the west flank of Mt. Tam to Stinson Beach. It had been a good day. They'd sat on a grassy slope above the Pacific Ocean eating sourdough bread and a nutty Jarlsberg cheese and Wren had never suspected she was with a woman who could so thoroughly emasculate a perfectly beautiful panzanella as Maia had just done. *Let it go!* she warned herself.

Maia had an exotic look about her, as if she were some part Asian. Wren knew very little about her. They had met only a week ago, the morning of that hike. Wren hadn't yet confessed her own secrets and she was sure Maia was holding back as well. She just hoped the as-yet unrevealed facts were bearable.

The waiter came to take their plates away, leaving a dessert menu. Wren took her hand back while she looked it over.

"Do you want to share something?" she asked.

"Okay. How about something chocolate? I'm a total chocoholic. The first time I tasted it, I thought, oh, my God, this is better than an orgasm. Actually, I couldn't have thought that because I hadn't had an orgasm yet, the first time I tasted chocolate."

Wren chuckled. "No, I wouldn't think so."

Maia looked thoughtful, staring into space. "No. It was about two months later that I had my first orgasm. You know, it's hard to compare those two things, isn't it? I mean, they're like apples and oranges. Or maybe chocolate and orgasms. Just different."

Wren blinked, trying to catch up. "How old were you when you first tasted chocolate?"

Two On The Aisle   3

"How old? Relative to?" Maia looked momentarily confused. "Oh, you mean in earth years?"

Maia laughed louder than usual with an edge of hysteria. She was apparently joking. Wren tried to laugh, but it came out as a small twitter because experience had taught her to be wary. Dating had become so disappointing, not to mention terrifying, that she was nearly ready to give it up. Why was it so hard to meet a pleasant, ordinary, sane woman in this huge city full of gay women?

"Twenty, twenty-one," Maia said.

"Twenty? You never tasted chocolate until you were twenty?"

Maia nodded. "It gave me the creeps. They don't have it where I come from and I had this instinctive fear of it, I guess."

"I thought you were from Denver."

Maia was distracted by something on the menu. "Look! Twelve layer Hungarian Dobos Torte." She read the description. "Rich layers of sponge cake sandwiched by alternating layers of chocolate buttercream and chocolate ganache, finished with a hard shell of caramel and sprinkled with walnuts and chocolate nibs." She looked up at Wren with an eager, lustful expression, nearly salivating.

If a woman ever looks like that while thinking of me, Wren decided, I'll ask her to marry me on the spot.

"I had it a couple weeks ago," Wren said. "It sounds wonderful, but it was a little disappointing. The cake was too dry. I think you'll be happier with the chocolate mousse pie. Dense mousse on an almond paste crust. It's extraordinary."

"Okay." Maia snapped her menu shut. "You must come here a lot."

"Not that often."

Josephine was too expensive to come to often. Especially when it was pleasure and couldn't be written off as a business expense.

"Back to where you come from," Wren said after they ordered coffee and mousse pie. "Where they don't have chocolate."

Maia again laughed the slightly crazy laugh. Then she peered soberly into Wren's eyes and spoke softly. "I feel I can trust you. I can trust you, can't I?"

This isn't a good sign, Wren decided, but nodded anyway and said, "Sure."

"Yes," Maia said decisively. "I know I can. I have unusual powers of perception and I can see what a sincere, honorable person you are. I want us to start off solid. No surprises. I believe in laying all the cards on the table up front and I hope you'll do the same with me."

The seriousness of Maia's expression suggested this evening, originally so full of promise, was about to go badly south. Wren prepared herself for *The Thing*, the inevitable confession, the horrible reality that would dash her hopes to the ground and stomp them into dust.

"The people who raised me," Maia said solemnly, "weren't my biological parents."

"Oh!" Wren breathed, hugely relieved. "You're adopted."

"No, not adopted. I was a changeling."

"A changeling?"

"A changeling is a baby who gets switched with another."

"Yeah, I know. But I haven't heard the term outside of fairy tales. Because in literature, the changeling is a non-human child who's left in the place of the human baby stolen by fairies, trolls or even the Devil. So, technically, you can't be a changeling unless you're a non-human."

Wren added a laugh just as their dessert arrived, a disconcerting imitation of the new crazy Maia laugh she had just been introduced to. The waiter set down the coffee cups and a plate of chocolate perfection with whipped cream and chocolate curls on top and poured them both coffee.

Maia tasted the chocolate mousse. "Umm. You were right about this. So good!"

"So you were switched with another baby?" Wren was still intent on clearing up the facts of Maia's origins. "A hospital snafu or something?"

Maia's mouth was full of chocolate mousse, some whipped cream on her upper lip. She swallowed and said, "No. Seriously, Wren. I was a changeling. I was left with these people as an infant. They were wonderful to me. They raised me as if I were their own daughter. In fact, to this day they won't admit what I know to be true, even though they must be heartbroken over losing their own child. Even I have no idea what happened to her." Maia swallowed another big spoonful of mousse. "My people communicate with me telepathically, but they never mention the other baby. I guess they don't want me to be distracted with worrying about her."

Wren shook her head. "You showed me a picture of your parents last week. You look just like your mother."

Maia nodded emphatically. "That was supposed to fool them, to make them think I was really theirs. It's the way it's done."

"The way what's done?"

"Aren't you going to taste this? It's delicious."

"Go ahead." Wren had lost interest in dessert.

Maia took another spoonful. "My parents, my real parents, are from Gravlax."

"Gravlax?" Wren sputtered in disbelief. "Cured salmon?"

"No. This is a different Gravlax. This is a planet in the Rambutan system."

Wren slammed into the back of her chair and laughed, thoroughly relieved to realize she was the butt of a joke. "Very funny! Rambutan, like the fruit. Good one!"

Maia stopped eating, looking thoroughly, deadly serious. "I'm not joking."

"Yeah, right." Wren picked up the second spoon and took a big scoop of mousse. "I suppose you're going to tell me the town you were born in was Kielbasa and your father's name is Radicchio." She shook her head, impressed, realizing someone must have tipped Maia off about Wren's secret identity as a food critic.

Maia still wasn't smiling.

"Is this one of those hidden camera shows?" Wren looked around to see if she could find a TV crew disguised as waiters. "Picking the capers and olives out of the panzanella, that was supposed to drive me nuts, right?" She poked through the freesias in the vase between them, looking for a microphone.

Maia looked genuinely perplexed. Either she was a good

actress or she was out of her mind. Wren stopped eating and put down her spoon, worried that she had just encountered the reason she and Maia would not be waking up tomorrow morning in one another's arms, joyfully celebrating the beginning of their life together.

A loud disturbance from the kitchen attracted the attention of everyone in the restaurant. Sounds of banging metal, breaking glass and raised voices reached them, overwhelming the low-playing classical music and halting dinner conversation. Everyone stopped eating to listen. The only intelligible word amid a string of French-sounding curses was "dry," uttered with a slightly rolled "r." It came like a staccato refrain: *Dry! Dry! Dry!* Or the call of a scarlet macaw, emphatic and high-pitched, a chorus of exclamations followed by a round of questions: *Dry? Dry? Dry?*

A chef in kitchen whites came running through the swinging door, looking terrified and shrieking in Italian. Following him was a man Wren recognized as the owner of Josephine, John Bâtarde, the famous French chef. He wore a three-piece suit and carried a huge and beautiful torte on a plate above his head. He clutched a rolled up newspaper in his other hand, squeezing it so tight his knuckles were white, like he was trying to strangle it. His ginger mustache was crooked from the snarl on his mouth. His round face was red with wrath and his little eyes blazed with fury. He looked truly scary.

"He dares to call my Dobos torte dry!" Bâtarde yelled at no one in particular. "Dry! Dry! Dry!"

Suddenly realizing he was referring to her review of Josephine in today's paper, Wren shrunk into her chair, willing herself to disappear from Bâtarde's intense gaze. *Oh, crap!* she thought, trying to recall exactly what she'd said about the torte in an otherwise radiant report.

"Threlkeld's days are numbered!" he declared. "Nobody insults my cake and gets away with it!"

With that, the great chef flung the cake blindly into the air where it smacked into a ceiling fan. He then turned and stomped back into the kitchen as twelve layers of cake and chocolate frosting were swiftly chopped and sprayed around the room

Two On The Aisle   7

by the turning blades. Wren instinctively put her arms over her head as cake rained down on them and the plate bounced from one to the other of the fan blades before falling to the floor and breaking into shards. As the screaming in the restaurant subsided, she realized the danger had passed and peeked out to see traumatized diners with cake in their hair and frosting on their faces.

She was unscathed, but a fist-sized chunk of cake had landed next to her coffee cup.

Maia pinched off a sample and tasted it. "You're right," she said. "It's a little dry. Apparently some food critic thought so too. But the chocolate frosting's really good." She looked thoughtful. "When my people return to take us back to Gravlax, I'm insisting we bring cacao trees back with us."

CHAPTER TWO

I pray thee, gentle mortal, sing again:
Mine ear is much enamour'd of thy note.
So is mine eye enthralled to thy shape;
And thy fair virtue's force perforce doth move me
On the first view to say, to swear, I love thee.

—*A Midsummer Night's Dream*, Act III, Scene 1

If Sophie had been paying attention to the sidewalk in front of her instead of gawking at the two intriguing lookalike women hugging one another in the plaza of the Oregon Shakespeare Festival theater complex, she would have seen the step up and would have avoided tripping over it and landing backward on her butt while her overnight bag went flying on a course as true as one of Cupid's arrows straight toward the more appealing of the two women, landing directly at her feet.

But that wasn't how it happened. Sophie did not see the step and she did indeed trip over it, fell, and sent her luggage hurtling toward the young woman hugging her doppelganger. That woman, startled, looked up, found the source of the special delivery and locked eyes with Sophie, a serene look of neutrality on her face as they stared at one another, both of them immobile for a full five seconds before the woman reached down for Sophie's bag. She was about thirty years old, petite, dressed in black pants and a simple white shirt. Her hair was dark brown and short, straight with no part. Her bangs fell haphazardly over her forehead in a style that looked slightly mischievous, as though the result of deliberate disorder. She had a fresh, classically-shaped face with nearly straight-across eyebrows over wide, soulful brown eyes, a serious mouth and freckled cheeks. Such a sincere, vulnerable look.

That same face appeared on the other woman, but as a grotesque distortion. That woman was dressed in an Elizabethan costume with a fitted dress of blue silk, a gold braided cord wrapped around her waist, its tassels hanging loose in front. She wore a garish red wig, all brassy curls hanging down over her shoulders, and her eyes were enhanced with thick false eyelashes and dark violet eye shadow. Her lips were made fuller and more pert with a gaudy application of crimson lipstick. She was taller than her double by no more than two inches, but the shape of her face, her nose and the color of her eyes were identical. As appealing as the features were on the one woman, that was how repulsive they were on the other.

It was no wonder Sophie had been staring at this remarkable pair. On the left was a nightmare and on the right, a dream; yet they were twins.

Suddenly they both flew to her side, the pretty one clutching Sophie's bag.

"Are you all right?" asked the beauty, her bottomless sienna eyes overflowing with concern.

"I think so," Sophie answered, untangling her legs and taking stock of her condition. She felt a twinge in one elbow, but it wasn't much, probably just a bruise.

The woman reached down to catch hold of her hand. Sophie's fingers folded around the soft and delicate offer of support. No sooner did the woman start to pull than she was displaced by her ugly sister, who said, "Let me help you up." Her voice was as distorted as her face, strangely low and grating. She stood in front of Sophie and grabbed both her hands in her large, hairy-wristed ones, and pulled her to her feet. As Sophie stood facing the ugly sister, she saw, beneath the thick makeup, dark stubble and an unmistakable Adam's apple.

Suddenly, it all became clear to her. The ugly sister was a brother! His version of that face, which seemed bizarre and unattractive on a woman, was perfectly agreeable on a man. As her mind made the transition, she decided he was probably a handsome young man under all the makeup.

"Thank you," she said, acutely embarrassed. "I'm such a klutz."

"This is yours, isn't it?" asked the lovely woman, holding out Sophie's bag.

She took it. "Yes. Thanks."

The woman smiled and her eyes lit up with a radiance that took Sophie's breath away.

"You're sure you're okay?" she asked.

Sophie nodded. "I'm fine."

Satisfied, the curious twins walked off toward the theater. After watching them for a moment, Sophie turned and continued on her way to her hotel.

Coming into town always had its diversions. Ashland, Oregon was a smallish town, but a sophisticated one, its focal point being the Shakespeare Festival. Bohemians and stoners, street musicians and schizophrenics, sometimes schizophrenic street musicians, disenchanted exiles from California and enchanted visitors from Nebraska, winemakers and winos, fortune tellers and wandering minstrels all coexisted peacefully on these streets. It was a town that was a perpetual festival of art and the byproducts of artists' colonies everywhere—leftism, homosexuality, Unitarianism, free love and freer thought, good wine, environmentalism, activism of many flavors, organic gardening and, fortunately for Sophie, a larger than standard appetite for goat cheese.

Today, apparently, the diversions included an unlikely pair of twins whose faces continued to haunt Sophie as she walked along Main Street past the tourist shops, restaurants and art galleries.

She passed a fiftyish woman holding a sign above her head: *My Body, My Choice, My Drugs.* Sophie noted that the woman was close to her mother's age, but she couldn't quite picture her mother protesting for legalizing recreational drugs. An Ashland native, Olivia Ward had never been a part of this bohemian scene. Maybe she just hadn't had the leisure time for it. She had been a single mother of two girls, Sophie and her old sister Dena, with a full-time job, driving the school bus mornings and afternoons for thirty years. Now, Sophie thought with satisfaction, her mother was enjoying her early retirement. Even with all of her newfound free time, she wasn't likely to be doing or promoting drugs, especially not with her recently acquired devotion to healthy living. The most dangerous thing Olivia put in her mouth these days was Danish pastry. Ever since her stroke two years ago, she'd become a health fanatic.

Having grown up here, Sophie was used to the spirit of this town and found it fun. She was glad to have a reason to come into town now on a regular basis. The farm, her childhood home, with its quiet, even bucolic atmosphere, had seemed like the perfect refuge two years ago when she'd returned to it to nurse her mother back to health. It had been her relief from the fast-paced, frenetic lifestyle of an investment banker in Southern California. A respite too from life as Jan's significant other, a role that had provided more than enough drama all on its own. It was like a vacation, she'd thought at the time, anticipating a stay of a few weeks until her mother could manage on her own again. Yet, two years later, here she still was.

The once a week dose of crazy she got in town was just what she needed. This was her day to visit friends, eat out and shop as she made her deliveries to her handful of customers, the restaurants featuring Tallulah Rose chèvre. The farm suited her now, much more than it ever had as a child when her raging imagination had fueled a wanderlust for greener pastures and sparkling roads paved in gold. She'd seen the world and had learned for herself the lesson about all that glistens.

Sophie's attention was suddenly grabbed by a twenty-something girl in a filmy green, nearly sheer, form-fitting nylon bodysuit, standing on a low wall playing a mandolin. She looked like she was wearing a gigantic green stocking, so thin she may as well have been naked. Across the front, hanging from her waist, was a jagged piece of green cloth, covering her most private region. Sophie tried not to stare at her erect nipples or the dark line between her buttocks as she bent over to bow at a man dropping a dollar into her cup.

She reminded herself to stop walking if she was going to stare or she'd end up on her butt on the ground again. So she stopped and decided there was nothing wrong with staring. If the girl didn't want people to stare, she wouldn't be standing on a wall displaying herself. Along with a few others who were brazen enough to take the challenge, Sophie stood on the sidewalk pretending to listen to the girl's tune while regarding her sinuous curves encased in their green sleeve. The song she played was a traditional folk song, something Sophie vaguely recognized but couldn't put a title to. But as the girl began to sing, Sophie recognized "Annie Laurie."

"Her brow is like the snowdrift," sang the girl. "Her neck is like the swan; her face it is the fairest that er'e the sun shone on." The girl's voice was untrained, but pleasant. "For bonnie Annie Laurie, I'd lay me doon and dee."

As Sophie watched, the girl's face seemed to change into that of the young woman who had returned her overnight bag a few minutes before. The wide brown eyes, the freckled cheeks, the disobedient bangs, the vulnerable looking mouth. Moments into this fantasy, the face transformed again into the grotesque mug of the brother with its white stage makeup and violet eye shadow and thick masculine eyebrows. Sophie shook herself to dispel the image, then put some money in the mandolin player's cup before continuing on, singing quietly to herself. "For bonnie Annie Laurie, I'd lay me doon and dee."

CHAPTER THREE

Out of my door, you witch, you hag, you baggage, you polecat, you runyon!
Out, out! I'll conjure you, I'll fortune-tell you.

—*The Merry Wives of Windsor,* Act IV, Scene 2

Wren stood by herself outside the theater as her brother Raven changed into his street clothes inside. She reviewed the photos she'd taken of him on her phone, choosing one to email to her parents back home. He was in his costume, fully made up with the red wig, dress, the whole bit. She included the message, "Your lovely son, Beatrice." She smiled to herself, thinking what a kick they'd get when they saw it. She hoped they'd make it up here sometime this summer to see him perform.

Raven would be hilarious if the dress rehearsal was any indication. Tonight was opening night and he was understandably jubilant. Suddenly, things were going great for him. He'd landed this plum role with a major theater company and he had a handsome new boyfriend, Kyle, who seemed surprisingly palatable. Wren actually liked him, which may have been a first among her brother's partners. She hoped he would be long-term, but they'd only known one another six weeks, so they were very much in the throes of passionate novelty. It made her happy to see her brother doing so well and not just because he was so much easier to be around when he was happy.

She leaned against a lamppost, watching people pass, and her mind turned to the woman who had fallen on the sidewalk a half hour before. Wren had been thinking about her ever since, remembering her in vibrant detail. She was tall and sinewy with tanned, muscular arms. Her face was unblemished and unadorned, with high, pronounced cheekbones and a thin nose. Her hair was abundant, ash blonde, parted in the middle. She had a natural, wholesome look about her, casual and approachable, even while sitting on the ground in a state of flustered embarrassment. But it was her clever eyes, blue-gray, direct and riveting, that had made the most lasting impression. The way she'd held Wren's gaze as she bent over to offer her a hand had communicated worlds to her, worlds of possibility.

She watched a young man ride by on a unicycle. This town had its allure. It was a welcome diversion from San Francisco. During the week she'd been here, she had found it totally charming. She had always thought of herself as a city girl. But there were certain small towns, like this one, that had a city kind of personality without the city kind of isolation. Why was it, she thought, that the more people you lived among, the more alone you felt?

But Ashland, like San Francisco, wasn't all fun and games. There were a handful of derelict people on the downtown streets, making their living off soft-hearted tourists. One of them stood nearby, accosting theater patrons on their way to and from the box office. She was a woman with long, ratty hair, wearing a well-worn and voluminous brown cape that covered her completely from her neck to the ground, perplexing attire for a summer day. Her face was arresting, pale and gaunt with dark circles under her deep-set eyes. She was speaking to passersby, but Wren was too far away to hear her words.

Wren was well accustomed to homeless people. There were so many of them in a big city like San Francisco they became part of the landscape, sometimes tragically unseen. San Francisco, like Ashland, had a large tourist population and Wren had sometimes observed visitors photographing the street people as if they were another of the many attractions, like a sea lion or sidewalk musician. Of course, it wasn't always easy to tell the difference between a weekend street performer and a homeless person. In fact, Wren was beginning to question her initial assessment of the odd woman she was watching. Her arm gestures were theatrical. She didn't seem to be begging for money so much as putting on a show. She raised a closed fist above her head and shook it emphatically. Maybe she was a religious nut, haranguing the crowd like those obnoxious end-of-the-worlders preaching at the captive audience at Powell and Market streets back home. An unfortunate hazard of waiting in line for a cable car ride.

Then, just as Wren thought she had the woman pegged, she took hold of a man's hand and traced a line on his palm with her finger. A fortune teller?

Wren considered moving closer, as her curiosity was now piqued, but as she took her first step in that direction, a tall woman in a smart black dress burst out of the theater and hurried toward the cape-wearing woman, yelling plenty loud enough for Wren to hear every word.

"Get away from here!" she commanded, making shooing motions with her arms. "I told you never to set foot on this property again. Leave immediately or I'll call the police. Better yet, I'll have one of my boys throw you in the river!"

The woman from the theater was obviously angry, not just in a general indignation sort of way. She was livid, barely able to control herself. She continued the shooing gesture as the other woman began to move off. "Out of my sight!" she screamed.

The woman in the brown cape turned Wren's way as she made her unhurried exit, appearing unruffled. She stopped for just a moment, looking directly at Wren, her pale eyes boring intensely into her. Wren was surprised to see the woman was young, her own age.

16   Robbi McCoy

She reached out a long, bony index finger, pointing at her. "While you here do snoring lie," she breathed in a melodramatic and menacing voice, "Open-ey'd conspiracy his time doth take. If of life you keep a care, shake off slumber, and beware."

The theater woman was now stamping her feet and screaming. "Get out of here, you crazy witch!"

Wren stood frozen on the spot, as if the woman's pointing finger had control of her motor function.

"Awake! Awake!" exhorted the woman. She then lowered her arm, releasing Wren, and scurried off down the street.

The other woman now calmed herself and made a general apology around the courtyard. She pushed her long black hair back from her face with both hands and Wren noticed for the first time that she had a narrow white streak through it, possibly natural, in the style of Lily Munster. As she disappeared into the theater, Raven came out. He walked up to his sister, his face all smiles.

"All ready!" he announced.

His makeup was gone, his own dark hair slightly damp and well tempered. He wore jeans and a turquoise T-shirt with the theater logo on it.

"Sorry," he said, taking hold of her arm. "Did I scare you? You look terrified."

"Uh, no." Wren shook herself. "It wasn't you. We just had a bit of a ruckus. There was a strange, homeless woman. Or a lunatic. Not sure. A Shakespeare-quoting homeless lunatic. Kind of scary, actually. That woman who just passed you, she chased her away."

"Cleo? She's our artistic director. Plus all-around bouncer." He laughed. "She's not afraid of anybody, but I'm surprised you'd be frightened by a homeless person."

Wren laughed, shrugging off her anxiety. "I know! Silly. It was nothing, really." She hugged his arm closer. "I want you to know I'm having a fabulous time and I'm really happy to be here to share your success."

"'The world's mine oyster!'" he quoted, then grinned, his boyish face full of joy.

Wren was always aware that they were twins and as much

alike in appearance as a boy and girl could be, sharing the same dark brown hair, the same brown eyes with their long, thick eyelashes, the same small nose. They were very nearly the same size. He was five-six and she was two inches shorter. Raven was fine-featured and somewhat girlish, especially when it suited him. If they dressed alike and had similar haircuts, Wren suspected most people would have a hard time telling which of them was the man and which the woman. That had been more true when they were kids, before the manifestations of hormones took over, when they really could be and sometimes were mistaken for one another.

As often happens with twins, Wren and Raven had always been close, had often been one another's best friend, and felt one another's absence or presence keenly depending on their circumstances. For the past few years, they had been separated by geographical distance as Raven wandered in his search for the things young people everywhere search for: fame, fortune and love. They hadn't seen one another much in the meantime, but kept in touch with phone calls and frequently found themselves calling one another at the same time to find one another's line in use. After being separated for so long, Wren was delighted Raven had gotten a gig so close to her for the summer. She hoped it would turn into something more permanent.

Suddenly a pixie appeared beside Raven, a cute impish boy with coarse red hair completely covering his ears, freckled cheeks, long, thin limbs and a generous mouth that stretched across the entire bottom half of his face. He wore a white, short-sleeved shirt under a colorful paisley print vest with a navy blue tie tucked into it.

"Hey, Raven," he said in a thin voice, bouncing on his toes.

Raven laid a hand on the boy's shoulder. "Max, this is my sister Wren. Wren, this is Max, my understudy. He also appears in our play as A Boy."

Max reached a long arm out and shook Wren's hand firmly. "You look just like Raven!" he remarked, his eyes full of spark. Max looked no more than twenty, with a slender build and delicate features.

18   Robbi McCoy

"We're twins," Wren said, then realized that was an unnecessary explanation.

"I'm going shopping for tonight's after-party," Max said. "Do you want anything?"

Raven opened his wallet and handed over some money. "Yeah. I'd like some fruit juice. Orange, grapefruit. Something to rehydrate. Thanks."

Max took the money. "Where are you off to?"

"I'm taking my sister to lunch at Sprouts. See you later."

"Right. Break a leg tonight." Max skipped away.

"Sprouts?" Wren asked.

"It's great. Vegetarian. Fresh, local produce. Your kind of place."

"Perfect. Your understudy seems very young."

"Twenty-six. I know, he doesn't look it. He's a good kid. Very green, very eager. And not likely to get his big break this summer."

"Not unless you literally break a leg."

Raven laughed. "Not going to happen. This is my big break too."

They proceeded to Main Street with its red and gold theater banners hung from lightposts and the occasional half-timbered building reminiscent of sixteenth-century England. This was the district of Ashland's Shakespeare Festival where shops sported names like Ye Olde Tobacconist or Covent Garden Tearoom. Any anglophile would be happy stopping into the Boar's Head Tavern for fish and chips. A life-size wooden statue of William Shakespeare stood outside the Stratford Inn, one hand on his hip, the other thrust upward in front of him in a classic actor pose. Wren jumped up next to the statue and posed so Raven could take her picture.

"I'm so glad you got here before the play opened," he said as she rejoined him on the sidewalk, "so we could do some sightseeing together. It's been fun, but as of tonight, I belong to the theater." He twirled his hand above his head dramatically. "Ready for lunch?"

She took his arm. "'Lead on, MacDuff!'"

"Speaking of Hamlet," Raven said, "that's my goal, to play

him. Can't you just see me dressed all in black, the brooding Dane with his unrelenting angst?"

"Hmmm." Wren eyed him, enjoying his expression of brooding angst. "I don't know. I can definitely see you as Ophelia."

He whacked her playfully on the shoulder. "Okay, okay, I get that. I wouldn't turn her down either."

Looking at one another with the pure delight of being together, they both burst out laughing.

CHAPTER FOUR

All the world's a stage,
And all the men and women, merely players;
They have their exits and their entrances;
And one man in his time plays many parts,
His acts being seven ages.

—*As You Like It*, Act II, Scene 7

Sprouts had eight square tables arranged in a tight pattern behind a wall of glass providing a view of the street. A small coffee bar was tucked into one corner with self-serve coffee, tea and pastries. Prominently displayed on the back wall was a carved wooden sign that read, "No Shakespeare!"

When Wren brought that to Raven's attention, he shrugged good-humoredly. "I'll try to restrain myself."

Ellie Marcus, who introduced herself as the owner of Sprouts, also served as their waitress. She was a pleasant, ordinary looking woman about their age with a round face and surprised looking eyes. Something about the angle of her eyebrows, Wren decided. Her honey brown hair was piled asymmetrically on top of her head and held there with a silver clip. She brought them fragrant rustic bread and a round of rosemary butter to spread on it. Wren opened the menu to a list of vegetarian dishes that awakened her appetite and curiosity.

"This looks great," she said.

"I knew you'd like it!" Raven bounced gleefully in his chair. "The restaurant scene here is surprisingly vibrant."

"It's a tourist town, so not that surprising. I'm hoping to find a few gems up here. That Ginnie's Café was fabulous. The boysenberry pancakes, my God!"

"I'm sure it caused quite a stir when your review of Ginnie's appeared in the local paper this morning. Can't you just hear the clamor?" He lowered his voice to an emphatic whisper. "Eno Threlkeld is in town! Hide your cheap wine and limp broccolini!"

Wren glanced around to make sure nobody was within hearing distance. Ellie was by the coffee bar, setting out a fresh pot of coffee.

"Do you think they know me up here?" Wren asked. "It's kind of off the map."

"Maybe off the geography map, but not off the culinary map. Like you said, it's a tourist town. Food is important here. In fact, they're having this big cooking competition in a couple weeks, a cupcake bake-off."

"Cupcakes?"

"Yeah, just like on TV. The winner gets to cater dessert to the theater's annual fundraiser, the Midsummer Night's Dream Gala. Biggest party of the summer."

"Sounds like fun."

"You're invited. Hey, maybe you could get in on that bake-off somehow. A big-city critic would help publicize it. I know they're bringing in some celebrity chef to judge it."

"The whole secrecy thing kind of makes me unavailable for public appearances."

"Oh, sure. Duh!" Raven shook his head in self-derision.

"Who's the celebrity chef?"

"Don't remember."

Ellie came by to take their order. Wren chose the Burmese red rice salad and Raven ordered vegetable lasagna.

"Not a Shakespeare fan, eh?" Raven asked, gesturing toward the *No Shakespeare!* sign.

"If by not a fan," Ellie answered, "you mean despising everything about Shakespeare, then, yes, I'm not a fan."

"Ouch!" Raven said, wincing.

"Are you an actor?"

"Yeah."

"I thought so. My father was an actor too. Shakespeare was his thing. Drummed the goddamned crap into us from infancy. From birth, even. The story goes, at his first sight of me, he said, 'A daughter and a goodly babe. Lusty and like to live.'"

Raven snickered. "That's actually sort of sweet."

"If you'd lived it, you wouldn't think so. The only bedtime stories my sister and I ever heard were Shakespeare plays with the occasional Molière or Marlowe tossed in for grins. Not just comedies, but the histories and tragedies too." Ellie snorted in disgust. "Can you imagine doing that to a little kid? I can tell you the plot of all of them, frontwards and backwards. Even *Coriolanus.*"

"And you don't like any of them?"

"Not a one. Mistaken identities running rampant, love at first sight, all those twins! Men disguised as women, women disguised as men and nobody knowing the difference. Gimme a break!"

"You mentioned a sister?" Wren asked. "Does she hate Shakespeare too?"

"Unfortunately, no." Ellie rolled her eyes before moving on to another table.

Raven shrugged and grimaced.

Wren took a drink of her iced tea, noting the slightly floral edge to it and wondering what sort of tea it was. She couldn't place it. She usually didn't ask questions in a restaurant because if she happened to write about it later, in a review, the person she'd spoken to might put two and two together and remember their conversation, thereby remembering her. She'd learned to carefully conceal her professional identity from restaurant staffers. If they knew she was a critic, they'd immediately begin pandering to her and suddenly a perfectly acceptable asparagus risotto would have shaved black truffles on it and her dessert plate would be adorned with rose petals as though she were being wooed by a besotted lover.

The opposite was also true, she reminded herself, remembering the scene in Josephine from six weeks before when John Bâtarde had been so angry with her review, he'd threatened her destruction and thrown a cake into a fan. Fortunately, he had no idea who Eno Threlkeld was. Yes, secrecy was essential.

When Ellie brought their meals, they both turned their attention to food. After a few bites of her red rice salad, which was excellent, Wren stuck her fork in Raven's lasagna and helped herself to a generous bite. "Um, very tasty."

He sat back and took a swallow from his water glass. "I know you said you weren't seeing anyone. Not even a little bit?"

She shook her head. "Not even a little bit. I'm just so tired of that scene. All the drama. The screaming, the tears, the gnashing of teeth."

"Maybe you should try dating women rather than Godzilla."

Wren nodded appreciatively. "The problem is, you don't know they're Godzilla at first. Almost all women have the uncanny ability to appear completely sane, reasonable and wonderfully easygoing for exactly three weeks. And by then, you're hopelessly entangled and it takes months, even years, to escape." She shook her head morosely, remembering her nightmarish dating history. "I'm some kind of freak magnet. Freaks and flakes. It never fails."

"That sounds like a breakfast cereal." Raven punctuated the air with his fork. "Freaky flakes."

"Exactly!"

"You're exaggerating. You're just too picky."

"Oh, no, no, no!" Wren waved her hand between them. "You don't know what I've been up against. Let me give you an example. Erica. Second date. The woman served me a fabulous, home-cooked meal with English peas from her own garden. She's perfect, I'm thinking. She says she wants me. I want her.

I'm taking off her clothes. Her body is gorgeous. I'm ready to dive into her."

Raven nodded encouragingly, raising his eyebrows expectantly.

"Then comes the inevitable freaky deal breaker. She wants me to wear a costume."

"A costume? What kind? I'm all for costumes."

"Snow White. The black wig, the blue and yellow dress, high-backed collar, the classic Disney cartoon version."

"Oh, I love it!" Raven quacked.

"She tells me she can't have sex with anybody other than Snow White. Just not possible. Her therapist has been trying to get her to branch out a little, maybe try Dorothy from the Wizard of Oz or Wonder Woman."

Raven tried unsuccessfully to look serious. "What happened?"

"What do you think happened?"

"You put the costume on?" He burst into laughter again. "Come on, Wren, it wouldn't have been that bad, would it?"

She smiled indulgently at him. "I couldn't do it. Maybe it was my failing."

"Yes, maybe. *I* could have done it." He popped a tiny roasted red potato in his mouth.

"That was one of the more interesting whack jobs. I won't even mention the run-of-the-mill crazies." She also decided not to mention Maia from Gravlax, the most recent of her dating nightmares. Too recent. It gave her a shiver to even think of it.

Raven sputtered out a laugh. "Oh, my! You have had an interesting dating life, haven't you?"

"Which is why I'm happily single for now. I'm enjoying the peace and tranquility."

Raven dropped his fork, which clattered against his plate. "Peace and tranquility? My poor misguided sister!" He thrust an arm before him and spoke with his stage voice. "Rage and blow! Think not to contain thy passions. Without passion, life is an empty wine flask, a slice of unbuttered bread, a monochromatic rainbow." He lowered his arm and faced her with a scowl. "Otherwise, get thee to a nunnery."

Ellie stopped what she was doing, stared hard and threateningly at Raven, then pointed to the *No Shakespeare!* sign.

He nodded sheepishly toward her. He was keyed up today, preparing for his performance, keeping himself in tune like an orchestra during warm-up. Wren leaned back in her chair, thinking how much she liked Raven's company.

"No nunnery for me, thank you," she said flatly. "I'm sure it's temporary, but I'm not in the market for a relationship."

"Who said anything about a relationship? I was talking about dating. Why are women incapable of sleeping with someone without making a lifelong commitment of heart and soul? Why can't you just have a good time? Enjoy the moment, then let it go." He made a fluttering gesture through the air between them. "Men are superior when it comes to enjoying sex. Women seem to have to be in love before you can do it. It's physically impossible otherwise. In fact, I believe it violates the fourth law of thermodynamics."

"Very funny!" she said sarcastically.

She thought back over the last few years, her doomed relationships and bungled dates, trying to remember such a thing as casual sex with no hope for something more. She came up blank. "You make a one-night stand sound like a noble accomplishment."

"In a way, it is. Why shouldn't two consenting adults be able to enjoy one another's company without all of the emotional traps? A purely physical encounter is a thing of beauty. It's simple and satisfying. It asks nothing of you. It doesn't hurt your heart or your mind. You're the one complaining about relationships, after all. You shouldn't have to swear off sex because you're too emotionally immature to avoid falling in love with every person who kisses you."

"Are you calling me emotionally immature?"

"No. I'm speaking in generalities. About women...in general." She noted the twinkle in his eye. "Of which you are one."

She took another bite of her rice, eying him across the table. Ellie stopped to refill their glasses.

"How's your lunch?" she asked.

"Fantastic!" Raven answered. "I think this has officially become my favorite restaurant in town."

Ellie smiled with genuine appreciation and said, "Thank you. That's so good to hear."

A commotion near the door drew their attention. A heavily clothed woman with long, tousled blonde hair was entering the restaurant. Wren immediately recognized her as the person Cleo had run off the theater property earlier.

"What delightful distraction is this?" Raven asked.

"Oh, my God!" shrieked Ellie, darting over to the woman in the doorway as her wild eyes flitted over the people in the room. Wren stiffened as the woman's stare locked on her, followed by a toothy, frightening grin.

Ellie had hold of the sleeve of her cape and was pulling her toward the kitchen. But the woman resisted, standing her ground, still staring at Wren. Ellie tugged more emphatically, throwing apologetic smiles around the room.

Before she disappeared into the kitchen, the intruder, still eying Wren, proclaimed, "By the pricking of my thumbs, something wicked this way comes!"

Wren felt stunned, wondering if the woman had followed her here, was targeting her for some reason. "What the hell was that?"

Raven patted her hand. "Your next date would be my guess." Then he burst out laughing.

She took a deep breath as the rest of the diners returned to their meals. A minute later Ellie came hurrying over. She leaned down to Wren, whispering. "I'm so sorry. That's just my weird sister Cassandra. I've told her over and over to leave my customers alone. I hope she didn't upset you."

"Your sister?" Wren said uncertainly. "Oh, no. It's okay."

"Are you sure? I can take you in the back and get her to apologize."

"No!" Wren shrieked. Then more calmly, "No, thanks. I'm fine. Just a little unexpected."

The door bell tingled again. Wren spun around to look, illogically expecting the ghost of Christmas past or some such horror. She was relieved to see an ordinary woman pushing through the door, pulling a Styrofoam box on a wheeled cart. Maybe not an entirely ordinary woman, she thought, recognizing the woman from an hour ago outside the theater, the one who'd fallen on the sidewalk. Yes, it was definitely the same woman. Her clothes, jeans and a cotton shirt, didn't distinguish her, but Wren held the image of her face in her mind. She recognized those remarkable blue-gray eyes.

"Oh, hi, Sophie!" called Ellie, hailing the newcomer with a wave.

Sophie.

Sophie smiled a greeting to Ellie, then the two of them went together toward the kitchen while Wren watched Sophie from behind, noting with appreciation how her hips moved as she walked. Those hips had a special way of turning with each step, like a dance. They had a mesmerizing quality that held Wren's attention until they were gone from view.

A captivating woman, she thought with a sigh, but if she were gay by some extraordinary stroke of luck, she was probably just another freaky flake.

CHAPTER FIVE

This bud of love by summer's ripening breath,
May prove a beauteous flower when next we meet.

—*Romeo and Juliet*, Act II, Scene 2

Sophie held her breath as Ellie sliced a wedge off the chêvre log and tasted it like the connoisseur she was, with a seriously determined slant to her compact mouth and a distracted stare in her eyes. The cheese sat like an anxious debutante awaiting its coming out ball—creamy white with its flecks of purple sage, its claim to fame. Or perhaps its undoing, if all did not go as Sophie hoped.

"Ummm," Ellie said as her tongue teased out the depth of flavor from the sample.

Was that a good Ummm or an undecided Ummm, Sophie wondered, watching Ellie's face for the answer.

They both stood at a gleaming stainless steel counter in the kitchen of the restaurant. Johanna, the cook, was at her station with her chef's knife, preparing some quiet wonder. That was the difference between the kitchen at Sprouts and most other restaurant kitchens. The food here was nearly silent. There was a noticeable absence of sizzling and spitting and splattering. It was fresh and simple and mostly uncooked.

In the back at a small table, Ellie's younger sister Cassandra sat over her lunch, eating noiselessly, her wild hair surrounding her face like a mane. Seeing Sophie looking at her, she waved. Sophie smiled and nodded. "One of the witches from *Macbeth* again, is it?" she said to Ellie.

"She's been on that for a while now. It's always been one of her favorites. I wish she'd go back to Desdemona. I mean if she has to be somebody from Shakespeare. She rocks Desdemona. Or even Lady Macbeth. But, you know what, I can't complain. I'm just relieved she's off the Caliban kick. That sucked big time!"

Sophie laughed, remembering a few months ago when Cassandra had wandered the streets of Ashland in the guise of "a freckled whelp hag-born—not honour'd with a human shape." It was a trial for Ellie to have such a loathing of Shakespeare's works and have a sister who lived perpetually in them. It was a legacy from their actor father, Anthony Marcus, each daughter responding to his vocation with opposing attitudes on the Bard.

Ellie was Sophie's first and best customer, one of the restaurant owners who bought as much of the small-batch chêvre as she could turn out, which wasn't a lot. Quality over quantity, that was the philosophy at Tallulah Rose Creamery. Sophie had known Ellie since they were kids. They were the same age and had gone to the same school. Ellie had always been single, not just unmarried, but unpartnered. Sophie was nearly certain she hadn't even been on a date since high school when she had agreed to go to the senior prom with the first boy who'd asked her, not because she was interested in the boy, but because, like so many teenagers, Sophie included, she was interested in not being different. Ellie was one of those rarities, a woman with no drive to couple. She was reasonably good-looking and certainly pleasant enough to attract a mate. She just had no desire to do so.

Ellie turned her round face to Sophie with an appreciative smile. "That is truly inspired."

"So you like it?"

"I love it! I think I could do some sort of bruschetta with that. With those yellow heirloom tomatoes we've been getting and a fruity balsamic vinegar. What do you think?"

"Yes. I like that. I thought it might go well with corn too, you know? Maybe some sort of corn cake."

Ellie's eyes widened as she nodded. "Fantastic idea. Johanna! I want you to taste this purple sage."

Johanna's large hands worked a mandolin at a rapid tempo, slicing perfect rounds of zucchini. A ruddy-faced, solidly built woman with massive arms and legs, she turned toward them with a frown.

Ellie waved her over. "Come here. Sophie's brought us something new."

Johanna begrudgingly wiped her hands on a towel and trundled over to stare at the cheese. Ellie sliced off another piece and handed the knife to her. Sophie and Ellie stood perfectly still as they watched Johanna's tongue take command of the sample, giving it short shrift before swallowing.

"Good," she said and that seemed to be the end of her commentary.

"Sophie suggested corn cakes," Ellie said. "What do you think? Could you do a corn cake that would complement that?"

"I could," Johanna grunted, "but I don't think that would impress Eno Threlkeld."

"Eno Threlkeld?" Ellie looked taken aback. "Why do you bring him up?"

"He wrote a review of Ginnie's Café. It was in the paper today."

"Our local paper?"

Johanna nodded.

"We don't usually get Eno Threlkeld's column in our local paper."

"They picked it up because it was a local restaurant."

"Was it a good review?" Ellie asked.

Johanna nodded again.

"That was lucky for Ginnie, then," noted Ellie. "But she does a really nice breakfast, nobody can deny."

"Who's Eno Threlkeld?" Sophie asked.

"He's a top restaurant critic based in San Francisco," Ellie explained. "Very influential."

"And he's in town," Johanna pointed out.

"At least he *was* in town at some point," Ellie corrected. "Maybe he was just passing through."

"Maybe he was and maybe he wasn't. We should be prepared, just in case."

"Prepared how?" asked Sophie.

Johanna glanced dismissively at her. "By not featuring things like corn cakes."

"I like corn cakes," Sophie muttered defensively.

"A good review from Eno Threlkeld," Ellie noted, "would be a feather in our cap. His column goes out to hundreds of newspapers every week. So much of our business here is from tourists, something like that can make a real difference."

"Be on the lookout for him," Johanna warned.

"How do we do that? Nobody knows what he looks like. He's not going to walk in and introduce himself."

Johanna went wordlessly back to her mandolin while Sophie handed over several logs of goat cheese to Ellie.

"That should get us through most of the week," Ellie said, closing the refrigerator.

"Do you have any of Katrina Olafssen's aebleskiver? My mother'll kill me if I don't bring any home."

"Oh, I'm sorry," Ellie said. "We're out. Bad timing. She'll bring me a new batch tomorrow."

"Maybe even better timing, then. I'm spending the night, so I can stop by in the morning and get some fresh."

"Perfect."

Cassandra gave a disconcerting grunt, causing them both to look at her. She seemed to have finished her meal and sat unoccupied with a vacant look on her face.

"How's Cassandra doing?" Sophie asked.

"Same as usual. Therapy doesn't seem to be doing a damn bit of good. She just terrorized some woman out front. I wish she wasn't so…weird."

"Don't you think she'd be okay again if she could get back

on the stage? Don't you think the problem is that her dream was shattered?"

"Maybe, but she isn't going to get back on stage, not as long as Cleo Keggermeister is in charge. Bitter old hag." Ellie's tone was angry. "And none of this would have happened if my father hadn't encouraged her to act in the first place. It wasn't enough he had to destroy his own life. I'm just grateful I was immune to his romantic ideas."

Sophie smiled. "Romantic ideas, not your weakness."

"It's a good thing one of us is living in the real world," Ellie stated flatly.

"Do you ever hear from your father?" Sophie asked.

"Not for a long time." Ellie looked exasperated, as if the very idea of her father pained her. "Last I heard, he was in trouble with some loan shark in Venice. He said if he didn't make a payment, the guy was gonna cut his heart out or something like that. I couldn't help him. I had just bought this place. I had nothing. I was in debt up to my ears myself. I haven't heard from him since. I don't know if he's dead or alive. I guess he gave up on us when I didn't come through with the cash." Ellie sighed forlornly. "I know Cassandra misses him. They were so close. But I couldn't care less. Good riddance, I say. The man was a bum and a philanderer."

Sophie patted Ellie's shoulder, hearing the emotional ambivalence in her voice.

"Whatever." Ellie swatted the air dismissively. "You staying for lunch?"

"Yes! I understand you serve some incredible goat cheese."

Ellie laughed. "You know, I still can't believe you're a goat farmer. All through high school, all you could talk about was getting off the farm, going to the big city, living a life where there was absolutely zero chance you'd ever step in a pile of animal shit again."

"I remember. But that's what rubber boots are for. Besides, there are a lot worse things to step in. At least shit is honest."

Ellie gave her a sympathetic look. "When your mother had that stroke, we all expected you to sell the farm and take her to L.A. to live with you. Instead, you gave it all up to come here."

"Giving it all up wasn't as hard as you make it sound," Sophie said. "Life in the city, at least for me, was stressful and depressing, even if I was making a boatload of money. Since I've been here, I've felt so much saner. I feel healed. In fact, I think I've come to prefer the company of goats to people."

"What a thing to say! Not all people, I hope."

"Not all people, no. But there are a whole lot of people in Southern California I do not miss."

Sophie thought briefly of her ex, Jan, and stiffened against the wave of pain that thought brought with it. The pain was much less intense and came less often than it once had. Jan and all she represented, good and bad, was fading into a dull blurry background buzz.

"I, for one, am glad to have you back," Ellie announced firmly.

Before returning two years ago, Sophie hadn't seen Ellie or any of her childhood friends since high school. She'd been in such a hurry to get out of here, to go off and explore the larger world. And she had. She'd gone to college in Southern California, gotten an MBA, pursued a career in finance, a lucrative and competitive field that had used her up.

That had been where she'd met Jan, and the two of them had built a comfortable life together, full of friends and social events, a hectic, expensive life. What Sophie had not known was that Jan had been routinely sleeping with those friends, that a humiliating number of their social circle were her secret lovers. She'd slept with clients too, and not just women. Her explanation, when Sophie finally caught on, was that it was "just business" or "just fun" and that none of it was serious. None of it meant anything. The only person who mattered, she had said, the only person she loved was Sophie. As Jan's second chance turned into a third chance, Sophie became more and more broken. She gradually realized she had no true friends and that feeling eventually spread to include Jan.

Ellie wasn't the only one who was surprised that Sophie was now a goat farmer. When she'd come back to Oregon, there had been no plan other than helping her mother recuperate. As Olivia got better, Sophie got comfortable. The farm felt more like home than she'd ever expected. She couldn't remember an actual day when she decided to stay. She just never decided to leave.

Her mother needed her. That was what she told everyone—Jan, her employer, her "friends" in L.A. The truth was, she needed her mother and everything her mother represented, a sense of belonging and unconditional love. The fact that Jan had let her go and had not asked very convincingly for her to come back was proof that it had been the right decision to stay. But the most telling thing of all was the day she woke up alone in her room in the old farmhouse and realized it had been three months since she had cried. Her life in L.A. had been a string of tearful episodes knit together with makeup sex and periods of stony indifference. There had been so many tears, silent ones as she sat alone in the apartment wondering how to stop caring, and angry ones during the many arguments that shook their walls and their affection. Then she had come here and had quit crying. A kind of numbness had descended on her for several weeks. Gradually, she had started feeling again, feeling good, hearing herself laugh, eventually realizing she hadn't been happy for years. She and her mother recovered together, one of them physically and one of them psychically. There was no longer any question she had done the right thing by staying here.

Olivia Ward had never been a serious farmer, but she did have a horse, a few chickens and two goats, Tallulah and Rose. To fill in the time while her mother recovered, Sophie had started making goat cheese. After experimenting with a few recipes, she had given some to Ellie to sample. Ellie had raved and said, half jokingly, that if Sophie were selling, she'd be buying. That's how it had happened, and that's when Sophie really settled in, buying four more goats to supplement the original pair.

She and her mother had lived in harmony for the last two years, much greater harmony than she would have expected given her rebellious teenage years. She had fought her mother over every tiny decision and couldn't wait to be far, far away from her. Par for the course with mothers and daughters, she was sure. After all those years apart, Olivia hadn't seemed so much like the enemy anymore. Yes, it had all worked out remarkably well. Sophie was happy here.

Two On The Aisle   35

"Take any table you want, Sophie," Ellie instructed, so she chose a seat next to the front window.

As she opened her menu, she caught the eye of a woman she immediately recognized as one of the twins from the theater. For a second, her heart seemed to stop as those deep brown eyes gazed into hers, inviting her in. When their stare broke off, Sophie noticed the young man at her table. In the next heartbeat, her spirits sank until she recognized him as the woman's brother, looking completely different in ordinary clothes and without his makeup. He was a slim, handsome man with delicate features and gay mannerisms. If the brother was gay, maybe the sister was too, Sophie reasoned, realizing almost immediately that wasn't logical. More of a hope than a hypothesis. Then she had to ask herself why she was hoping this stranger was gay. She was probably just another theater tourist in town for the weekend, not, as Sophie had immediately fantasized, an angel from Providence sent to rock her world.

The woman smiled warmly at her, acknowledging with a nod that she too recognized her.

Ellie came by to take Sophie's order just as the door opened and a small, fresh-faced person with shaggy red hair bounded in and darted to the twins' table. Ellie gawked, open-mouthed, at the little freckled urchin. She seemed completely transfixed, her hand poised in midair as if she'd been turned to stone. Sophie waited a few seconds, watching Ellie with perplexed curiosity, before tugging lightly on her sleeve. Ellie roused herself and her eyes gradually focused on Sophie.

"I'm ready to order," Sophie said.

"Okay," Ellie said distractedly, but before Sophie could utter a word, she was off like an iron filing to a magnet, darting to the twins' table. "Hi," she said, taking hold of the boy's hand and shaking it, "I'm Ellie. Are you staying for lunch?"

"No!" interjected the male twin. "He's just leaving."

The boy smiled sheepishly, then was gone, out the door in the blink of an eye. Ellie wandered slowly back to Sophie's table, her eyes on the door.

"Did you see that beautiful boy?" she asked.

Stunned, Sophie studied Ellie's face, seeing a look there

that was completely unfamiliar, a look of enchantment. Was it possible that at the age of thirty, Ellie had suddenly seen the face of love? And was it possible that the face of love was a skinny, redheaded pixie?

After Ellie took her order and disappeared into the kitchen, Sophie glanced again at the young woman and her brother. Odd that she and Ellie were having the same experience today. Sophie hadn't felt this sort of elemental attraction to anyone for a long time, certainly not since moving back home. Despite a momentary fantasy, she didn't want to encourage it. She didn't want to invite all of those severe and tormenting feelings back into her life. She'd been feeling such a sense of peace here, as if she'd recovered herself after being lost for years.

She didn't miss her old life or any of the people in it. Except now and then, on a warm night when she couldn't sleep, she missed the closeness of a woman. Just loneliness, that's all it was, the type of undirected loneliness that came along on a summer breeze and lingered for a few hours before it blew away again.

CHAPTER SIX

O, she did so course o'er my exteriors with such a greedy intention,
that the appetite of her eye did seem to scorch me up like a burning-glass!

—*The Merry Wives of Windsor,* Act I, Scene 2

"That boy idolizes me," Raven said after the pixieish Max had gone. "If he ever does get a chance to be on stage, you'll see, he'll use all my tricks. I've taught him how to walk, how to talk, how to bat his eyes. He wouldn't make a bad Beatrice, not at all. But for now he'll have to be content with being billed as A Boy."

Wren turned to look at Sophie again. She thought her smile, which seemed a bit self-conscious, was adorable. They each held one another's gaze for a moment. Wren was transfixed by those piercing blue-gray eyes.

"What are you looking at?" Raven asked, irritated that he was no longer the center of attention.

"Oh," Wren said, setting her fork down. "Sorry." She lowered her voice. "That woman by the window is the one who fell outside the theater earlier."

He glanced at Sophie. "Ah, so it is." He gave her a tiny wave. Then he looked back at his sister. "What were we talking about? Oh, yes, set design. You're going to be impressed. I know you're used to great theater. San Francisco, well, what do you expect, right? But I don't think you'll find much to scoff at."

"I have no intention of scoffing," Wren assured him. "I'm expecting brilliance."

"You don't need to go that far. You'll make me nervous. But thank you." Raven smiled in that charmingly ingratiating way he had, creating dimples.

She reached over and pinched his cheek. "I'm very proud of you."

Wren caught Sophie's eye again. Sophie smiled, this time more fully, then she self-consciously tucked her hair behind her ear and turned her attention to the people passing by on the sidewalk. Wren wondered what it was about this stranger that intrigued her so much. She was attractive, but not beautiful, not the sort of beautiful that would turn heads on the street. Her beauty was centered in her eyes, in the depth of expression there. And in the way she moved her head and her long-fingered hands, with deliberation and grace.

Wren realized Raven was talking to her. She looked at him, startled to find him making a grimacing face at her.

"What?" she asked.

"I just said I'm treating you to lunch." He waved the bill at her. "And you don't have the decency to say thank you."

"I'm sorry. I didn't hear you. Thank you! You're a sweet, super awesome brother!"

"That's better." He glanced at Sophie, then back at Wren, raising one eyebrow à la Mister Spock. "Is there something interesting going on here?"

She waved her hand dismissively. "No. Nothing."

"Methinks it were something, lady." He folded his hands over one another on the table, looking smug. "I know that distracted look."

She shook her head. "She's just interesting looking, that's all. She's probably straight."

He pursed his lips together thoughtfully, looking surreptitiously at Sophie. "I don't know. This might be a lesbian hangout. A vegetarian restaurant. Possibilities there. If they've got hummus on the menu, that cinches it. Do you remember seeing hummus?"

"Hummus?" blurted Wren. "What you know about lesbians could fit in a fairy's pocket."

"Oh!" He looked offended. "Nay, sister, not so. I say she's family."

Wren glanced again at Sophie, who was still staring out the window. "You think so?"

"I do."

Wren shook her head. "Look, it doesn't matter."

"You don't want to go over and talk to her? I'll make myself scarce."

"No," she said firmly. "Why are you so concerned about my love life?"

"I just don't want you to be lonely and sad," he explained. "With only your vibrator for company."

She stared.

He shrugged. "Kyle found it when he was cleaning your room."

Her mouth dropped open.

"I hate to think of you alone in your room," he said, looking forlorn, "just you and your limited supply of batteries..."

"Then don't think about it!"

He laughed. "Believe me, I don't want to!"

"And tell Kyle to stay out of my room!" She wiped her mouth and put the napkin in her plate. "Are we ready to go?"

"Yeah. Too bad you aren't writing a review of this place. Then we'd get dessert."

"Maybe next time. My column's done for this week."

"You were very nice to Ginnie." Raven counted out his money, sticking his tongue out in concentration as he calculated the tip.

"I was, yes, but no more than she deserved. I'm sure she'll

like it. I sent her an email telling her to be on the lookout for it today. I mean, Eno sent her an email."

He nodded, pulling theater tickets out of his wallet. He handed her one. "This is yours. I've got a few left over. What should I do with them?"

"Give them away. No point wasting them."

"You're right."

Raven climbed onto his chair and stood his full, not so impressive height, announcing, "Ladies and gentlemen, I'm giving away free tickets to tonight's performance of *Much Ado About Nothing*, a comedic masterpiece, in which I steal the show in the character of Beatrice. These are orchestra seats. Best in the house."

Ellie stood near the door to the kitchen, her hands on her hips, frowning at Raven's theatrics, but allowing him to continue.

Sophie raised her hand. "I'll take one," she said, approaching their table and glancing briefly at Wren.

"Ah, my good lady," Raven exclaimed, bending over to hand her a ticket. "A most excellent choice for an evening's entertainment."

She curtseyed slightly and said, "Thank you, good sir," before returning to her table.

"Is that Shakespeare?" asked a young man in baggy jeans. "What's it about?"

Wren noted the almost imperceptible look of frustration on Raven's face before he adopted a theatrical smile and said, "It's a comedy, sir. A Shakespearean comedy full of wit and whimsy. Two pairs of young lovers, a semi-effectual villain, improbable misunderstandings. Ultimately and predictably, all lovers are united to live happily ever after."

"Okay," said the man without enthusiasm. "Gimme two."

"Here you are, sir," Raven said gamely. "Two on the aisle. Enjoy the show!"

CHAPTER SEVEN

Now, by the world, it is a lusty wench!
I love her ten times more than e'er I did:
O! how I long to have some chat with her!

—*The Taming of the Shrew*, Act II, Scene 1

Before the play began, Sophie checked the playbill to learn the name of the young man playing Beatrice: Raven Landry. Interesting name, she thought. She was still intrigued by the fascinating resemblance of Raven to his twin sister whose name she still didn't know. She'd been unable to keep from staring at them all through lunch and was still preoccupied with the sister as she found her seat and settled in for the performance. She was seated on an aisle on the left side of the orchestra section with an excellent view of the stage, which, at the moment, was hidden by opulent red curtains.

She was both startled and overjoyed when the very woman on her mind, wearing tan chinos and a matching tailored jacket, walked past her and sat on the other side of the aisle two rows ahead. She slipped off her jacket, revealing a sleeveless coral tunic beneath and a bare arm so exquisite Sophie caught her breath at the sight of it. How opportune, she thought, staring unabashedly at the woman's small foot in chic brown sandals as she crossed her legs and made herself comfortable. Like Sophie, she'd changed for the theater, but her hair was still mussed, confirming that the look was deliberate. Why not? It suited her, the touch of feistiness.

Sophie had wanted to look at her even more in the restaurant, but every time she tried, she found the woman looking back at her as if they knew one another. Sophie was sure she didn't know Raven's sister. She didn't think she could forget meeting someone so... She sighed. She wasn't sure what it was about her that made her want to stare. Like her brother, she was fair-skinned and dark haired. Like her brother, she moved fluidly and rapidly. She had an androgynous look about her, except for her mouth, which was lush and feminine and her eyes, which were thick-lashed and capped by those unusual, linear eyebrows. No great mystery, is it? Sophie asked herself. She's lovely to look at. She's the kind of woman she had always been attracted to, the kind of woman she could see on a street and immediately want to touch. That kind of woman didn't cross her path very often. Like most things in life, the rarer they were, the more precious they seemed.

They were seated in the outdoor theater, Sophie's favorite. Above them was the open sky, settling gradually into dusk. As the curtain rose, she reluctantly turned her gaze to the stage.

Because Raven was playing a woman's role, she had guessed all the parts would be played by men, a throwback to the original Elizabethan custom. But while both Benedick and Beatrice were played by men, Hero and Claudio were played by women, so the two pairs of lovers were same-sex couples, a very campy approach to this play and one that was a hit with the audience judging by the laughter and applause. Raven Landry was wildly entertaining, flinging the skirt of his dress flagrantly this way and that as if it were a matador's cape. Sophie was glad he was good. She wanted to like him.

When the little redheaded boy she'd seen earlier in the

restaurant appeared onstage, looking identical to before except for the simple costume of white shirt and brown pants, Sophie remembered with renewed wonder how Ellie had been struck by him. He ran off stage to fetch Benedick's book after his scant two lines and was heard no more. If Ellie knew he was an actor, she would quickly lose interest. Of that, Sophie was sure. Ellie's disdain for the theater and those associated with it was vast and uncompromising. It seemed she had transferred all her rage at her father to the thing he had loved most.

While watching the play, Sophie found herself glancing often at Raven's sister, watching her laugh at the antics onstage. What would she think, Sophie wondered, if she knew how I was staring? At least she would probably be pleased to know it's with admiration. Definitely admiration. Maybe a little bit of lust too, if she were being honest with herself. The very cerebral Sophie Ward wasn't beyond lusting after a beautiful young woman, though that had been a rarity in recent years. She couldn't remember feeling this way since before Jan, during college when lust was in every girl's heart. In the last two years, she hadn't thought much about sex and hadn't met anyone who triggered those thoughts. Until today. Another piece of evidence that she was totally over Jan.

At intermission, Sophie walked out to the snack bar to get a bottle of water. She turned from the counter to find Raven's sister standing right behind her, observing her with a cunning smile.

"Hi," she chirped. "We meet again. How do you like the play?"

"It's hilarious. Your brother— The man playing Beatrice, he *is* your brother?"

"He is. That's Raven. My name's Wren."

She held out her hand and Sophie shook it, then they moved aside to get clear of the snack bar. Sophie felt exhilarated to be speaking to this woman rather than just admiring her from a safe distance.

"I'm Sophie," she said. "Wren, like the bird?"

"That's right. Wren and Raven."

"Oh! I just assumed Raven was a stage name."

"No. It's his real name. My parents are birding fanatics."

Sophie heard herself snort out a laugh. "Do you have any other siblings?"

"Yes. An older sister named Robin."

Sophie laughed more freely this time.

"I've always thought she got the best deal." Wren's luscious mouth curled into a crooked smile. "A normal name."

"I don't know. I think Wren and Raven are very interesting names. Exotic and romantic."

"Yes. I like it better now than I did as a kid. You know how that goes."

"Well, your brother's doing a wonderful job. They all are."

"Are you a big Shakespeare fan?" Wren asked.

"I like it, sure. I suppose if I were really a fan, I'd make more of an effort to see it, especially since we have such good theater right here in Ashland. Living here, you can't really escape Shakespeare. The town is sort of a live theater experience. You might run into a scene from *Romeo and Juliet* just walking down the street. It sometimes seems a little redundant to go to the theater."

"I hadn't thought of it that way. The town's a little surreal, I guess, as a place to live. A perpetual Renaissance faire."

"Downtown is, but the rest of the town is ordinary. There are regular neighborhoods, schools, places you can live your entire life and never see a man in tights."

There was that smile again, Wren's easy smile, natural and engaging, forcing Sophie to stare at those luscious lips.

"Men in tights, yeah," Wren said, "or a woman in the middle of summer in a heavy, floor-length cape."

"You met Cassandra earlier, didn't you?"

"Is she okay? I mean...sane?"

"She's okay. Harmless, anyway. Up until four years ago, she was a member of the company."

"She was an actor here?"

"Right. I heard she was pretty good. Not from her sister. Ellie never, ever goes to a Shakespeare play. Cassandra, on the other hand, lives for the theater. Well, she did. I'm sorry I never got to see her perform."

"What happened?" asked Wren.

"She clashed with Cleo Keggermeister," Sophie explained, giving Wren a drastically abbreviated version of the story. "She runs the show here."

"Yeah, I actually know who she is."

"Several years ago, Cleo fired her and banished her from the property for life."

"That would explain what I saw this morning."

"She hasn't been herself since." Catching the irony of her statement, Sophie laughed tensely. "Literally."

"That's sad." Wren shook her head. "I'd better get in line," she said, "if I'm going to get something to drink before intermission's over."

Sophie said goodbye and found a quiet spot to make a phone call home.

"Is everything okay?" she asked after her mother picked up.

"Fine," Olivia said. "Everything's fine. I milked the goats, fed the chickens, made myself a little dinner."

Anyone not knowing Olivia before wouldn't notice anything odd about her voice, but Sophie did notice the slight slur, the lingering effect of the stroke. She had recovered remarkably well, almost completely, regaining most of the movement in her left side, her face and arm. For a while now, Olivia had been able to do everything she'd been able to do before the stroke. More even, because she had thrown herself so completely into recovery that it went well beyond simply recovery. At the age of fifty, Olivia had radically changed her lifestyle, taking up serious regular exercise and improving her diet. She'd never been a slouch, but now she was a genuine health nut. She was far more healthy now than she had been just prior to the day Klaus found her lying on the kitchen floor, semiconscious, paralyzed on her left side. Her neurologist was impressed with her determination and astonished at her recovery. Just shows how important the right frame of mind can be, he had said. Dr. Connor, a kayaking fanatic, had even gotten Olivia out on the river a few times, a sport she was growing more and more fond of, judging by how quick she was to accept his invitations.

"What are you doing tonight?" her mother asked.

"I ended up going to a play, *Much Ado About Nothing*."

"Is that the one where the two sets of identical twins with the same names get each other all mixed up?"

"No. I think that's *Comedy of Errors*."

"Is it the one where two pairs of lovers fall in and out of love with each other in the woods and a bunch of fairies are flitting about? And somebody named Bottom is turned into an ass?"

"That's *A Midsummer Night's Dream*. No, this is the one where two pairs of lovers, despite several unlikely misunderstandings, get together in the end."

"That's not much of a description, Sophie."

"It's not much of a play!" She laughed. "At least as far as plot goes. Very aptly named. There's a dimwitted constable named Dogberry. Does that ring a bell?"

"No," Olivia said flatly.

"Let's see." Sophie searched her mind for something distinctive. "John the Bastard frames Hero so her fiancé thinks she's seeing another man. He calls off their wedding at the last minute."

"Oh! John the Bastard! I remember." Olivia chuckled. "I'm glad you're having some fun. Did you sell any of that sage cheese?"

"Sold the entire batch," Sophie reported. "I think it's going to be a hit. I have the one delivery in the morning, then home. I should be back before noon."

After her call, Sophie made her way back to her seat. As she sat down, Wren turned around and smiled at her. She returned the smile and they both settled in for the rest of the performance. The sky above was aglitter with stars now that the sky had darkened. There was a cool breeze wafting through the theater, welcome after the hot summer day. Though the audience was now in semidarkness, Sophie could see well enough to watch Wren pull her jacket on, cross her legs at the knee and settle back in her seat.

Although she was facing forward, caught up in the play, Sophie sensed that they both remained acutely aware of one another's presence. By now she had the impression that Wren was as interested in her as she was in Wren. There was something telling in the way she held Sophie's gaze and in the undercurrent of tension between them.

She began to imagine some next step, some gesture to insure they might see one another again, get to know one another, maybe become friends. Then, later on, who knew what else?

Suddenly she was thinking about Tallulah and Rose, her mother's original two goats, and their immediate and absolute dislike or attraction to any new animal who came into the farm. Like the little tan one, Tater, that they both adored from the moment she walked into the yard. A touch of a nose, a sniff of a butt and they were lifelong enemies or the dearest of friends. Humans liked to think of their relationships as much more complex than those of animals, but there was no denying there are people you meet you have an instant rapport with or take an instant disliking to. That was what was happening here. Sophie was experiencing an irresistibly strong attraction to Wren Landry, even without the benefit of sniffing her butt.

Feeling flushed and embarrassed, Sophie quickly glanced at Wren, but she was facing the stage and appeared not to have received that thought transmission. Relieved, Sophie sat back and tried to focus on the play.

CHAPTER EIGHT

See how she leans her cheek upon her hand!
O that I were a glove upon that hand,
That I might touch that cheek!

—*Romeo and Juliet*, Act II, Scene 2

Wren was on her feet, clapping emphatically, as Raven and his fellow actors took their bows. He looked triumphant in his showy orange curls and azure gown, his eyes shining with unmistakable joy. Wren waved both arms above her head, trying to get his attention. At last he noticed her and waved.

As soon as the clapping died down, the audience was on the move, heading out of the theater. Wren stepped into the aisle and stared, shocked, at the empty seat where Sophie had been. She scanned the crowd ahead. She felt suddenly desperate, not to mention stupid. She should have gotten her phone number at least. She didn't even get a last name. Wren wasn't sure what she wanted from Sophie, but she knew she wanted something, some further contact. Maybe just to see her self-conscious smile again or watch her walk with those hips in that swaying dance that left Wren feeling so fluttery.

She pushed through the crowd of theater patrons until she was outside where she could watch from a controlled vantage point. She examined every woman who emerged from the theater until she realized Sophie must have made it out ahead of her. Still she stood there, powerless, hoping there had been some delay, that Sophie had stopped at the gift shop or the restroom and might still appear. How could I have let her get away? she berated herself. As she stood intently watching the doorway, growing more and more angry at herself, someone tapped her shoulder.

She spun around to see Sophie. She was so relieved, she grabbed hold of her arm and clung to it.

"There you are!" Wren cried. "I thought you'd already gone."

"I was looking out for you." Sophie looked down at her sleeve.

Realizing she was gripping Sophie's arm, Wren abruptly let go.

"Hey," Sophie suggested, "would you like to get drinks or coffee or something?"

Her smile seemed both warm and genuine. With that invitation, Wren relaxed considerably, knowing she wasn't alone in wanting more.

"You know," she said, "I'm really hungry. Shakespeare always makes me ravenous."

Sophie laughed lightly. "Really? I wouldn't mind a snack myself. There's a little hole-in-the-wall hot dog place I know. They're simple, but good. Could you go for that?"

Hot dogs? Wren thought, smiling to herself. It had been a long time since she'd had a hot dog. It wasn't the sort of thing people normally suggested to her, assuming that because she was a food critic, she would turn her nose up at something as humble as a hot dog.

"That sounds perfect!" she said gratefully.

Sophie suggested they walk through the park, so they took a

path beside a creek, winding through dense trees, the way lit at regular intervals by overhead lamps.

"It looks so different here at night," Wren observed. "You do know where you're going, right?"

"Uh-huh. I spent many hours here in my youth."

"Oh, you grew up here? You're a native?"

"Yeah. My sister and I used to hang out here after school waiting for our mom to get off work. She was a school bus driver. When we were in grammar school, we rode the route with her mornings and afternoons. In high school we waited here, playing soccer with other kids or reading under a tree or whatever. I know this place like my own yard. I know all the secret spots."

They crossed a wooden bridge over the creek.

"What are all these secret spots you know about?" Wren prodded.

Sophie laughed quietly, as if to herself. "I've got to admit, most of my secret spots are well known to every high schooler."

"Oh, it's like that. Make-out places."

Sophie's expression was slightly embarrassed. "Mostly, yeah."

They passed a small duck pond where a young couple sat on a bench on the far side, kissing. Wren wondered if Sophie had brought her here to suggest romance. Or was this just her shortcut to the hot dog place? Sophie wasn't easy to read.

A few minutes after emerging from the park, they were seated at a small round table with sheets of waxed paper for plates and two regular hot dogs with mustard. The lemonade was freshly squeezed and surprisingly good. The hot dogs were also good and just right for the occasion. Wren and Sophie sat smiling at one another across the table.

She seems strangely tense, Wren thought, as if she knows I'm wondering what it would be like to kiss her.

A streak of mustard squirted out of Sophie's bun as she took a bite, smearing yellow along the side of her mouth. She put down the hot dog and wiped her face with her napkin, laughing nervously. "What are you doing in Ashland?" she asked, wadding the napkin in her hand.

"Visiting my brother. Came to cheer him on. I live in San Francisco."

"Oh. That's a beautiful city. I've been there a few times on business." Sophie wrapped her long fingers around her lemonade glass. "I used to live in L.A. Worked at putting other people's money to work. I moved back here two years ago. Not here in Ashland, but nearby. On a farm, a dairy of sorts."

"A farm? Cool. I've always lived in the city, but I've always thought I had a farm girl in me somewhere. Really satisfying kind of life, I imagine."

Wren took a sip of lemonade, amused by Sophie's apparent discomfort. She fidgeted with her napkin, tearing the edge of it between her thumb and forefinger. Wren took this as a good sign. If Sophie was nervous, she must be interested. Wren was unquestionably interested. She wasn't thinking beyond that. She just knew she liked to look at Sophie and listen to her voice. She liked her face and the way her mouth went completely thin and straight when she was contemplating a thought. Her lips were expressive, especially when she wasn't speaking. They had a multitude of postures. Wren was certain she hadn't yet seen them all. Sophie wasn't a chatterer by any means. Wren had to prompt her with questions. She seemed contemplative and naturally reticent.

"What drove you to come back?" Wren asked.

"It just all got to be too much. Too much pressure. Too much hypocrisy. Just a lot of bullshit, really."

Wren decided there was a heartbreak in there somewhere.

"No bullshit on the farm?" she asked, suppressing a smile.

"No." Sophie's look of appreciation proved that she got the joke. "No bulls or even cows. It's not that kind of dairy. Goats. There are six producing does and one kid. I make goat cheese."

"No kidding! Commercially?"

"Yes." Sophie laughed lightly in a self-deprecating way. "Just small batches by hand. *Handcrafted* as they say on the menus. I sell it to restaurants. Sprouts, for instance."

"You just get more and more interesting," Wren said with honest admiration. "A goat farmer."

With that thought, an image of Little Bo Peep entered Wren's mind and she nearly choked on the last bite of her hot dog. She took a drink of lemonade, trying to wash away the image. Sophie looked nothing like Bo Peep. She was an attractive, smart, interesting...goatherd. The phrase "freaky flakes" entered her mind. Not fair, she thought. There was nothing freaky or flaky about a goat farm. Artisan cheese was a big business these days. Perfectly legitimate.

Wren anchored her elbow on the table and rested her chin on her hand, adopting what she hoped was a dreamy expression. "'I should leave grazing, were I of your flock, and only live by gazing.'"

Sophie giggled and blushed, a reaction that delighted Wren, but she quickly adopted a sterner expression and quipped, "Then you'd starve to death. And, frankly, you seem to have a healthy appetite."

Wren smiled and stirred her lemonade with her straw. "What kind of living does a goatherd make these days? Is it profitable with such a small herd?"

"It's just a hobby right now. I made some good investments before and that's enough to live on. Cheesemaking is still new. But I'm having fun with it. The goats are so cute and playful. And the cheese, it's a science and an art. It gives me a creative outlet."

"What kind do you make?" Wren leaned back and crossed her legs, watching Sophie's embarrassed smile, an entirely charming expression.

"French style. I haven't gotten into the aged cheeses at all. Maybe, eventually, I'll try feta. I'm still experimenting. I don't even have a label yet."

"But you're going to keep at it?"

"I think so, yes."

"What type of goats do you have?"

"Nubians."

Wren nodded. "Their milk has a higher butterfat content than most other dairy goats. Makes a rich cheese." She drained the last of the lemonade in her cup. "Do you use bovine rennet or a vegetable enzyme?"

Sophie looked so surprised that she balked for a second

before answering. "Vegetable enzyme. Ellie would insist on that, even if I didn't. No added animal protein."

Wren realized that in her enthusiasm for the subject, she had gotten a little close to revealing her own expertise.

"How do you know so much about cheese?" Sophie asked.

Wren laughed, trying to sound nonchalant. "Oh, I love cheese! I've even tried making mozzarella a couple of times. Just for fun, you know. Nothing serious."

Sophie watched Wren silently before asking, "What do you do?"

Wren fell back on her standard cover story, something that usually didn't generate much interest and worked well for her because in reality it was her sister Robin's job. "I'm a real estate agent with the Touchstone Agency."

"In San Francisco?"

"Yes. Things have been slow the last few years. It's not as good a job as it once was."

"I can imagine. Do you like it?"

"Sometimes more than others. It has its moments."

Wren didn't enjoy lying to Sophie, but they were strangers and she was an unknown factor. The effectiveness of her job depended on its secrecy. It was just the way things were. Over the past few years, there had been many times she'd thanked herself for keeping this secret from a date.

"Summer isn't the best time to take a vacation from real estate, is it?" Sophie asked.

"No, you're right. It's the busy season, but this was such a special thing. Raven's big break, you know. I wanted to be here for him."

"You two are close, aren't you?"

"Yes. We are. Always have been."

"Is it true what they say, that twins have some kind of psychic connection? Like you can read each other's minds?"

"Totally true. If I focus hard, I can see what he's up to in my mind. For instance, right now—" She squinted in a show of serious concentration. "He's half drunk on merlot, eating mini tacos, and singing a round of 'Sigh no more, ladies' with his actor chums."

"You can see that?" Sophie's mouth fell open in astonishment.

Wren chuckled. "I'm kidding."

"Good! I'd hate to think he could also see everything you're doing." She reddened a little. "I mean, like, uh..."

Wren laughed and decided to rescue her from completing her sentence. "You mentioned a sister. Does she live around here?"

"Arizona. She's divorced and living with a guy named Hank who milks rattlesnakes to supplement his disability check." Sophie rolled her eyes. "He's got some kind of back problem."

"You don't like him?"

"Honestly, I've never met the dude. I haven't even seen Dena for two years. We don't have that much in common."

Sophie looked irritated with herself as she wadded up her shredded napkin and tucked it deliberately under the edge of her waxed paper as if to put it out of reach of her nervous fingers. Then she let her hand rest on the table and gazed at Wren, her face assuming an expression of satisfaction, her blue-gray eyes lingering on Wren's mouth.

Wren slid her hand on top of Sophie's where it lay on the table, clasping their fingers together. They looked into one another's eyes silently, communicating their mutual attraction. Wren then noticed the clerk leaning against a wall, looking impatient, and realized they were the only patrons left in the place. She took her hand back and nodded toward the teenage boy.

"I think he's waiting for us to leave," she said.

A few moments later, they were on the sidewalk in the cool night air. It was late and silent except for the muffled sounds of a television from a nearby bar.

"My hotel's right there," Sophie said, pointing across the street.

"Your hotel? How far away is this goat farm?"

"Not far. I've got a delivery in the morning, so I decided to stay and have a mini-vacation. I'm glad I did. I had a great time tonight."

Wren looked deep into Sophie's eyes. "Me too."

"How will you get home? Should I drive you?"

"I'll walk over to the theater. Raven will still be there.

Opening night party. He won't be ready to go home for a while yet."

Sophie nodded. "All right. Thanks for the company."

"Sure." Wren felt nervous now too, but summoned her courage. "Do you think I could see you again? Can I have your phone number or something?"

They stood facing one another on the abandoned sidewalk. Sophie's expression was unreadable, passive. For a moment Wren thought she'd made a blunder. She realized she'd never even asked Sophie if she was gay and she'd never told her she was either. Maybe her request for a second date had been a surprise. But that wasn't possible, Wren told herself, not after the sexual tension evident between them all evening. No way she wasn't both gay and interested. But there were all kinds of possible unknowns here. Sophie could have a hundred reasons for not wanting to see her again. Maybe she was seeing someone else and a flirtatious chat over a hot dog was all she could allow herself.

"I know we just met," Wren said, trying to overcome the awkward silence, "but I feel…something. I've been feeling it all day. I thought you might be feeling it too and maybe you'd like to see where it takes us."

Wren was taken off guard as Sophie put a hand to her face, curling her long fingers behind her ear, then leaned in and kissed her. Suddenly her very expressive mouth was taking possession of Wren's, sending desire coursing through her. Wren wrapped her arms around Sophie's neck and returned the kiss, exploring her warm and generous mouth as their bodies pressed closer together. Wren let herself get lost in the sensations of Sophie's mouth and arms until the sound of a slamming door forced them apart.

It was the hot dog clerk, leaving for the night. He stood outside the door in the light of a streetlamp, turning his key in the lock. He then looked their way and muttered, "Get a room," before turning and walking in the opposite direction.

Wren turned back to Sophie, whose mouth was pressed into an uncomfortable smile.

"I already have a room," she laughed. "Do you want to come in?" She sounded a little surprised at her own question.

CHAPTER NINE

I'll make my heaven in a lady's lap,
And deck my body in gay ornaments,
And 'witch sweet ladies with my words and looks.

—*Henry VI*, Part III

Sophie fumbled with her key card, inserting it upside down and then backward before realizing her hand was shaking so much she could no longer get the card in the slot. *Calm down, you idiot*, she told herself.

Wren reached over and slipped the card from her hand, standing close beside her, so close Sophie could feel the heat from her body. She calmly slid the card in its slot and pushed open the door.

On the walk across the street, Sophie kept asking herself what she thought she was doing, picking up a stranger. She had never done anything like this and didn't believe she was doing it now. Even kissing her, which had happened almost without her conscious knowledge, had been strange and terrifying, but totally wonderful. She had obviously lost her mind.

The fact that Wren was so calm only made her more nervous. Was this so routine for her? As Sophie stepped into her room, she decided she was making a horrible mistake. She'd make up some story, some excuse to get Wren to leave. Like she didn't feel well. Or she had a jealous girlfriend, the murderous type. Or maybe *she* was the murderous type. She wasn't sure how she could convey that, short of standing over Wren holding a butcher knife or something equally bizarre. *No, no!* Sophie said to herself. You don't have to go quite that far. Just tell her to leave, politely. She'll appreciate the honesty of a simple request, an admission that you had a momentary loss of sanity and have now recovered, nearly recovered. Recovered enough to know this was a big mistake!

After switching on the entry light, Wren stood facing her and took hold of both her hands. "What can I do to make you more relaxed?"

Sophie swallowed hard. "Leave." Then she laughed a laugh that sounded nothing like herself.

"Seriously?" Wren asked, looking puzzled.

Sophie shook her head, completely disarmed by Wren's beautiful, defenseless looking mouth. "No. No." She squeezed Wren's fingers reassuringly. "I don't want you to leave."

"I'm glad to hear it. I don't want to leave."

Wren's voice and expression were so composed, so unruffled. How could she be so at ease? Maybe *she's* the ax murderer, Sophie considered, then felt like kicking herself.

"Do you want me to call room service?" Sophie asked, pulling her hands away. "Do you want anything?"

Wren's eyes held her like a tractor beam. "Only you," she cooed.

Sophie was ecstatic that the little scream of terror she heard in her head didn't actually come out of her throat. She didn't know why she was so jumpy except that Wren was so sexy and she wanted her so badly. That wasn't how things usually went, not even back in the days when she was dating, years and years ago. She normally took things very slowly. What was happening here was scary. But also exciting and intense. A charming, adorable woman was looking lustfully into her eyes. It was like a fantasy, many fantasies of beautiful, ardent strangers who swept in from nowhere, gave only pleasure, then swept out again, owed and owing nothing.

Wren removed her jacket and tossed it on a chair, revealing those lovely shoulders and arms. "You have been with a woman before, haven't you?" she asked, sounding concerned.

"Oh, sure! Hundreds of times."

Wren made a peculiar, surprised-sounding peep as her mouth fell open.

Oh, God! Did I actually say that? "I mean, yes," Sophie rushed to clarify. "I'm exclusively into women. I'm sorry I'm behaving like an idiot. I'm just nervous. You and I...we've just met."

"I feel like I know you." Wren stepped closer, then reached up to caress Sophie's cheek. "I felt that way from the moment I first saw you."

Sophie felt her body going limp as Wren's fingers brushed her lips. There was something very special about this delicious woman, about the power she had over Sophie's body. Or was it just that it had been so long? Two years was a ridiculously long time.

Wren's eyes were dark, deep, pulling her in.

Sophie took hold of Wren's shoulders and pulled her tightly against her and their mouths came together hungrily. As they kissed, Sophie's nervousness dissipated almost instantly. In its place, a tremendous yearning grew, spreading through her limbs, making her fingertips tingle. She ached all over with desire.

She drew Wren to the bed where they lay together, kissing deeper and deeper while their hands caressed each other through and under their clothes. Sophie felt the smooth muscles of Wren's stomach and the firm little breasts pressing into her palms, begging for attention.

Wren rolled on top of her, lying between her legs while Sophie's arms held her tight and her hips pushed up against her urgently. Wren's hand slid down the front of her jeans, between her legs, feeling her through the fabric. Sophie knew the material must be soaked by now. She was on fire and aching in every nerve to be touched in the one spot she could find relief. She reached between them to unzip her jeans and helped Wren pull them off, then lifted her hips as the panties followed.

Wren lay close to her side, her hand sliding over that critical spot with a serious intensity that matched Sophie's insistent need. It was feverish, frenzied and over quickly with a final upward drive of her hips and a sharp cry of release. Then she lay back, breathing hard, astonished that it had happened so quickly.

Wren moved closer to her face and kissed her neck softly. "Not so nervous now?"

"No," Sophie said quietly. "Not nervous at all."

She turned to look at Wren in the dim light cast from the single bulb in the entryway. Her face looked sweet and tranquil. She was still fully clothed. Even her stylish sandals were still on. Sophie started laughing.

"What are you laughing at?" Wren asked.

Sophie looked up at the ceiling. "Nothing. I mean, just this. Nothing like rushing into it."

Wren laughed too, then said, "I enjoyed your enthusiasm. Immensely. You're a very passionate woman."

Maybe just desperate, Sophie thought.

"The passionate goatherd," Wren said playfully. "Sounds like a pastoral poem."

Sophie laughed again, feeling suddenly very comfortable with Wren. And very tender toward her as well. She turned on her side and drew her close, kissing her gently. Her mouth felt so wonderfully soft and luxurious.

They continued kissing as desire grew between them again. Sophie's hands explored Wren's body, slowly pulling the shirt over her head, undoing the zipper on her pants, and leisurely removing her clothes piece by piece until they lay side by side, naked in one another's arms, hanging on the verge of another urgent, ecstatic freefall.

CHAPTER TEN

Full fathom five thy father lies;
Of his bones are coral made;
Those are pearls that were his eyes.

—*The Tempest* Act I, Scene 2

Sophie arrived at Sprouts early, so early that the restaurant wasn't open and she had to use the back door. Johanna was alone in the kitchen, prepping vegetables.

"Hello, Johanna!" Sophie called cheerfully.

Johanna waved her knife in Sophie's direction without looking up from her board.

Hearing voices in the front, she went through the restaurant where Ellie and Katrina Olafssen were standing at the coffee bar beside a large basket of freshly baked aebleskiver.

"Good morning!" Sophie shouted to Ellie and Katrina. Then she went up to Katrina and gave her a hearty hug, pressing the little woman's cheek against hers. Katrina was a petite woman in her sixties. She had a lined face and tiny round eyes all crinkled around the edges as if she were perpetually straining to see something. Her reddish-gray hair was twisted into two braids that were wrapped together into a bun. She always wore a long drab skirt of heavy cotton and a white, long-sleeved blouse with lace at the cuffs and collar. Her getup was vaguely European, but also from some bygone era. She looked more like an anachronism than a foreigner.

Sophie poured herself a large coffee and took one of the delicate spherical pastries in a paper napkin. She dipped it in a dish of strawberry jam and took a bite.

"So good," she breathed. "You're a magician, Katrina!"

"Not magic," she answered in her light, heavily accented voice. "Just a good family recipe from the old country. Ja, I never changed a thing."

"And you never should," Ellie said firmly, taking one of the pastries for herself.

"Put six of those in a bag for me to take home, Ellie," Sophie instructed.

"For your mama?" Katrina asked.

Sophie nodded, licking powdered sugar from her lips.

"Your mama knows a good aebleskiver when she tastes one."

"I'm going out on a limb," Sophie laughed, "to say yours are the only ones she's ever had. Even so, I guess she does know a good one when she tastes it. And so do I."

"You're a sweet girl, Sophie. When you see my Klaus today, tell him to call me. I need him to bring another big bag of flour. I can't carry those anymore, not the big bags."

"I'll tell him," Sophie assured her.

"He's so strong, that one. He can carry two of those bags, one in each arm. He's a good boy."

"Yes," Sophie agreed, "he is." She put the last of the pastry in her mouth.

Katrina patted her arm and grinned meaningfully at her. "I'm glad you think so." Then she let out a little chortle and scurried toward the front door. "Tell your mama hi for me. Bye, Ellie."

With a tinkle of the bell on the front door, Katrina was gone. Sophie washed down her pastry with coffee while Ellie filled a white paper bag for her.

"What was that about?" Ellie asked. "That whole grin-and-tickle show?"

"Oh, she's got it in her head Klaus and I might make a nice couple."

Ellie's eyes opened wide. "What? Where'd she get that idea?"

"I think maybe she got it from Klaus."

"Uh-oh." Ellie rolled the top of the sack down and handed it to Sophie.

"It's been going on a while now," Sophie explained. "The little hints that he's working up the courage to ask me out. I've just been ignoring it, pretending not to notice."

Ellie shook her head. "You should put a stop to that before he gets hurt."

"I know. I will. But, you know, my mother likes Klaus. She may be encouraging him."

Ellie fell into a chair and stared. "Your mother? My God, Sophie, what's going on? How can she think you'd be interested in Klaus after Jan. I mean, she knew about Jan, right? That you had a very serious relationship?"

Sophie bit her bottom lip before saying, "She knew about Jan. But she never met her. In the beginning, I told her about Jan in a Christmas letter. You know how it was. I wasn't on good terms with my mother for years. There wasn't a lot of communication. When she read the letter, she assumed Jan was actually a Yahn."

"Yahn?" Ellie wrinkled up her nose.

"A man with a Scandinavian name. That's how they pronounce it. I didn't even know that's what she thought at the time. Here I thought I was coming out to her and she thought I was dating a Norwegian."

Ellie burst into honking laughs. "That's too funny!"

"It didn't seem so funny when I finally caught on."

"Since you've been back home, you haven't explained it to her?"

Sophie shrugged. "It just didn't seem to matter anymore. Jan's out of my life and nobody else is in it. It just hasn't come up."

Ellie put her hand over her mouth, trying to hide her grin. "Sorry," she said, removing her hand. "You've got to tell her. You've got to tell all of them."

"I will. I will. I don't want to hurt Klaus. I'm fond of him, like a brother."

"Right. And Katrina too." Ellie pointed an accusing finger. "You don't want to have her getting carried away with something that isn't ever going to happen. She's had enough heartache in her life."

"What do you mean?"

Ellie turned serious. "You don't know her story? The shipwreck?"

Sophie shook her head. "Klaus never mentioned anything about a shipwreck." She sat in a chair next to Ellie. "Tell me."

Ellie settled into her chair with her hands on her knees. "Katrina and her husband immigrated from Denmark and settled in Washington State near the coast. They had twin boys, Klaus and Eric. They looked so much alike as infants, Katrina stitched their initials on all their clothes so she could tell them apart." Ellie's face grew even more serious. "When the boys were two, the family went out in their fishing boat. A storm came up, and as they tried to make it back to the harbor, their boat was driven onto the rocks. Demolished the boat completely. Katrina managed to grab Klaus. They floated on a scrap of the hull to dry land and were rescued later that day by the Coast Guard. They were the only two to survive. Two days later, Katrina's husband's body washed ashore. Little Eric was never found."

"That's terrible!" Sophie observed, her thoughts turning to her friend Klaus.

"Yes, terrible." Ellie shook her head. "Katrina moved here with Klaus. She couldn't bear to live by the ocean anymore after what happened."

"I don't blame her," Sophie said. "Klaus has always seemed a little sad to me." She thought about Wren and Raven and how much they seemed to enjoy one another's company, how close they were. "Twins seem to have a closer bond than other siblings. I wonder if he feels that loss, like something's missing, even though he was too young to remember when it happened."

"I don't know, but Katrina certainly feels it. So don't you give her any more grief." Ellie slapped Sophie's knee as she got to her feet.

"No," Sophie said quietly, "I'll have a talk with Klaus, explain things to him."

"I'm sorry I've brought you down. You were in such a good mood when you came in."

Sophie brightened, thinking of Wren, who was probably still sleeping in their hotel room, her sweet face pressed into the pillow, her bangs pasted to her forehead. That was the last image Sophie had of her.

"Why *were* you in such a good mood?" Ellie asked, taking Sophie's coffee cup for a refill.

Sophie sighed deeply, recalling a line from *Richard III.* "'The sweetest sleep, and fairest-boding dreams that ever entered in a drowsy head, have I since your departure had.'"

Ellie spun around and pointed to her *No Shakespeare!* sign.

"Sometimes poetry is the only way to say it," Sophie said, apologetically.

Ellie stood with the empty cup dangling from her index finger. "Sweetest sleep, huh?" She looked suddenly enlightened. "You had a date!"

Sophie grinned and nodded.

Ellie planted herself back in her chair and leaned closer. "Tell me all about it."

"I might tell you a little about it," Sophie teased, "if you get me another cup of coffee."

Ellie was back on her feet instantly. Sophie wanted to tell her because Ellie was the only person she could tell. She wouldn't tell her everything, not even Wren's name, but she would tell her how uncharacteristically impulsive she'd been, how good it had turned out, how happy she'd felt this morning waking up beside that beautiful woman. And Ellie would be thrilled for her and impressed by her bold night of passion.

Then Ellie would ask her the obvious question: *Are you going to see her again?*

And Sophie would say she didn't think so. She'd say it was just one of those brief encounters, two strangers whose lives intersected for a few hours before they parted and went their own separate ways again. *Wasn't that what it was?* No expectations, no demands. Sophie had understood that and had done her best to play by those rules. Wren was on vacation, had been looking for a good time. And they'd had a good time. A very good time.

Then why, she wondered, was she starting to feel sad about it?

CHAPTER ELEVEN

Go to your bosom;
Knock there, and ask your heart what it doth know….

—*Measure for Measure*, Act II, Scene 2

It was late in the morning before Wren woke. When she opened her eyes, she saw she was alone in the bed. Maybe Sophie was in the bathroom or had gone out to bring back breakfast. She lay on her back, feeling spent and satisfied in a way she hadn't felt in a long time. She glanced at the clock. It was ten. Later than she had imagined. Then she saw a note on the pillow beside her and raised herself on her elbow to read it.

Sweet Wren, I had to make a morning appointment. I decided to let you sleep. After all, you worked very hard last night. I'll check out, so all you have to do is be out before noon. Thank you so much for an incredible night. Sophie.

So she was gone? Wren lay back on the pillow and closed her eyes, picturing Sophie, her graceful hands, her penetrating eyes, her smooth, gorgeous, emphatic hips. What an alluring woman. What a wonderful night! Apparently, that was all Sophie had wanted. She'd left no phone number. No mention of getting together again. Surprising, but probably best. Wren was only in town for two more weeks. Besides, as she'd told Raven, she wasn't interested in a relationship any time soon. No. This was perfect, she told herself firmly. One perfect, sublimely satisfying night.

She reached for her phone to read a text from Raven. It was simply a series of three exclamation marks. That was his response to the text she'd sent him last night during a private moment: *U won't C me 2nite.*

Eventually, she was able to rouse herself from the bed, take a shower and leave the hotel. She felt so energetic, she decided to walk home, enjoying the mild, clear morning. It was Saturday and people were crowding the downtown sidewalks already. She could hear the sound of rock music somewhere in the distance. She passed three young men sitting against a brick wall in the shade, sharing a joint. The pungent smell of marijuana hit her nostrils briefly and was gone as she kept a brisk pace. As she left downtown, entering a residential neighborhood, she saw fewer people. The street was peaceful. Some homeowners were doing yard work before the day got hot. Two cats, a gray tabby and a tortoiseshell, slept atop fence posts on either side of a garden gate, looking like mismatched post toppers. As she turned a corner, she entered a neighborhood of older homes, mostly restored Victorians like the one she was staying in. Their colors were cheerful—yellow, turquoise, lavender, mint green. These reminded her of Pacific Heights in San Francisco, splendid old houses lovingly cared for, beautifully detailed and extravagantly expensive. Here, she imagined, they were significantly more affordable, but no less charming.

This town, she noted again, was thoroughly delightful, such a bright mix of qualities, small but not small-minded.

She turned down another street and approached the house Kyle and Raven were renting, a three-story, green and blue Victorian with a round tower on the right-hand side, topped with a steepled roof. The entire façade of the house was crowded with tall, narrow windows. She skipped up the front steps between concrete posts and railings to the double doors with their etched glass ovals, taking a deep, floral-scented breath as she passed the rose bushes flanking the porch.

The boys were in the sunroom at the back of the house, having coffee, looking like they had risen late as well and were in no hurry to start the day. Though it was noon, Kyle wasn't yet dressed. He wore only a pair of white cotton sweatpants, his feet and chest bare. He was a well-cut man, Wren noticed, admiring his muscled abdomen. His striking black hair was perfectly tamed, as always, cut short on the sides and longer on top. She hadn't yet seen him with a hair out of place and had the impression he rose up from his pillow each morning looking just so. His long, thin nose gave his face an air of distinction. His family came from Italy and his complexion reflected his heritage. He had thick black eyebrows and dark eyes, and there was something emphatically European about him.

Raven wore a T-shirt and shorts and was sprawled across a white wicker chair. The sun poured in through the south-facing wall of windows, lighting this scene, like something from a Grecian urn: two smug, self-adoring young gods, flush with virility, lounging in paradise.

"Ah!" Raven cawed as Wren entered the room. "Look who's finally turned up, our merry wanderer of the night."

"You look like you had a wonderful time," Kyle observed. "You're beaming."

"I did," Wren said, throwing herself on a sofa. "Sorry I didn't make your party, Raven."

"You obviously had a party of your own to go to." Raven sat up. "Who was she?"

"Her name is Sophie Ward. She's a farmer." She poured herself a cup of coffee from the pot on the table.

"Farmer?" Kyle asked.

"Yes. A woman of the earth. A local girl."

"Ah, look how she blushes," Kyle announced, pointing accusingly at Wren.

Raven leaned forward to stare at her sternly and adopted his stage voice. "'Would you not swear, all you that see her, that she were a maid, by these exterior shows? But she is none:

she knows the heat of a luxurious bed: her blush is guilt, not modesty.'"

"Yeah, yeah," Wren said dismissively.

"So your girlfriend is from here," Kyle remarked. "A small-town girl."

"Not in the sense you mean. She lived in L.A. for ten years. Worked in finance. I get the impression she was very successful there, but she longed to return to the simpler life, so she came back."

"Seems you had plenty of time for conversation," Kyle said. "Is that what you did all night? Talk?"

Wren gave him an indulgent smile. "Hardly. Actually, she's not much of a talker, but she's a very good listener." She thought back over the night's conversation and realized she'd prattled on and on and had come away knowing very little about Sophie Ward. Was that deliberate, she wondered, or just natural reticence?

Raven flitted over and sat beside her on the couch. "Is my sister in love?" he asked, looking hopeful.

"After one night?" She laughed shortly, then took a swallow from her mug.

"As we've already established," he said, "women fall in love with anybody who can give them an orgasm."

"Or several," corrected Wren.

Raven clamped a hand over his mouth in mock offense, then glanced at Kyle with a bawdy expression of wonder.

"But that's simply not true," she stated flatly.

"When can we meet her?" Raven asked.

"She was in town just for the night. Gone back to her farm today."

"She's really a farmer?" Kyle asked.

"A goatherd, more accurately. She raises goats and makes cheese."

"So you have some foodie thing in common," noted Raven. "When will you see her again?"

Wren shrugged. "I don't know that I will. She didn't give me her phone number. I think it was just one of those things, you know? Two passionate strangers taking solace in one another's company."

Raven sputtered. "Oh, come on!"

"I know you don't think women are capable of it, but we had a fantastic night and that's that." Raven looked skeptical. "Seriously," Wren insisted. "Two ships passing in the night, sailing in opposite directions, never to cross paths again. A brief, enchanting encounter, whole and satisfying unto itself. No strings. No promises to keep. No regrets."

Raven turned to Kyle. "The lady doth protest too much, methinks."

Kyle nodded thoughtfully.

"It wasn't that blonde you were checking out at Sprouts, was it?" Raven asked, narrowing his eyes at her. "The chick I gave the ticket to."

Wren regarded him levelly and didn't answer.

Raven jumped up with a high-pitched hoot of triumph. "It *was* her." He sat back down and patted her foot impatiently. "What'd she say about the play?"

Wren rolled her eyes. "I should have known you'd manage to make it about you."

"What'd she say?" he persisted.

"She said she liked it. She said you were wonderful."

His face broke into a happy smile.

"I'm glad you had a good time," Kyle said, standing and hitching up his pants. To Raven, he said, "Hon, you need to get going. Matinee today."

"You're right," Raven said. He leaned over to give Wren a kiss on the cheek. "I'll leave you in Kyle's capable hands."

"I need to write a review for next week's column," said Wren. "Kyle can squire me about town to all the trendy spots."

"I can be your cover," Kyle said, looking thrilled. "We'll pose as a dashing young hetero couple."

"Can you pull that off?"

"I can." He lowered his voice. "I'll butch it up for you. I'll be a ladies' man."

Raven squealed and flung his arms around Kyle. "Oh, this does sound fun! I wish I could play."

When Raven and Kyle had gone, Wren lay back on the sofa and closed her eyes, remembering the incredible sensations of her night with Sophie. She knew it was going to take a while to come down from this high and she was in no hurry.

Now that she was alone with her thoughts, she reflected on Sophie's morning note. It was a very impersonal way to leave things, to walk out like that without saying goodbye or going to breakfast together or…anything. For some reason, Sophie wanted to make sure Wren understood it was just the one night, that it ended right there. It was unexpectedly cool, coming from a woman who had seemed so warm, nurturing and passionate.

I'm a big girl, Wren told herself. Emotionally mature. I can do this.

She *had* done it, she corrected herself. It was over.

She took a sip of her coffee, then began to wonder if Sophie was still in town or if she was back on the farm. She wondered what her life was like there with her goats, if she was lonely, if she would be happily surprised and ardently enthusiastic if Wren were to show up there uninvited. Or was it possible she really was content with just the one night? Certainly it was possible, if she could believe her own argument, that women were capable of being satisfied with a one-night stand, that a woman didn't have to follow some ridiculous imperative of nature that dictated she had to fall in love with anyone who gave her an orgasm. Or several.

That was a laughable idea in this day and age, and thoroughly without merit. She had had many an orgasm in her life with women she hadn't been in love with. A few, anyway. It was just like a man to equate sex with love. If she were to fall in love with Sophie, or any woman, for that matter, it would have nothing to do with orgasms. It would be because of her character, her personality, the things they had in common.

She leaned heavily into the cradling arm of the couch, summoning up an image of Sophie. If Wren were to fall in love, it would be because of the inexplicable pull of that other woman's gaze. Or the crease on the left side of her mouth when she smiled without parting her lips. Or the hesitation in her laugh when she was uncertain it was okay to find something funny. Or the relaxed, melodious rhythm of her speech that sounded like an oboe concerto when you lay drowsily in her arms with your eyes closed. It would be because of these and many other genuine mysteries that were thoroughly captivating about this one woman. There was no way to explain it, why one woman's earlobe was so much more remarkable than every other woman's earlobe. Or why her kiss sent you spinning and another's left you cold. No, there was no easy explanation for falling in love, but Wren knew well that the compelling mixture of emotions she felt toward Sophie had started manifesting themselves twenty-four hours earlier outside the theater when they had first looked into one another's eyes, long before they had ever touched.

CHAPTER TWELVE

Truly, shepherd, in respect of itself, it is a good life;
but in respect that it is a shepherd's life, it is naught. In respect
that it is solitary, I like it very well;
but in respect that it is private, it is a very vile life.

—*As You Like It*, Act III, Scene 2

Before her foot touched ground, Sophie heard the bleating of goats. Not the calm and sporadic comments they made to one another during a typical summer day, but urgent and distressed calls of alarm. She leapt out of the pickup and ran toward the goat pen as fast as she could, finding all the goats gathered around Tater, the little tan one, who stood with her head wedged between two runners of the fence, bellowing at the top of her lungs.

Tallulah, whom Olivia often called Chatterbox, started prattling at Sophie nonstop, as if explaining what had happened. She shook her head vigorously, making her long ears fly up and smack the top of her head. She could make dozens of different sounds, combining grunts, squeaks and brays into a language unique to her. Sophie was certain she thought she was the translator for the herd.

"Okay," Sophie said, in a soothing voice, "Everybody calm down."

She approached the fence, glancing around the yard and seeing no sign of her mother. As their gazes met, Tater stopped bleating, but her eyes remained terror-stricken. Sophie lay a gentle hand on her head, then entered the pen and straddled her, taking hold of her head in both hands and twisting it enough to angle her out between the boards. As soon as she was free, Tater hopped twice, then took off running full tilt to the other side of the pen.

Sophie laughed as Tater celebrated her freedom. Twopenny came up and butted gently against Sophie's knees, so she gave her a scratch behind the ears before exiting the pen. She left the gate open, allowing the goats to wander into the yard.

"There you go, kids," she joked. "Cut the lawn for me."

Poppy, the little black and white kid, followed her mother Rose out of the pen and over to the house where the green grass beckoned. The only goat born here, Poppy was as likely to follow Olivia or Sophie around as Rose. She seemed to consider them all her mother equally, which was hardly surprising, since Olivia often took the little kid inside the house and sat her on the furniture or her lap like a cat. It was her little joke that Poppy's first word, directed at Olivia, had been "Maa-Maa."

Sophie heard the sound of a horse galloping. Gambit, their chestnut gelding, raced in from the east, slowing to a trot as he neared the goat pen. Olivia was on his back, her hair loose and wild, the color of wood-fire smoke. She reined him in a few feet away. He was a midsized horse with plenty of spirit, intensely devoted to Olivia, the only rider he would take without a fuss. His fussiness was gradually diminishing in Sophie's case. She could now induce him to take the bit without much arguing if she preceded it with a sugar cube or piece of fruit.

"You're back," Olivia said, holding the reins slack in her hand. Tall and thin, she sat up straight in the saddle. She wore jeans, boots and a sleeveless blouse that displayed her browned, well-toned arms.

Twenty years from now, Sophie expected herself to look nearly identical to how her mother looked now. She was a tough, capable woman. Before the stroke, she'd had no trouble running this place by herself. She'd lived alone here since Sophie had left over ten years ago and seemed perfectly content to do so.

"Tater got her head stuck in the fence," Sophie reported.

"Silly fool." Olivia stood up in the saddle and swung her leg over to dismount. "It's always something with her. At least she didn't get herself stuck on the roof again."

Sophie laughed, remembering having to rescue a terrified Tater from the roof of the house a couple months earlier. After that, they'd had to move the wood pile away from the house to make sure it didn't happen again.

"How many orders did you get?" her mother asked.

"Five. I think the sage is going to be popular. People seem to like it."

"I like my cheese plain," Olivia said flatly.

"Yes, I know, but foodies are always looking for a thrill. A new color of carrot or a new flavor of chêvre."

"People are funny. A purple carrot tastes the same as an orange one. Did you know that?"

"I don't think I've ever had a purple carrot."

"I have."

"It would be pretty," reflected Sophie, "a medley of purple and orange carrots."

Olivia nodded. "Yes, they're pretty, like your lavender sprig on the top of the cheese. Like a pressed flower. That's why people like it, don't you think? Because it's pretty."

Sophie nodded and patted Gambit's velvety snout. "I brought you a little treat, Mom. I'll get it out of the truck."

"Aebleskiver?" Olivia's face lit up.

"Just baked this morning."

"I'll put Gambit away and go make a fresh pot of coffee."

Sophie ran to the pickup to get her bag of pastries. She found her mother in the kitchen taking mugs out of the cupboard, Poppy at her heels, while the coffee sputtered. As usual, she took the yellow mug down for herself, the one with a cartoon bus on it and the words, "World's Best Bus Driver" inscribed in blue. One of her long-time passengers had given her that years ago and it remained her favorite. That was the sort of gift the kids gave to Olivia over the years, and all of them remained as part of the familiar, permanent décor, from the plush school bus pillow in Olivia's rocker to the mustard-colored salt and pepper shakers on their kitchen table. It seemed those had always been here, a bus-shaped holder with smiling children for shakers, a boy for the pepper and a girl for the salt. For this reason, their kitchen was and always had been painted yellow. At her retirement party, the school transportation department had presented her with a bus-shaped cake, a realistic replica of the vehicle she'd driven for over twenty-five years, with the words Ashland School District in dark brown icing and the faces of children in every window.

Getting the coffee, Olivia worked around the huge stainless steel pot on the stove that Sophie used to heat the goat milk before curdling it.

"Here you go," Sophie said, putting the pastries on the table. "I'll be back in after I feed the chickens. Don't eat them all."

"Don't worry. I'll save you one." Olivia grinned. "By the way, Sophie, I'll be going out this afternoon. Warren's coming by to take me kayaking."

"Oh. That makes three weekends in a row." Warren, known as Dr. Connor to Sophie, was Olivia's neurologist. "That man does love kayaking, doesn't he?"

Olivia looked slightly embarrassed. "Yeah, a regular fanatic. It's great fun. Anyway, don't expect me for dinner."

"You won't be on the river that long, will you?"

"No, but people usually go to dinner afterward. There's a nice restaurant right there where we pull out."

"So it's a group of people you're going with?" Sophie asked.

Olivia frowned, as though irritated by Sophie's question. "Lots of people will be out on the river today. Such a nice warm day for it."

"True. I wouldn't mind going myself. You can rent a kayak there where you put in, right?"

"No!" Olivia spun around to face her. "I mean, yes, you can

rent them. But you won't have time for that today. You've got a new batch of cheese to start on."

Sophie nodded. "You're right. Maybe some other time."

She went to the back porch to pull on her rubber boots, then went to the shed to get a coffee can full of chicken feed. The shed smelled of lavender. Several bundles of it hung from the ceiling, drying. With no facility devoted to her cheese-making operation, she made the best of what she had, the house kitchen for making the cheese, the shed for herb storage. Three lavender bushes grew on the property and they had been her inspiration when she expanded beyond the plain chèvre. She kept a few bundles drying here at all times and loved the floral fragrance they imparted to the shed, which had previously smelled, not unpleasantly, of animal feed and straw. A few bundles of drying sage had now joined the lavender above her head. She wondered how many other farmers had such fragrant sheds full of potpourri.

When she stepped into the chicken coop, seven chickens gathered around her feet, clucking excitedly. She poured the feed into their pan and then filled their water dispenser with fresh water as they circled the food pan, pecking intently, two white and four red hens and one rooster. There were five eggs lying on the raised straw beds.

"One of you has taken a break today, I see." She sat on a stool and picked up one of the rust-colored hens, turning her on her back so her yellow feet stuck straight up. In the way of chickens, the hen went still and silent and lay in Sophie's hands like a hunk of wood, one round yellow eye watching her, blinking, but otherwise completely inanimate. This behavior always calmed Sophie. Whether the hen was silent or it clucked softly, as they sometimes did, Sophie felt the tension drain out of her while holding a chicken. After her return to the farm, the chickens had helped her to learn how to relax, slow down and focus her thoughts. The hen's eye was now halfway shut. Sophie began to feel the hypnotic effect of what she thought of as chicken magic. While you were lulling them into this lethargic state, they were doing the same to you.

Her life in L.A. had been frenetic, noisy and tense. For several weeks here she had to have the radio on all the time just for the noise, to drown out her own thoughts. But she had adapted, with the help of the chickens and the goats and the cheese making. Now she didn't mind the quiet. She could even fall asleep at night without the radio, with no sound other than the crickets and frogs. The thoughts in her head weren't disturbing like they had been at first.

Those first few weeks had been torture. She had lain awake in her room feeling like an exile from her life, wondering what Jan was doing and who she was with. In addition to the anxiety and pain of leaving Jan, she had also felt anger, mainly toward her sister Dena who had breezed in while their mother was in the hospital, then breezed out again, saying she had so many things to do, she had to get back to Tucson where Hank wasn't able to manage on his own for long with his bad back. He missed her so, she just couldn't ever leave him for more than a day or two, but she did want to come and make sure Mom was well cared for and to say how happy she was that Sophie was able to come up, which made her feel a lot better about leaving again.

That was how Sophie had been elected, rather than Dena, to stay on and help Olivia through her recovery period.

After a month, Sophie had begun to enter her own recovery period. Being away from Jan helped her see her more clearly, see what a user she was, and how that wasn't going to change, despite the continuous promises, continually broken. She was a chronic liar and a chronic cheat.

The one person Sophie talked to about Jan was Ellie. One day Ellie had said, "My God, Sophie, the whole time you've been telling me about Jan, you've never once said you loved her."

That had brought her up short. Of course she had loved Jan…once. But it had all turned so sour and left her full of anger and resentment. Nothing resembling love. Sophie recalled hearing somewhere that love, simple honest love, can't survive everyday life. Things are always changing. It's just the way of the universe. If it isn't expanding, it's contracting. If a mountain isn't going up, it's coming down. If you aren't falling in love, you're falling out of love.

Sophie looked at the pale yellow skin covering the hen's eye and realized she'd been so cynical back then. Over the last two years, her cynicism had softened, her anger had dissipated. People weren't mountains. They didn't have to obey laws of physics like an inanimate object. People could fall in love and stay in love. Just because it hadn't happened to her, didn't mean it couldn't happen. She was sure of it.

As Olivia's health had improved and she'd assumed more and more of her former chores, Jan had asked, "When are you coming home?" and Sophie had said, "I don't know." After a couple more months, Jan said, "Maybe we should move your stuff out there, if you don't know how long you're going to be." Then, somehow, two years had gone by and Sophie hadn't heard from Jan for quite a while. They never officially broke up. They had dissolved like a sand castle in the surf, sloughing itself off wave by wave until you couldn't tell anything had ever stood there.

Sophie wasn't angry any more. Hope and optimism had returned. She had become herself again. She believed in love again.

She put the hen down. It ruffled its plumage before diving for the feed dish. She wasn't tense today, had no need of chicken magic. She sighed, thinking of Wren, that sweet little bird with her own soothing magic. She wondered how long Wren would be in town. The note she had left her had been hard to write. As she'd sat at the desk in the hotel room writing that note, she could see the bed in the mirror, could see the tousled sheets and the top of Wren's head, her chaotic hair testifying to a boisterous night.

Her note had been calculatingly casual. She had wanted to say more. She had wanted to leave her phone number and ask Wren to call her. She'd wanted to make a demand. At least a request. To corrupt their beautiful night with strings. If Wren had wanted that, she would have asked. At some point in the many hours they lay together talking, there was plenty of opportunity to mention getting together again. But it never came up. Since Wren didn't mention it, Sophie didn't either. Besides, even if Wren were willing to see her again, it probably wasn't a good idea. It would be too easy to get used to her, to fall...under her spell. She thought again about the idea that love couldn't survive everyday life. *Love*, she scoffed. This wasn't about love. This was about sex. And it was marvelous sex, a gift given with no hint of everyday life to spoil it. Be grateful, she chided herself. Be elated!

Sophie rose from the stool, collected the eggs and joined her mother in the house for coffee and aebleskiver.

CHAPTER THIRTEEN

All my fond love thus do I blow to heaven.
'Tis gone.

—*Othello*, Act III, Scene 3

Kyle put an arm around Wren's shoulders as they admired a painting. The gallery owner stood nearby, available but unobtrusive. The watercolor was a vibrant tableau of carnelian tomatoes spilling from a shabby wicker basket, some of them smashed open, their watery seeds soaking into a newspaper. There was nothing "still" about this still life. Tomatoes continued to roll and bump into each other, urging the viewer to thrust out a hand to catch them before they escaped the edge of the frame. In a literal sense, it was the scene of an accident. Even so, to Wren it was more like a luxurious opportunity. She could tell the tomatoes were ripe, just picked, skins taut, unspoiled by refrigeration, bursting with lusciousness. Now that they had ruptured, they had to be eaten, immediately, and there could be no doubt that was a fortunate turn of events.

Wren admired an artist who could capture the desirability of a piece of fruit.

"Do you want it?" Kyle asked, his black hair shining metallic blue under the gallery lights.

"I think I do."

He nodded toward the owner and pointed at the painting. "My wife would like that one."

The man's mouth turned up into a generous smile, then he stepped forward and reached for the print, lifting it from its hanger. As he took it in the back to wrap it, Wren turned to Kyle and asked, "My wife?"

"I told you I could pull it off." He set his lips smugly.

"I hope that means you're going to buy it for me."

He took his arm from her shoulders. "Let's not get crazy."

"That's what I thought."

As an artist, Kyle was an ideal companion for touring the Ashland art galleries. Originally, when Raven had told her he was an artist, she'd had an image of a deadbeat lying around the house smoking European cigarettes and drinking Lambrusco while Raven brought home the bacon. But even if Kyle's work wasn't hanging in the local galleries, he was making money with his talent, taking jobs some artists would turn their noses up at. He wasn't above designing product packaging or advertising flyers. For holidays, he decorated store windows. On weekends, he became a sidewalk caricaturist. He was a working artist, the best kind to rent a house with. His dreams of greater things remained intact, but didn't overshadow the need to buy food. Wren liked him more and more, seeing him as the perfect balancing influence for Raven's more flighty personality.

After she paid for the print, they walked out into the warm June evening, arm in arm, Wren's new piece of art wrapped in brown butcher paper and tucked under Kyle's right arm. People looked at them as they walked along the sidewalk. Wren knew they made a striking couple. Kyle was an unarguably handsome man. He was clearly enjoying the charade, as much an actor in his way as Raven was.

"I'm so glad we get to spend some time together," Kyle said, "to get to know one another. When I heard you were coming up, I was thrilled because ever since I first knew Raven was a twin, I've been curious about you. He's always going on about 'the special bond of twins.' He clearly feels his life is blessed in an extraordinary way. I kind of understand. There will always be one person who's known him from the beginning, from the womb, more intimately than anyone else ever will. That *is* a special bond."

"Do you have brothers and sisters?"

"No. I'm an only child. My parents both died when I was just a baby, so no chance for siblings."

"I'm sorry. Was it an accident?"

He glanced away and sighed. "Uh, I'd rather not talk about it. Ancient history." His smile, meant to reassure, was unconvincing.

"Well, I'll be happy to be your sister as well as Raven's." She gave his arm a heartening squeeze.

"There!" he said. "That look you just gave me. I've seen it on his face. Uncanny! It's unnerving to see a woman with the features and mannerisms of the man I love. That's probably why I took an instant liking to you." He quietly studied her face, then asked, "Ready to eat?"

"Way past ready."

"I'm trying to think of a suitable restaurant, some place worthy of your column." He nodded toward a Japanese place with dark wood paneling on the outside. "Something like that?"

"I'd like to go to Sprouts," she said decisively.

"Really? Raven said he took you there already. You want to go to the same place twice?"

"I haven't reviewed it yet. Besides, I really want to taste Sophie's cheese and that's the one place I know that serves it."

"Sophie's still on your mind, is she?" He grinned knowingly. "All right. Let's go to Sprouts, although the macho man I'm pretending to be may have to grumble at having leaves and twigs for dinner."

Sophie had indeed been on Wren's mind almost continuously ever since their blissful night together. She'd been wondering again this morning if she should search for her and try to see her again. But she was wary of starting something. She didn't know Sophie well enough to know if she was the sort who could say goodbye at the end of a vacation affair. Wren had been put on guard by her brother's irritating teasing about how women inevitably fell in love with anybody they slept with. The generalization was ridiculous. But it did sometimes happen. She didn't want to take a chance it would happen to Sophie. She didn't want to hurt her. It probably wasn't worth the risk. But Sophie's incredibly expressive lips were invading her dreams. If she wasn't going to taste Sophie's mouth again, then at least she could taste the fruits of her labor. That was the reasoning that led her back to Ellie's restaurant.

Sprouts wasn't as busy tonight as it had been over the weekend. There were only two other couples there, so they had their choice of tables and chose one next to the front window.

No sooner had they taken their seats than a Dalmatian with a blue leather collar slipped in through the front door as another customer left, running through the room and sliding on the slick floor as he made his turns. The dog ran to one end of the room, then ran back, wagging his tail wildly and looking thoroughly gleeful. Kyle leapt to his feet and tried unsuccessfully to grab the dog's collar as he sped past.

The door opened again and in burst Ellie's weird sister Cassandra, looking even more crazed than she had the previous times Wren had seen her. She was still wearing her long brown cape, still had dark circles under her eyes, still hadn't bothered to brush her hair.

"Spot!" she hollered at the dog, who ignored her and continued running under tables with his nose to the floor, sniffing emphatically. Wren made herself as small as possible in her chair, hoping Cassandra wouldn't notice her, but it was a vain hope. As their gaze met, the woman stopped short and stared with her haunting, sallow eyes.

"You!" she accused, stretching out her menacing index finger as Wren stood to face her, her legs trembling. "'Fair is foul, and foul is fair!'" she hissed.

To no avail, Wren glanced around for Ellie to enforce her

Two On The Aisle   85

No Shakespeare! sign. Her attention was unwillingly drawn back to Cassandra, who locked her stare ruthlessly onto her. Wren stood speechless and terrified until the dog came skidding to a halt at Cassandra's feet. She reached down and grabbed him by the collar, opening the door with her other hand, then gave him a powerful heave through the open doorway.

"Out, damned Spot! Out, I say!" She turned to narrow her eyes wordlessly but meaningfully at Wren before following Spot outside.

Kyle put an arm around Wren, hugging her close. "Are you okay? You look scared stiff."

"That crazy woman keeps harassing me."

"You've seen her before?"

"The other day when Raven and I had lunch here. The same thing happened." Wren sat down shakily. "Fair is foul and foul is fair? What the hell?"

"She's obviously nuts. Don't let it bother you." He patted her hand, then opened the menu. "Hey, let's eat. I've never been in on a restaurant review before. Can I order what I want, or do I need to order something specific?"

Wren pushed Cassandra from her mind. "You can order what you want as long as it's different from what I order. And you have to let me taste everything."

She scanned the menu, shaking off the lingering uneasiness over Cassandra's burning stare. "I really want to taste Sophie's chèvre, so I think I'll start with this roasted beet salad with goat cheese and toasted walnuts."

"That sounds yummy," Kyle said with a distinct lilt to his voice.

Wren looked over the top of her menu at him with a disapproving shake of her head. "That was way too gay."

"Oh, sorry," he said, expanding his chest and lowering his voice. "Beet salad. Yes, my love, I'm sure you'll enjoy that. I think I'll go for something meatier, like this grilled portobello mushroom."

Wren laughed. "For my entrée, I'm going with the butternut squash ravioli."

Ellie came out with a basket of bread for their table, then

took their order. Wren glanced at the unoccupied table where Sophie had sat the other day. In her mind, she could see her there still, wielding her fork with her elegant long fingers, those same fingers that had been so instrumental in her satisfaction later that night. Feeling suddenly liquid, Wren slid partway down in her chair before shaking off the sensation and righting herself. She swallowed a gulp of water.

"I've been meaning to ask about your pseudonym," said Kyle. "How did you come up with it?"

She spread her napkin in her lap before answering in hushed tones. "Eno Threlkeld is an actual person, a boy who went to high school with us. He and Raven were good friends. What Raven liked about him, I'm sure, was that he was so big. He was tall and broad. As you know, Raven was a squirt."

"Still is."

"Yes. And flagrantly gay, even as a child. He endured a lot of abuse. Eno was kind of a misfit too. He was the only child of an older couple. His father was a fisherman. He smelled sort of fishy all the time. I do remember that, and that may be the real reason he wasn't all that popular. Eno was a bodyguard for Raven, protecting him from bullies. That lasted until high school graduation when Raven and I went away to college. Haven't seen him since."

"So you named your alter ego after a fishy boy?"

"Yeah, I guess so. When I was casting about for a pen name, I happened to be touring the Lake District in England and came upon this little Norse village of Threlkeld. It reminded me of Eno. I thought it would make a good name. The kind of person it conjures up is so unlike me, don't you think?"

"Yes! Practically the opposite of you. Like a brawny marauding Viking."

"Eno wasn't a marauder, by any means. He was gentle and kind, but he did look like he could pound you into sawdust. I don't think old Eno would mind my using his name. I hope not, anyway."

Ellie came out with their appetizers, setting a beet salad in front of Wren and a grilled portobello mushroom in front of Kyle.

"Weren't you in here last week?" Ellie asked Wren. "With your twin brother?"

"Yes, that was me."

"Here with her husband tonight," Kyle offered.

Ellie turned to Kyle, who beamed at her with a close-lipped smile.

"Yes, darling," Wren said, patting his hand. "By the way," she said to Ellie, "your sister was in here again."

Ellie looked taken aback. "She was?"

"Just a few minutes ago, with a dog."

"She brought Spot in here? I'm so sorry about that. I've told her a hundred times I don't want that dog in here." Looking frazzled, Ellie retreated to the kitchen.

Wren observed her salad, admiring its appearance, then scooped up a taste of the goat cheese with her spoon, letting it spend some time on her tongue.

"How is it?" Kyle asked, staring expectantly at her.

She swallowed. "Disappointing. Very ordinary. Even a bit gritty. It doesn't have the richness I would have expected from Nubians either. I mean, it isn't terrible, but it's nothing special." She tasted one of the beets and a piece of oak leaf lettuce. "However, the salad, as a composition, is lovely."

"So is this mushroom. Have a taste." He pushed his fork toward her and she scraped the bite off with her teeth.

"Yes, that's good. Not too much vinegar. Good quality, fruity olive oil." Wren returned to her salad. "This is a great restaurant. Everything's so fresh and simply prepared. They don't go overboard with trying to be cute or anything. Which makes me even more disappointed in this cheese. I had high expectations."

"Just because the woman was good in bed doesn't mean she can make cheese."

"You're absolutely right!" Wren laughed at her own illogical assumption. "Besides, she's new at cheese making. She'll get better."

The bell on the door tinkled. Wren spun around to see Raven's understudy Max coming through the doorway. He looked nervously expectant, scanning the room before committing himself to coming all the way in. With his hair tamed and combed back, he looked slightly less waif-like than usual. He was also dressed more formally than before in tan slacks and a crisp white button-down shirt with a striped tan and yellow tie.

Ellie appeared from the back. Seeing Max, she halted mid-stride. They stood fifteen feet from one another, wordlessly staring. Ellie turned red and stuttered, then recovered enough to approach Max and offer him a table. He seemed to have gone completely mute. He sat, a silly smile on his face.

"That's Raven's understudy," Wren informed Kyle. "Have you met him?"

"No." Kyle peered around Wren to get a better look. "Scrawny little thing, isn't he?"

Max noticed Wren, recognized her and waved. She returned his greeting with a smile.

"He looks all of eighteen," Kyle observed.

"'He wears the rose of youth upon him,'" Wren quoted. "According to Raven, he's twenty-six."

Kyle shrugged and cut into his mushroom.

The next time Ellie came by, to take their empty appetizer plates, Wren said, "I have a question about the chèvre."

"Tallulah Rose, yes."

"My husband here was just wondering if they were open for tours or tastings. It's local, right?"

"Yes. But they don't have anything like that. They've only been in business a short time. I was surprised we still had some of the cheese left. We run out every week before we get the new batch on Fridays. It's a small family farm. Just a few goats and the two of them."

Wren started. "The two of them?"

"Just Sophie and Olivia. They do everything themselves. They do plan to increase production, eventually. We're looking forward to that."

Wren nodded. "Thank you."

Ellie headed over to Max's table as Wren let this new information sink in. "Olivia" echoed in her brain like a ricocheting bullet.

Kyle reached across the table and put his hand over hers. "Are you okay?"

"I had no idea she was with someone." She remembered how nervous Sophie had been last Friday and how Wren had chalked that up to excitement or timidity. It hadn't occurred to her it might be because she was cheating on someone.

"Hmmm." Kyle frowned. "So she makes a lousy cheese and she's a liar."

"Oh, no, no! She didn't lie. She never said she was single." Wren stared at her plate. "I never asked."

"You look upset."

She forced a smile. "No, I'm not. I...I didn't expect anything more out of it. Just a good night's fun."

Kyle looked skeptical, then took his hand away. "Why were you asking those questions anyway? I thought you liked to keep a low profile when you're working."

"Yes, but I was thinking of going out there, visiting Tallulah Rose Creamery. I was just trying to get a little more information."

Kyle put his fork down. "Ah, now I see. Now the truth comes out. I know why you're so disappointed that her cheese is ordinary and she has a partner. It wasn't just a good night's fun. You want to see her again."

Wren sighed. "Okay, I'll admit I wouldn't mind another one-night stand."

"Technically, it isn't a one-night stand if you do it again."

"You know what I mean."

Kyle smiled. "I don't believe you. Once, maybe it's just sex. Twice between two women and you're headed for the altar."

"You boys are exasperating! I won't be able to prove you wrong now, will I, because obviously I'm not going to have another chance with her."

"Ahhh." He looked sympathetically sad, thrusting out his bottom lip. "At least you can give her cheese a bad review."

Wren laughed shortly. "You're right!"

Despite what she had said to Kyle, she really was disappointed. She had no right to be, she knew. She'd be a hypocrite to take a morally disapproving stance now. There had been nothing between them to suggest they would ever see one another again. Sophie's morning note should have made that clear. Goodbye. Thanks for the good time. Then she went home to her goats and her Olivia. No harm done. It was none of Wren's business, nor her problem, why Sophie had cheated. But that tiny prudish, judgmental part of her was already waggling its finger and the romantic, idealistic part of her was searching for an explanation. Which was why it now seemed right that her review of Sprouts should come down with a certain measure of hard justice on Tallulah Rose Creamery.

CHAPTER FOURTEEN

...I could a tale unfold whose lightest word
Would harrow up thy soul, freeze thy young blood;
Make thy two eyes, like stars, start from their spheres;
Thy knotted and combined locks to part,
And each particular hair to stand on end
Like quills upon the fretful porcupine.

—*Hamlet*, Act I, Scene 5

"Lavender?" Sophie asked. "Is that really a flavor people want in a cupcake?"

Klaus stood beside her in the kitchen holding a tray containing a half dozen vanilla and lavender-flavored cupcakes frosted with white-chocolate ganache, white chocolate curls and a sprinkling of tiny lavender flowers for garnish. They were gorgeous little works of art. Behind him over the kitchen counter hung several balls of goat cheese in cheesecloth nests, dripping their milky whey into a plastic tub.

Klaus Olafssen was a big man, muscular and brimming with health and vigor. He had a bright, enthusiastic smile that was oddly innocent looking, boyish, actually, bursting out from his wide, clean-shaven jaw. His sandy, untamed, naturally wavy hair hung down on his forehead into his vivid blue eyes, eyes that always looked a little melancholy to her. She recalled the tragic story of how he had lost his father and twin brother to the ocean.

"You could just as well ask the same thing about goat cheese," he answered. "If you asked people what flavor goat cheese they want, what are the chances somebody'd say lavender?"

Sophie smiled. "Okay, you have a point."

"Will you try it?" Klaus asked, pushing the tray closer.

"Sure. Try to stop me." Sophie picked up a cupcake and peeled down the wrapper. In the past few weeks, she'd eaten more cupcakes than she had in her entire life. She was one of Klaus's regular taste testers as he prepared for the big Cupcake Extravaganza, a bake-off he was seriously determined to win. The winner would create the dessert centerpiece for the annual Midsummer Night's Dream Gala, a fundraiser for the Shakespeare Festival. It would be quite a coup if he could pull it off.

Sophie bit through the frosting and into the cake, giving the bite her full attention. "That's really good. Moist, delicate. The lavender is subtle. Prominent vanilla flavor."

"Too much?"

"Maybe a little strong. You could cut back on the vanilla just a smidge and give the lavender center stage. But the white chocolate frosting is the perfect complement to this cake. You're getting so good at this."

"Thanks, Sophie. I appreciate the help. I really want to win this thing." He ran his hand through his hair, brushing it back from his forehead. "What's your favorite so far?"

"That's tough. I'd say it's between this one and the lemon cake with the lemon curd filling. You have to make three flavors, right?"

He nodded.

"Well, then, definitely the lemon and the lavender. I'd stay away from chocolate. It's hard to get any flavor from a chocolate cupcake other than chocolate. These lighter flavors are more surprising, more playful, so maybe the raspberry trifle. One of your early flavors. It was incredible and I think you'll get extra points for highlighting local produce."

"That's very good advice. Thanks."

The muscles in the back of his huge arms flexed as he set down the tray of cupcakes. It was kind of funny, Sophie thought, that this big man produced such dainty little cakes.

"Get your mama to taste these too." he said. "I want to hear what she thinks."

"I will. No problem there. She's got such a sweet tooth. I swear that woman could live on nothing but cake. But she's not home right now. She's kayaking with Dr. Connor."

"Yeah, Dr. Connor. He's a great guy. I heard he joined Doctors Without Borders. He'll be going off to someplace we never heard of soon."

"I remember Mom mentioning that. That's the kind of adventure made for a bachelor like him."

"Your mama and Dr. Connor. They make a nice couple."

"Oh, no, it's not like that!" Sophie objected, thrown by the suggestion of her mother being romantically involved with her doctor. "No. It's just the kayaking. He's an experienced kayaker himself and he thought it would be good exercise for her. Strengthen her muscles. All part of the recovery regimen."

"So it's therapy?" Klaus asked.

"Right. Therapy."

The way Klaus looked at her, his face full of indulgent affection, unnerved her. "Both of our mothers are such strong women, aren't they?" he remarked.

"Yes, they are. Very capable. By the way, I just heard what happened to your father. And your brother Eric. Such a sad story. I feel so bad for your mother."

He nodded gloomily. "I often wonder how different life would be if I had a twin brother. Sometimes I have the eerie feeling that he's not really gone. Like when people lose an arm or leg and say they still feel pain in the missing limb. That's how I feel about Eric, like he's still attached to me somehow. It's like he's right here in my head sometimes. It's kind of funny to say

I miss him because I can't remember him at all." He sighed. "I don't have any memory of my father either."

"Nor do I of mine."

"I don't think you've ever mentioned your father before."

"My father was a mystery man," Sophie said, recalling her favorite photo of him, a dashing, swarthy man with an olive complexion and dark eyes, a man who had taken her mother's heart by storm, but had been a near stranger, even to Olivia. "His name was Claude. He and my mother weren't married. He was a drifter. Came and went like the wind. I was barely three by the time he was out of our lives."

"Do you think your mother still misses him?"

"I know she doesn't. She hasn't mentioned him in years and when she would talk about him, years ago to satisfy our curiosity, she said he was actually sort of an oaf. He could turn a young girl's head with his looks, but she was sure he never would have made a decent husband or father. She was over him even by then. Which is a good thing considering what happened. After he left us, he hooked up with a rich widow."

"Really?" Klaus lifted his eyebrows. "So is he going to leave you a fortune?"

Sophie laughed. "Even if things had turned out well for him, I doubt that would have happened. Unfortunately for Claude, his rich widow turned out to be his fatal mistake. Her name was Gertrude. Her first husband died under suspicious circumstances. A month later, my father married her. The sheets of her marriage bed not yet cooled, as they say."

"Sounds dicey," Klaus observed.

"Gertrude's son thought so too." Sophie shook her head. "That kid was bad news. A pale, melancholy boy. Sort of a sociopath and self-absorbed diva. A real ham, if you know what I mean."

Klaus raised his eyebrows to indicate his understanding.

"He freaked out when his mother remarried so quickly. Called her a whore. Accused my father of murdering his father. Went berserk. A touch of an Oedipal complex in that boy; that's always been my interpretation. I wouldn't be surprised if he's the one who killed his father."

"What happened?"

"The kid went on a murder spree. By the time it was over, his mother was dead, my father was dead, and he was dead too."

Klaus gasped. "Horrible!"

"It must have been. Mom thought it was too terrible to even tell us until we were in our twenties. But Claude was just a name to us. It was just a story about someone else's family tragedy. Like a stage play."

Klaus shook his head sadly, but then brightened and said, "Another thing we have in common, isn't it? Being raised by single mothers."

Sophie shuffled her feet uncomfortably, recognizing where his thoughts were headed. "Where are you going with this whole cupcake thing?" she asked, deliberately changing the subject. "What if you do win the bake-off?"

He looked embarrassed, his fair skin reddening. "It's sort of my dream, Sophie, to bake for a living. You know, a lot of the restaurants in town don't make their own desserts. They buy from local bakeries. That's what I'm hoping to get into."

"I had no idea. You've never mentioned it before."

He nodded vigorously. "I'd feature Mama's aebleskiver and those apple dumplings she makes. Then develop some specialties of my own, like my lime curd tarts. I'm not bad at éclairs either. I should bring you one sometime, after the cupcake thing is over. If I can win this competition, it'll be the boost of confidence I need to go for it."

"I hope you win, then, but you don't really need that. If it's your dream, just do it. I'm sure you'd be a big hit."

"We'll see what the judges think." He stood. "Not to take anything away from your opinion, Sophie, but this is a hard business to get into, and I'd at least like to know how I measure up with the pros." He looked suddenly shy. "If I rented a professional kitchen in town, there might be room to share it, like with a cheese maker or something." He nodded toward the dripping cheesecloths over the sink.

Sophie laughed nervously. "Oh! That's very sweet of you, Klaus, but I'm okay with this at the moment. It's kind of nice to be able to hang out around the farm, not have to go to an office...or a kitchen somewhere."

He looked at his shoes and she held her breath, wondering how to talk to him about the futility of his romantic ideas without hurting him.

He looked up, looking resolute. "I guess I should get to work. What do you want me to do today?"

"How about clearing some of the dry brush over by the east fence?"

He pulled a pair of leather gloves from his back pocket. "Right. See you later, Sophie."

She heaved a sigh of relief, telling herself she had to bite the bullet and just tell him she was gay. But apparently that wasn't going to happen today.

After she had finished turning all the cheeses over, she took a folded note from her pocket. On it was the phone number of the Touchstone Real Estate Agency in San Francisco. She'd looked it up on the Internet and written it on this piece of paper two days ago and had debated calling ever since. Today she had managed to persuade herself to do it, to call Wren and find out if she, like Sophie, might be interested in getting together again. If Wren wasn't yet back at work, maybe she could find a way to get a message to her through her company.

Assumptions had been made, perhaps on both sides, and assumptions could be wrong. Wasn't that the lesson in almost every Shakespeare comedy? That simple misunderstandings could put everyone on the wrong path, create all sorts of plot complications that could have been avoided simply by somebody asking a direct question? Or in this case, making a phone call. Nothing to lose by finding out if the assumption was wrong. And everything to gain. Maybe Wren was thinking about her too. Maybe they both wanted more than a one-night stand. And maybe Wren was afraid to make the first move because she assumed Sophie didn't want to see her again.

The more she thought about it, the more she wondered why she had ever assumed Wren wouldn't want to see her again. Because she didn't give her a phone number or an email address? Because she didn't ask for another date? But she herself hadn't done those things either, and it was she who had left that morning while Wren was still asleep, leaving no encouragement. So it was up to her, she decided, to make the first move. Because she hadn't been able to get Wren out of her mind for more than a few minutes at a time. Because her body ached at the memory of that beautiful, seductive creature she had momentarily possessed and who had possessed her more completely than she had guessed at the time. With each day that passed, her desire for Wren grew stronger.

She dialed the number. A woman answered promptly with "Touchstone Agency."

"Hi," Sophie said cheerfully. "I'm trying to get in touch with one of your agents. She gave me her card, but I've misplaced it, so I'd like to get an email address or a phone number."

"What's her name?"

"Wren Landry."

"Wren Landry? There's no one here by that name."

"Are you sure? That's Wren like the bird, W-R-E-N."

"I'm sure we don't have an agent with that name. I know everyone here."

"Oh." Sophie hesitated, puzzled.

"Maybe she's with another agency," the woman suggested.

"Yes," Sophie said slowly. "That must be it. Thank you."

She lowered herself into a kitchen chair, leaning on her elbows on the table, staring down at five white cupcakes with brilliant flecks of purple flowers on top. Here's the proof, she thought. No Shakespeare comedy, after all. The assumption had been correct. Wren had withheld her contact information on purpose and the information she'd given was false.

Sophie's disappointment was huge. She had apparently managed to convince herself that there was more real feeling and more substance between them than there really was. Wren had been looking for a diversion. That's all.

If she had sat there another minute, she would have been in tears, but she was distracted by the sound of goats bleating and realized it was time to feed the animals. Just as well, she thought, anticipating a few minutes of chicken magic.

CHAPTER FIFTEEN

My story being done,
She gave me for my pains a world of sighs:
She swore, —in faith, 'twas strange, 'twas passing strange,
'Twas pitiful, 'twas wondrous pitiful...

—*Othello*, Act I, Scene 3

Sooner or later, every visitor to southern Oregon ends up on a jetboat tour of Hellgate Canyon. Wren was no different. On Tuesday, Raven had a break from performing, so Wren and the boys boarded the wide, blue tour boat along with a couple of dozen other people for a two-hour tour of the river. Their boat was named *Fish Hawk*, an informal term for osprey, and they were lucky to spy a couple of those raptors during the tour, gliding on thermal currents and occasionally swooping close to the water in search of a meal.

Hellgate Canyon, so-called because of its rocky narrows, was beautiful with its thick stands of conifers and rugged volcanic flanks. In the canyon, the water was deep and greenish, squeezing through the narrow walls. The tour guide pointed out a bald eagle high in a dead tree, its signature white head easy to pick out against a deep blue sky. Everybody in the boat peered up at the same time to glimpse it.

Wren and Raven played the game they had played since they were small, racing to see which of them could be the first to identify any birds they came across. Their parents had often taken them on nature walks and had encouraged this game. There were very few birds native to the Western United States they couldn't peg. Though Kyle couldn't compete in the game, he seemed to enjoy watching them. In fact, the young couple sitting in front of them, who introduced themselves as Antonio and Nicola, also got drawn into the game and listened for Wren or Raven's call-out, then followed their pointing finger to catch sight of their discoveries.

As their list of birds mounted, Wren thought how much her parents would have liked this tour. Raven got credit for a double-breasted cormorant, three turkey vultures and a belted kingfisher. Wren spied a pair of mergansers, a Cooper's hawk and an American Dipper. When they were close enough to shore to recognize songbirds, Raven spotted a Western Bluebird. Then he turned to look at her, silently communicating what was on his mind. Together, in unison, they yelled, "Wrentit," then fell against each other and broke into euphoric giggles.

As children, even when he didn't see a wrentit, Raven would often say he did, just so he could say it. As an adult, Wren was as happy with this immature joke as he was, not for its silliness, but for the shared experience of childhood. But as a teenager, especially in the presence of other teenagers, she had been mortified by the teasing and had hated that there was no equivalent affront for him. He had liked anything to do with ravens. He drew temporary tattoos of them on his skin, once in the middle of his forehead, after which he'd had his head scrubbed until he cried. He had spent most of his ninth year quoting "Nevermore" at every possible opportunity, causing their father to perpetually regret ever reading Poe's poem to them.

Wren chuckled to herself, remembering her mother's

exasperation one night at the dinner table. "Do you want some more carrots?" she had asked Raven. "Nevermore!" he crowed for the fifth time during the meal. Their father warned him to stop it or he'd be sent to his room. But he couldn't help himself. Not ten minutes later, when Wren brought up a math test scheduled for the next day, their father said, "Maybe you two should take some time out after dinner to study." Wren had known without even looking at him that Raven was about to say it. "Nevermore!" He had been banished to his room for the rest of the evening.

It was a bright, clear day and she and Raven and Kyle all wore shorts, T-shirts and sunglasses. The jetboat shared the river with fishing boats, rafts, kayaks and canoes, lots of colorful watercraft out for a fine summer day's recreation. They passed an entire flotilla of river runners on their way back to the dock in Grant's Pass.

"If you really want to see some birds," Kyle suggested, "there's a forty-mile hiking trail along the shore. I've done a few miles of it. Nice way to see the river."

"This isn't a bad way either," Wren noted. "I wouldn't mind taking it a little slower, though."

"Maybe we can go rafting while you're here," Raven suggested. "There are some class four and five rapids on this river."

Wren laughed. "I might want to work up to that." She pointed to a couple of kayaks near the north shore, sliding cleanly along parallel to the jetboat. "That looks like fun."

The lead kayak was red and piloted by a middle-aged man wearing an Indiana Jones style hat. Behind him was a bright yellow craft paddled by a woman in a T-shirt and straw hat. Both of them wore orange life vests.

Suddenly the woman in front of Raven, Nicola, leaned over the side of the boat and started waving and hollering at the kayakers.

"Miss Ward! Miss Ward!" she hollered.

Recognizing Sophie's last name, Wren looked more carefully at the kayakers. "Give me your binoculars," she demanded of Kyle. He handed them over and she peered through, focusing on the woman in the yellow kayak, disappointed to see it wasn't

Two On The Aisle   101

Sophie. The woman was lean and muscular, wearing a sleeveless shirt, stroking smoothly side to side, driving her craft steadily through the current. From this distance, with her face shaded by her hat, her age was indeterminate.

Nicola stood up and waved both arms wildly, though they had all been repeatedly warned to remain seated. "Miss Ward!" she hollered again, cupping her hands around her mouth.

"Who is it?" Antonio asked, sounding irritated.

"It's Olivia Ward," Nicola explained. "Really nice lady. I haven't seen her since high school."

At the name "Olivia," Wren jumped up to get a better look through the binoculars. The kayaker had stopped paddling to look for the commotion. Nicola leaned over the edge of the boat and waved frantically. The woman in the kayak caught sight of the hysterical waving girl and raised her arm in greeting.

Wren leaned against the railing to keep the kayakers in view as the jetboat pulled out ahead of them. Just then the captain decided to make one of his wildly popular U-turns, spinning the boat rapidly around in a circle and tossing both Wren and Nicola over the side into the river. Wren landed headfirst in the shockingly cold water and went under, feeling the current whisking her downstream. She climbed back to the surface thirty or forty feet from the jetboat in time to see several young men, including Antonio, Kyle and Raven, all three shirtless, diving off the edge of the boat. One of the crew members was yelling and running back and forth on deck.

"Don't jump!" he commanded, but nobody was listening. "Man overboard!" he screamed to the captain.

The jetboat engine went silent and someone threw a life preserver, but Wren was already too far downstream. Reminding herself to stay calm, she let herself float with the current as she swam methodically toward shore, hoping none of those would-be rescuers were in trouble. The water was cold but bearable, and not too deep. Seeing the bottom beneath her, she stepped down into the sandy gravel and walked the rest of the way onto dry land.

She stood dripping, the binoculars still around her neck, and located the jetboat upstream. As she watched, Kyle appeared, swimming toward her. She waved. A minute later he walked out of the river and gave her a hug.

"You're okay," he observed.

"I'm fine." She shivered, her skin covered in goose bumps. "Where's Raven?"

"Don't know." Kyle lifted the binoculars off her.

"That was stupid, all you guys jumping in like that."

"I know. But what do you expect when a couple of girls fall overboard? Everybody wants to be a hero." He scanned the river through the binoculars. "There he is!" He waved at a dark bobbing head. "Raven!" he hollered. "Over here!"

Raven turned their way and fought hard against the current until he made it into the calm, shallow edge a few feet further downstream, where he pulled himself out. They ran to meet him, finding him grinning from ear to ear amid labored breathing.

"That was fun!" he shouted.

Wren slapped him playfully just as the two kayakers paddled by.

"So what was that all about?" Kyle asked.

Wren pointed at the yellow kayak. "That's Olivia Ward."

"Olivia Ward?" Raven asked.

"Olivia of Sophie and Olivia."

"That's Sophie's partner?" Kyle asked, staring after the kayak.

"Wife, I'm guessing," Wren said. "Same last name."

The jetboat came along then to pick them up. They climbed up the ladder and into the boat, then they rounded up the rest of the miscreants, all of whom had made landfall safely. Wren picked up Raven's T-shirt from the seat where he'd left it and dried her hair with it.

"Hey!" he objected, grabbing it from her. He wrinkled his nose at his wet shirt, then rubbed it across his own hair.

The boat proceeded to the dock with no further tricky maneuvers. Once they were secured, the captain came over the loudspeaker with a stern lecture for everyone who had misbehaved, telling them they had ruined the tour for everyone and endangered many lives with their foolish antics. Wren,

Raven, Kyle, Antonio and Nicola all stood on deck sopping wet, their heads bowed, taking their rebuke while the other passengers filed off the boat glaring at them. When the captain was finished, they too disembarked.

As they walked along the dock, Wren noticed the two kayaks that had triggered all the mischief. They were unattended, tethered at water's edge. There was a restaurant nearby, up a flight of wooden stairs. It was built partly on the riverbank, partly on pilings and had a large open deck overhanging the river. Other than the jetboat dock, there wasn't much else here to stop for. Wren guessed the kayakers had pulled out for a meal.

"Who's up for lunch?" she asked.

"Me!" Raven sang, raising his hand like a kindergartener.

"Me too," Kyle said. "There's nothing like a heart-pounding adventure to rev up an appetite."

Raven pulled on his damp shirt, then the three of them climbed the stairs to the entrance of the building.

"Let me seat you outside," suggested the hostess, "where you can dry off."

They were led through the dining room where Wren rapidly scanned the tables, looking for Olivia Ward. She finally spotted her at one of the outdoor tables as they followed the hostess single file into the bright afternoon sunshine.

"Can we have that one?" Wren asked, pointing to the closest unoccupied table to Olivia and her companion. It was too far away to overhear their conversation, but would afford her a much better view of them than she'd gotten on the river.

Wren took the chair facing Olivia's table and the boys both positioned themselves with a view out to the river, oblivious to Wren's purposes. They seemed more than usually caught up with one another, giving Wren the opportunity to study Olivia and friend by peeking at them over her menu. They were both about fifty, she decided. She was shocked to see that Olivia was old enough to be Sophie's mother. Her companion was handsome with a full head of dark, graying hair, small, penetrating eyes and firm, clean-shaven chin. Olivia's hair was turning gray from some light natural shade, ash blonde, maybe, the same color as Sophie's hair. She was thin and fit with light-colored eyes and a long face, pronounced lines on either side of her mouth, around her eyes and across her forehead. She was eating a salad, talking animatedly with her companion.

The waitress, a girl who introduced herself in a high, squeaky voice as Ariel, came by for their order. Having been using the menu as cover rather than reading material, Wren took her first glance at the menu while the boys ordered. Her eye landed on a wild-caught Oregon Chinook salmon salad and she ordered that.

"You guys are all wet," Ariel observed. "You been swimming?"

Kyle nodded soberly. "Yeah, we took a little dip."

Ariel giggled. "Most people wear swimsuits."

"It was spontaneous," Kyle informed her.

She squinted her face up in a silent laugh before departing.

Wren looked past the boys to Olivia's table, and was surprised to see her table mate with his hand over hers in an affectionate and familiar gesture. Wren stiffened, then cautioned herself not to jump to conclusions. He might be her brother. Or a dear, close old friend.

Ariel arrived at Olivia's table, picking up salad plates. Her grating voice rose loud enough for anybody on the deck to hear as she slapped the air, laughing, and said, "Oh, Dr. Connor, you're so funny!"

Dr. Connor, Wren repeated in her mind. Not that a name told her anything.

"Ah!" said Raven as Ariel returned to them a few minutes later. "Food at last!"

She set their plates down, then said, "Can I get you anything else?"

"Ariel," Wren said as casually as she could, "is that Dr. Connor over there?"

"Yes. That's him. Do you know him?"

Wren ignored the look of alarm on Kyle's face. "I do, but not well. I was considering going over to say hello, but don't want to intrude. He seems to be having such a good time with his...wife?"

Both Kyle and Raven had now turned completely around to stare at Olivia and Dr. Connor.

Ariel knit her brows together. "You must not know him very well at all. Everybody knows he's a widower. It's nice to see him out with a woman. After all these years, he deserves some happiness."

"No, I don't know him well," Wren confided. "His wife died a long time ago, did she?"

Ariel's mouth twitched noticeably as she threw a covert glance at Dr. Connor. She sat in the one empty chair at their table and pulled it up close to Wren. "A long time ago," she confirmed.

Raven and Kyle also focused their attention on Ariel, and the four of them formed a small, huddled group of near-whisperers.

"His wife's name was Cordelia," Ariel began. "She was the youngest of three daughters. The other two were greedy, heartless women who put a contract out to have Cordelia murdered so they could have their father's fortune for themselves."

Wren gasped. "Murder?"

"The father was a stupid old fool who was easily manipulated. They duped him, took everything he had, then turned him out to live on the streets."

"What thankless children!" Kyle exclaimed. "Unbelievable."

"They got it in the end, though," Ariel whispered. "Both sisters were in love with the same man. One poisoned the other one, then she killed herself."

"Murder and suicide!" Raven exclaimed.

Ariel nodded solemnly. "Their father, by then blind and insane, died of grief. The whole family, gone, just like that." She sputtered a pfffft. "And poor Dr. Connor a widower."

All four of them turned their heads to look at Dr. Connor, who looked perfectly happy as he leaned over and gave Olivia a romantic kiss on the mouth. Wren audibly caught her breath. Ariel jumped up and ran off to resume her duties.

"I thought she was Sophie's wife?" Kyle said. "Looks like she's somebody else's lover."

"Not unlike Sophie herself," Raven observed quietly, looking askance at Wren.

"Look," she said, defensively, "I didn't know about any of this last weekend when she asked me to her room."

Dr. Connor sat with Olivia's hand in both of his, smiling fondly into her face.

"Do you think he knows about Sophie?" Raven asked.

"Do you think she knows about Wren?" Kyle responded.

"'Oh, what a tangled web we weave,'" Raven quoted, then held up his index finger and said, "You know, a lot of people think that's Shakespeare, but it isn't. It's Sir Walter Scott from an epic poem called *Marmion* about a sixteenth-century battle between England and Scotland."

"Raven," commanded Wren, grabbing his wrist and nodding her head toward Olivia and Dr. Connor. "Focus."

"What do you mean, Wren? This is none of our business. If Sophie's wife has a boyfriend, maybe it's payback, you know? Simple justice on her cheating ass. Just be glad you aren't involved. That looks like a big mess and it's bound to blow up in everybody's face. Now let's eat. Leave them to their ruin."

Raven was right. It was none of her business. She tasted her salad and tried to keep her mind and eyes off Olivia. But it was impossible. She found herself inventing explanations, some of which left her feeling buoyant, like the one where Sophie and Olivia had already broken up and were still living together out of habit or convenience. The real explanation didn't have to be sordid or disastrous. It didn't have to cast Sophie in an unflattering light. But there were many other possible explanations that left Wren discouraged.

When Olivia and Dr. Connor stood to leave, Wren bolted up from her chair, ignoring the startled looks on the boys' faces, and dashed over to confront Olivia. She seemed to be driven almost against her will to this rash action, and had no idea what to say, but once she was standing face to face with the woman, she had no choice but to speak.

"Hi," she said, thoroughly embarrassed. She glanced back at her table to see the boys staring at her with open mouths, motionless, looking like they were waiting for a bomb to go off. She turned back to Olivia. "You're Olivia Ward, aren't you? I'm a friend of Sophie's. My name is Wren, like the bird."

Olivia smiled. "How do you do, Wren. I don't think I've ever heard Sophie mention you."

"No, we don't see much of one another any more."

Olivia turned to Dr. Connor. "This is my friend Warren."

Dr. Connor shook Wren's hand. "You're one of the girls who fell off the jetboat."

"That's right."

His eyes twinkled good-naturedly. "Glad you didn't drown."

"Me too." She turned back to Olivia. "How is Sophie?"

"She's great," Olivia replied. "Thriving. You should come out to the farm for a visit and meet the goats. Sophie's raising goats now, you know. Making cheese."

"I heard. Totally fascinating."

"I'll tell her I ran into you."

"Oh, no!" Wren objected, glad that her brain was able to work faster than her mouth. "Uh, don't bother. You know, now that she's on my mind, I think I'll just give her a call. I'll mention I met you here, you and Warren." Wren smiled at them both in turn with what she hoped was a suggestive undercurrent. "We've been sitting right over there for the last half hour." She pointed to her table where her brother and Kyle suddenly looked extremely guilty and pretended to be in the midst of a conversation with one another. "I won't keep you any longer," she said to Olivia. "You and your…date were on your way out."

Olivia looked slightly alarmed. "Look," she said quietly, "do you mind not saying anything to Sophie about seeing me here with Warren? I mean, no details at least."

"You mean details like the hand holding and kissing?" Wren asked, glad to have gotten the upper hand.

"Uh-huh. Like that."

Wren observed Olivia's face for a moment. "Okay. I suppose you're the one who should tell her about that."

Olivia nodded. "Yes, exactly." She was firm, not the least bit apologetic.

When they had left, Wren returned to her table.

"What do you think you're doing?" Raven scolded.

"Did you find out anything?" Kyle asked.

Raven snorted. "Like the woman's going to spill all her intimate secrets to a stranger! Of course she didn't find out anything."

"On the contrary, Mr. Smug Mug," Wren said. "I found out plenty."

"You did?"

"I did. Olivia Ward is having an affair with that dashing doctor on the sly. Sophie doesn't know and Olivia wants it to stay that way."

Raven's eyes widened. "I'm impressed."

"You know," Wren said, feeling pleased with herself, "when you think about it, I know a heck of a lot more about what's going on with Sophie and Olivia than either of them do."

"What're you going to do with this information?" Kyle asked.

Wren picked up her fork. "I don't know," she said decisively, then stabbed a piece of salmon and put it in her mouth.

There wasn't much she could do with the information. She began to feel lousy. She felt sorry for Sophie, thinking about what would happen when she found out her wife was having an affair, potentially more than an affair, with that handsome Dr. Connor. A bad business.

CHAPTER SIXTEEN

That he is mad, 'tis true: 'tis true 'tis pity; And pity 'tis 'tis true.

—*Hamlet*, Act II, Scene 2

Wren stormed out of the den and into the sunroom where Raven was having his morning coffee and reading the local newspaper. It was Friday and Kyle had gone out early to set up his drawing station downtown, hoping to get a jump on the weekend crowd.

"You wouldn't think he'd want to provoke me like this," Wren said, waving a piece of paper at Raven. "I can get back at him any time by reviewing one of his restaurants."

"Who are you talking about?" he asked, picking up his coffee mug.

"This pompous ass, John Bâtarde."

Raven wiped his mouth with the back of his hand. "John Bâtarde? That name sounds familiar."

"I'm not surprised. He's got a half dozen restaurants. A big star in the world of food. I think he even had a TV show for a while."

"No, that's not it. Somewhere recently..." Raven frowned, trying to remember, then he shook his head and said, "You should try one of these pastries. They're fabulous."

Wren eyed the plate of round doughy treats on the coffee table. "Are those aebleskiver?"

He shrugged. "Kyle found them somewhere in town." He picked one up and popped it whole into his mouth.

"I haven't had those in a while. But I think I'll pass. Since I've been here I've done nothing but sit around and eat and drink."

Wren sat in the comfy overstuffed chair next to the sofa and gazed out the sunroom window to the backyard. Raven and Kyle were not the gardening types. The yard was going wild. Tea roses were taking over the back fence and dandelions dotted the spotty lawn. In a bare patch that had been someone else's vegetable garden, a few tomato and zucchini plants had appeared from last year's forgotten seeds. Wren had taken pity on them and watered them a couple times, though she knew when she left they would be doomed. But she couldn't bear to see a plant die of thirst. Especially a volunteer from a seed that had survived the winter and found a way to realize its destiny all on its own. Such a hardy, optimistic little thing, a seedling.

She missed having a garden. A foodie without a bare patch of land to raise herbs and vegetables lacked authenticity. The Farmer's Market was great, but couldn't do much to satisfy the inclination to pluck a fresh sprig of rosemary to garnish a steak plate or snip a couple of chives to float on a bowl of butternut squash soup. Those spontaneous little touches that make food special have to come out of your own garden. She sighed fatalistically.

"Bâtarde has it in for me," she explained, "ever since I reviewed his flagship restaurant Josephine earlier this year. I said his twelve-layer Hungarian Dobos Torte was dry."

"Was it?"

"Yes, it was. The rest of the meal was great, which I acknowledged with ample enthusiasm, but the torte was dry. I also said it had good flavor, but all he heard was the dry part. The thing is, he didn't even make the damned thing. He doesn't cook in his restaurants. But it's his recipe, his signature dessert… literally. It's called John Bâtarde's Hungarian Dobos Torte. I mean, his name is part of it. I was actually in Josephine the night he read the review. He had a violent temper tantrum. He's been sending me hate mail ever since, threatening to destroy me."

"The bastard!" Raven hit the table with his fist.

"He should have gotten after his pastry chef, not me. I've built my reputation on honesty. I don't pander to anyone. I would never give a bad restaurant, or a bad torte, a good review just to be nice."

"Oh, no kidding!" Raven waved the newspaper at her. "A person can't even sleep with you and expect a good report."

"That's the review of Sprouts?"

He nodded. "Your goatherd isn't going to be happy about this."

She shrugged, knowing he was right. "I'm not in the business of making people happy. When Eno says nice things, people are all like, yeah, he got that right. But any little criticism and I'm some kind of freaking moron who doesn't know a cruller from a…aebleskiver." She leaned forward to look more carefully at the delicate spheres covered with powdered sugar. "Bâtarde, for instance," she continued, sitting back in her chair. "I said lovely things about his crab quesadilla and his pumpkin seed fritters. But none of that registers. All he notices is the one tiny negative comment."

"The ingrate!"

"After the review came out, he sent me an email asking what right I had insulting his torte. What right? I'm a food critic, for God's sake! But I didn't say that. I answered with my usual reply, that I call them as I see them."

"Seems fair."

"Actually," Wren admitted, "my exact words were, 'Sorry, Cookie, that's the way the torte crumbles.'"

Raven winced.

"Yeah," Wren admitted, "maybe not as tactful as I might have been."

112 Robbi McCoy

"I'll bet that really ticked him off."

"Big time. He demanded retribution. He demanded I show myself and tell him to his face his torte was dry. He threatened to ferret me out and destroy me. He called me a fraud, a coward, an ignorant, unqualified yokel."

"Ooh! Brought out the big guns, did he?" Raven laughed.

"Right. These people take their food very seriously. Sometimes it just gets so tiresome."

"Sick of it all?"

"Sometimes I am, yeah. I've been doing this so long now, it seems like so much of the same thing over and over. I suppose that's why I brushed him off like that. Just tired of the whining from these self-important kitchen divas who think of me as the enemy. They have the ludicrous viewpoint that if they could just get rid of the critics, their food would be flawless."

"That reminds me of that famous line from Henry the Sixth." Raven hopped up with sudden liveliness. He stood on the couch, bouncing on the cushion and raised one fist above his head. "The first thing we do, let's kill all the critics!"

"Lawyers!" Wren objected loudly. "Not critics! Let's kill all the *lawyers.*"

"Oh. You're right. Sorry." Raven sank back to a sitting position. "If you weren't a food critic, what would you do? You love writing about food."

"There are other ways to write about food. I've got a half-written book somewhere, for instance. And I do write feature articles once in a while. It's just that I've built up such a following as a critic. I'm Eno Threlkeld." She chuckled. "Hear my name and tremble."

"That's not really a joke, is it?"

"No, not entirely." She shook her head. "But I'm tired of being the bad guy."

"The majority of people don't see you that way. Most people can take the bad with the good, as long as it isn't mean-spirited."

"Most people, maybe," Wren conceded. "Bâtarde, no. But I hadn't heard from him in a while and thought maybe he'd gotten over it."

"But he hasn't?"

"Far from it. He's totally obsessed now with avenging his Dobos Torte."

In her mind, she could see the short round Frenchman shaking his fist at her, his ruddy face contorted into a hateful glare, his mustache askew from the snarl on his lip.

"I wouldn't be surprised if he really is insane," she said, shaking her head. "His mother went mad. Of course, she had reason. The family history, very sordid."

Raven looked up with interest. He was always in the mood for a scandalous family tale.

"When Bâtarde was a kid," she explained, "his father, Mack Bâtarde, murdered his boss. Stabbed him to death."

"No kidding? How do you know about this?"

"I'd heard rumors, so I looked it up in old newspapers."

"What was the motive?"

"Old Mack had his eye on the top job in his company. He wanted the guy out of the way."

"He couldn't just wait his turn like anybody else?"

"He was corrupted by ambition and goaded on by his wife Elizabeth. They called her Beth. Actually, she was the one who cooked up the plot to begin with. Very greedy, cold-hearted woman."

"She sounds lovely," Raven noted.

"They tried to frame one of the security guards at the company, but it didn't hold up. After his deed was discovered, Mack Bâtarde went on a murderous rampage. He slaughtered the wife and kids of a colleague."

Raven's eyes widened dramatically. "Why?"

"It's kind of hard to understand his motivation, actually. I mean, he starts out this fine, upstanding citizen, admired by all, then all of a sudden he's a treacherous lunatic murdering his friends, driven by greed and paranoia."

"Like he was cursed or bewitched or something?"

"Maybe." Wren shrugged. "So this guy whose family he killed came after him."

"I don't blame him."

"Killed Bâtarde in revenge. Very bloody business. Meanwhile,

114   Robbi McCoy

the guilt and stress were preying on Mrs. Bâtarde. She starts wandering aimlessly through the halls in the middle of the night, scrubbing at her hands, talking to herself. Completely bonkers."

"What happened to her?"

"There's a little bit of confusion over that. There was so much going on at the time, her death is almost a footnote, but most accounts said she killed herself. A colossal tragedy for several families by the time it was over."

"Wow." Raven settled back into his chair, balancing his coffee mug on his knee. "So Bâtarde, Junior, was left an orphan, just like my darling Kyle."

"Yes, except that Kyle turned into a beautiful, even-keeled person and Bâtarde is utterly unreasonable and a little scary. That reminds me, what's Kyle's story? How did he become an orphan?"

Raven shook his head. "That's a story for another day. I don't think we can handle two family tragedies in one sitting." He dismissed Wren's unvoiced objection with a wave of his hand. "Read me Bâtarde's note."

She tucked her legs up in the chair and read from the page in her hand. "'Threlkeld, you coward, if you're not running scared yet, you soon will be. I know where you are. You've slipped up and I'll soon have your head on a platter.'"

"Yuck!" Raven said, wrinkling up his face.

Wren continued reading. "'Two reviews in ten days. I'm so close now I can taste your lily-colored liver.'"

"Is this guy some kind of cannibal?"

"Food-related images sort of go with the territory."

Raven waved his hand. "Go on."

"'You're cornered and you'll soon be unmasked. You're finished, Threlkeld! You will rue the day you ever insulted a dessert of mine. Dry, indeed! Prepare yourself to be butchered!'"

Wren wadded up the paper and tossed it toward the trash can, missing.

"Maybe you should call the police," Raven suggested. "He sounds dangerous."

"It's just bluster. He still doesn't know who I am or how to find me. As long as that's true, he can't do a thing to me. Besides, I can't call the police without revealing myself. For all I know, that's his game. He's been trying to flush me out all along with threats and insults."

"So he knows you're in Ashland."

"I suppose. He must have seen that review this morning. Anybody could figure it out after the last two columns. If that's all he's got, he's as far from nailing me as he's ever been." She picked up one of the pastries and took a bite. "Oh, God, this is good!"

"Told you."

She nodded and finished the pastry, then stood. "I'm going over to the theater to see if I can snag some seats for a show tonight."

"I have a couple tickets for tonight's performance. You don't have to buy them."

"Sorry, Raven, I'd like to see something other than *Much Ado* this time." As she anticipated, he made a pouty face. "How many times can I watch you swat Benedick with your fan and still laugh?"

He smiled. "All right. I've heard good things about that Noel Coward's *Private Lives*."

"Oh, I love that play! I'll try for that. Has Kyle seen it?"

"No, not yet."

"Where can I find him?"

"He'll be set up on Main or Second, where the action is."

She nodded, then nipped another pastry before heading toward the doorway.

"Wait," he called. "Before you go, I just remembered where I heard that name before, John Bâtarde."

She stopped and faced him. "Where?"

"He's the celebrity judge they invited in for the Cupcake Extravaganza!"

Wren stared, surprised and wordless.

"He's here!" Raven declared. "Here in town."

CHAPTER SEVENTEEN

I was the more deceived.

—*Hamlet*, Act III, Scene 1

Sophie packed her Styrofoam cooler with dozens of rounds of chêvre and some ice packs, then fitted the lid on securely as she heard her mother's voice calling her, full of urgency.

"Sophie! Sophie!"

She ran out to the front porch to find Olivia standing there with the newspaper in her hand. Thrusting it at her, she said, "Look at this."

Sophie took the paper and folded it back to its original shape. "What am I looking at?"

"An article about Sprouts. Page seven. They dissed our cheese."

Sophie sat on the loveseat and found the review, written by Eno Threlkeld, the critic Ellie and Johanna had told her about. It was a glowing review of Sprouts and Sophie was all ready to rejoice...until she reached the part about the cheese.

The chèvre in the beet salad, from Tallulah Rose Creamery, a new, local dairy, was passable, tangy and properly ripened, but the texture was gritty and the flavor was unbalanced, leaving a slightly bitter aftertaste.

Sophie was stunned.

"Who is that guy?" Olivia asked. "He obviously doesn't know anything about cheese."

Sophie slumped back into the cushion. "Unfortunately, he's a big wheel. A critic from San Francisco."

"I thought our cheese was good. Didn't Ellie say it was the best she ever had?"

"Yes, she did." Sophie sighed. "I don't know, Mom. Maybe the standards are just that much higher in the big city. Maybe we're only good for Ashland. For San Francisco, maybe we're just…passable."

"So what are we going to do about it?" Olivia stood above her, her mouth set in a determined line.

"I don't know what we can do about it. This is his opinion."

Olivia sat back in her chair. "Maybe nobody'll read it," she said hopefully.

"I doubt that. This came from the Associated Press. That means everybody sees it. A lot of papers will pick it up."

Olivia went silent and sat looking at the floorboards, crestfallen. There was nothing Sophie could do to cheer her up. She felt too defeated herself, over both the lousy review and her discovery that Wren had lied about her employer. Was that even her real name? Fat chance! Who was named Wren? Sophie's original guess that Raven was a stage name had likely been correct. Wren had probably come up with that take-off on the spot. Very clever of her. She must have had a good laugh over it later. Sophie could easily imagine her telling her brother about it: "I told her my name was Wren and that our parents were birding fanatics." They'd both probably doubled over at that.

Sophie was aware that the Wren of her current imagination was a much more callous woman than the Wren she had spent the night with. But she was far too familiar with duplicity to question the possibility that both those women could coexist in one body.

118   Robbi McCoy

Going into town to deliver her new batch of cheese didn't make Sophie as happy as it would have before the Threlkeld review. But she felt somewhat better after the owner of the Blue Moon told her, "Don't pay any attention to that review. Your cheese is gorgeous stuff. I don't know what his problem is."

Sophie then walked from Main Street down Second Street, coming across a handsome young man set up for drawing caricatures. He was seated at a table across the street from Sprouts. A board behind the table displayed samples of his work. He was clean-shaven, neatly and casually dressed, wearing a suede, Robin Hood-style cap with a long pheasant feather out the back. He drank from a tall paper coffee cup, sitting back in his folding chair with his legs crossed, unengaged. Sophie stopped. She'd always wanted to have her caricature drawn, but had never taken the time to do it.

He jumped to his feet and smiled, showing his perfect teeth. "Hi. Would you like me to draw you?"

Sophie nodded and sat at the matching folding chair across from him.

"I'm Kyle," he said, putting aside his coffee.

"Sophia," she replied. "But everybody calls me Sophie."

"Beautiful name." He reached over and shook her hand. "Greek. Meaning wisdom."

"That's right. And what does Kyle mean?"

He clamped a fresh piece of drawing paper on his easel. "It's Gaelic. Means narrow or straight. Ironically, I am neither."

Sophie laughed. "I'm sure there are people who would say the same about me being wise."

He smiled warmly, then nodded toward his sample board. "Do you have anything in mind? We can do you in Elizabethan style with the ruffled collar. That's very popular."

"No, I think something more just regular me."

"Okay. Find a comfortable position. This'll take about fifteen minutes."

Sophie sat back in the chair. "I like gardening. Maybe you can put a big, floppy sun hat on me."

He nodded, making the first light marks on his paper. "Are you in town for long?"

"I live here," she said. "Not a tourist."

"I don't get many locals. Seems like a nice place to live. I've been here just a few months myself, but am considering staying."

"The town has a lot to offer," Sophie observed. "Especially for an artist."

After another minute, Kyle focused on his work, dropping the conversation, while Sophie sat still, casually watching the street activity. Across the street, Sprouts was open for lunch. People strolled up to read the menu. Some went in, some went on. A few people on their side of the street stopped to watch Kyle at work, which made Sophie self-conscious.

Kyle's estimate of fifteen minutes was exactly right. Just as Sophie was feeling like she needed to stand up and jump up and down, he announced, "Done!"

She got up and came around to look at his drawing. It was delightful. She was charmed. She clapped her hands together.

"You like it," he guessed.

"I love it!" The drawing was like her, yet not like her. Cute and funny with a hat as large as the rest of her altogether, her oversized head and her undersized body.

She paid him and he rolled up the paper and put it in a cardboard tube.

"Thank you so much, Mr. Straight and Narrow," Sophie said. "Your work is fabulous."

"I bow to your wisdom, milady." Kyle bowed from the waist, took her hand and brushed it lightly with his lips.

"Do you do other sorts of work?" Sophie asked. "For hire, I mean."

"If it pays," he said, "I'll consider it. What do you have in mind?"

"A product label. Would you do something like that?"

"Sure. I'm actually doing one right now, for a winery. Take my card and give me a call." He handed her a business card.

She glanced at the card, then tucked it away, thinking she'd found the solution to her label problem for Tallulah Rose Creamery. By now, a young couple was waiting their turn.

"Thanks, again," Sophie said.

As Kyle greeted his next customers, Sophie wheeled her Styrofoam cooler across the street to Sprouts, feeling much better than she had when she'd driven into town this morning. She slipped inside to find Ellie standing at the coffee bar talking with a young man. Sophie recognized him from a week ago. He was the boy who'd played the part of "a boy" in *Much Ado About Nothing*, the redheaded moppet. He took Ellie's hand tenderly in his and said, "'Where thou art, there is the world itself, and where thou art not, desolation.'"

Ellie put her free hand to her throat with a sharp intake of breath as the boy kissed her hand. He then abruptly turned and ran past Sophie and out the door.

Ellie noticed Sophie. "Hi," she said, her eyes unfocused, still clutching her throat.

Sophie approached her. "Did I just hear that boy quote Shakespeare at you?"

"Henry the Sixth, Part Two," she confirmed breathily.

This was interesting, Sophie thought, observing Ellie's face closely. "That's okay with you?"

"No harm done," Ellie said with a wave of her hand.

"True," agreed Sophie. "What's his name?"

"Max."

"You do know he's an actor, right?"

"Yes, I know. He told me. Not exactly my favorite people, as you know. But he's not a full-time actor and you know how many would-be actors give it a try and end up being house painters or plumbers. Actually, he works in a nursery."

"A nursery?"

"Plants. That kind of nursery."

"Oh." Sophie was still stunned at seeing Ellie being romanced. "Are you dating?"

"No! I barely know him. He's come by a couple times. Today he brought me a rose." She picked up a long-stemmed red rosebud from the coffee bar and held it to her nose.

"But you're interested?"

Ellie tilted her head coyly.

"Wow," Sophie breathed. "I never thought I'd see the day. You actually *are* interested. That's wonderful! He's a cute little guy. Buzzes around kind of fast. You might have a hard time keeping up with him."

Ellie laughed. "He hasn't asked me out."

"He will. There's not much point quoting poetry at a girl unless you're headed that way."

"I don't know what it is," Ellie said with a goofy smile, "but I can't stop thinking about him. He's just so sweet. Shy and quiet. Hard to imagine him on stage."

"I'm very happy for you, Ellie. Astonished, but happy."

Ellie took a deep sniff of her rose again before turning toward the kitchen. "Come on back and let's unload your cheese."

Sophie rolled her cooler into the kitchen. The chef preparing vegetables was someone she didn't recognize, a middle-aged woman who paid no attention to them.

"I hope you brought me more of that sage," Ellie said. "People loved it."

Sophie pulled the lid off her cooler. "I'm glad to hear you're still enthusiastic about my cheese."

"Of course! Why wouldn't I be?"

"Don't tell me you haven't seen the Threlkeld review."

"Yes, I've seen it. It was my restaurant he reviewed, after all. I'm so sorry about what he said about your cheese." She looked distraught. "I mean, I'm *really* sorry."

"It isn't your fault," Sophie said.

Ellie bit her bottom lip. "Well—"

"What do you mean, well?"

"It sort of is my fault. But I've fixed the problem." Ellie gestured toward the stranger at the prep station. "That's Maria. She's our new cook. I fired Johanna this morning as soon as I found out what she did. She was an excellent chef, but—"

"Fired Johanna?" Sophie interrupted. "Why? What does she have to do with it?"

Ellie looked apologetic. "She took it upon herself to serve store-bought chèvre when we ran out of yours."

"What?" Sophie stared. "But it says right on the menu, Tallulah Rose Creamery."

"Yes, I know. It was my firm policy that when we were out, we were to stop serving the dishes. But she thought that was a mistake. She thought that if somebody wanted a beet and chèvre salad, they should get it. She decided nobody would know the difference."

"She never did like me," Sophie said dejectedly.

"I had no idea she was doing that until this morning when I found the cheese in the refrigerator. Some supermarket brand. Some mass-produced stuff from California. Apparently, we ran out of yours even earlier than usual this week."

"Is that what Threlkeld got, the store-bought stuff?"

"I have to assume that. Why else would he be so unimpressed with it? If you taste that stuff she was serving, you'll understand. His opinion was right on. Johanna doesn't respect her customers. She thinks they're unsophisticated ninnies, that they can't tell a good goat cheese from a bad one. I couldn't believe she did that, especially knowing Threlkeld was in town."

"You fired her for that?"

"Yes! Not just the cheese. She's made other decisions that were in direct defiance of me. She's taken way too many liberties, as if she thought this was her restaurant, but this was the final straw. I'm proud to feature Tallulah Rose Creamery on my menu and I damned well know the difference. And so do my customers."

Sophie hugged Ellie, feeling grateful. "Thank you!"

"There's nothing to thank me for. I'm responsible for your bad review. I wish that Eno Threlkeld would make himself known so I could have another shot at him."

"You still have no idea what he looks like?"

"No. Johanna was serving her store-bought stuff Tuesday through Thursday. He must have come in during that time."

"Even if the review still stands, I feel a whole lot better knowing this." Sophie took a deep breath. "I was beginning to wonder myself if my cheese was merely passable."

"Trust me on that, Sophie. It's much better than passable. It's your perfectionist nature that insures that. You're not very fast and you don't produce very much, but what you do make is heavenly."

"Thanks," Sophie said.

"I'm sorry about the mix-up. I've told Maria we're going to

be putting your cheese front and center for a while. We'll come up with some new dishes and make sure it shines, give it the place of honor it deserves. So give me as much as you can."

"I can give you three extra this week." Sophie unpacked the cheese from her box. "I've been working harder than usual to make more. But, ultimately, it's up to the goats and the supply of milk."

Ellie put the cheese in the refrigerator. "What've you got there?" She indicated the cardboard tube.

"It's a caricature." Sophie opened the tube and unrolled the drawing, holding it up for Ellie.

She laughed for several seconds. "That's wonderful! You'll have to frame it and hang it up. "Who did it?"

"A guy across the street."

She led Ellie to the front window where she pointed out Kyle who was no longer drawing, but standing beside his easel as a woman fluttered up and gave him a hug. Sophie all but choked. It was Wren hanging on Kyle's neck.

In the many days since their tryst, she'd forgotten how lovely Wren was. She was surprised by the rush of emotion that swept over her at the sight of that face, even the slant of her forehead and the way her dark hair curled around her ear. She vividly remembered lying beside her as she slept, staring at that delicate and lovely ear, feeling overcome by its simple beauty.

So Wren was still in town. It occurred to Sophie that maybe she lived here. If everything else was a lie, maybe her story about living in San Francisco was also a lie.

"I should have him do me too," Ellie said, standing beside her.

Sophie roused herself from the quicksand she felt herself sinking into. "Yes, you should."

Her gaze was drawn back to the couple across the street. They were looking at one another, talking animatedly. Neither of them glanced her way. Which was just as well. She didn't know what she would do if Wren actually looked at her.

"Attractive couple, aren't they?" Ellie noted.

"Couple? Why do you assume that?"

"I'm not assuming. They were in here for dinner the other day. They referred to each other as husband and wife."

"Oh, no, that couldn't have been her," Sophie said. "It must have been another couple. Or he was with another woman."

"No." Ellie shook her head. "I know it was her. That's the same woman who was in here with her twin brother last week. You were here that day too. Maybe you remember them. They looked so much alike, it was hard not to notice."

Sophie's stomach knotted up.

"No, that's ridiculous," she began, then stopped abruptly because she realized she knew nothing about it one way or the other. All she knew about Wren was what Wren had told her and she already knew at least some of that was a lie.

"Is something wrong?" Ellie asked. "You look pale."

"I need to sit down," Sophie said, feeling weak in the knees. She let herself sink into a chair at the nearest table.

"What is it?" Ellie asked.

Sophie tried to compose herself. "That's her. That's the woman I—"

Ellie looked confused for a moment, then she suddenly seemed enlightened. "Your date!"

Sophie nodded.

"Oh, my God! Oh, my God!" Ellie slapped her hand over her mouth and gradually calmed herself. "Why? Why would you sleep with that gorgeous man's wife? Maybe I should say *how*? If I had a husband who looked like that… Not to imply you're not all that, Sophie." Ellie laid a reassuring hand on Sophie's shoulder.

Sophie shook her head forlornly. "I had no idea she—"

"You didn't know about him?"

"Of course I didn't know about him! If I'd known about him, do you think I'd have—"

Ellie looked stricken, glancing back through the window at the couple across the street.

"I don't know why I'm surprised she's a liar and a cheat," Sophie said bitterly. "In my experience, that's very common."

"Look, Sophie, you don't know anything about them. It's possible her husband doesn't mind. There are couples who have arrangements like that. Maybe she likes to be with a woman now and then."

Sophie stared, frowning her discontent.

"I can see I just don't know the right thing to say," Ellie said. "Sorry, but this isn't a situation I'm familiar with. How about this instead?" Her face turned into an exaggerated scowl. "That bitch! Using you like that. Who does she think she is? I hope her hair falls out and her teeth rot."

Sophie forced a smile. "That's a little extreme. After all, I used her too. It was mutual. I knew what I was doing, sleeping with a stranger. That's part of the bargain, that you don't know why she's in your bed. You're just grateful for it."

"Oh, so now you're defending her. You see, I can't win here." Ellie stamped one foot on the floor with mock indignation.

"It bothers me more than it should," Sophie said. "It reminds me of Jan. Cheating. Lies. But you're right, I know nothing about Wren's marriage. If that's her name. Did she tell you her name?"

"No."

"Are you really sure they're married?"

"All I can tell you is he referred to her as his wife and she referred to him as her husband. I didn't ask to see a marriage license. They seemed very fond of one another. Talkative, laughing." Ellie cringed. "Oh, maybe that isn't what you want to hear either, is it?"

"The thing is, I really liked her. I thought she was sweet and sincere. Why am I such a terrible judge of character?"

"I'm sorry, Sophie. I need to get back to my customers. Sit here as long as you want. Have a cup of tea."

When Kyle had said he was neither straight nor narrow, Sophie had assumed he meant he was gay and open-minded. Maybe he was bisexual. Wren apparently was. Maybe that was something they had in common.

As Sophie watched unobserved, Wren snatched the cap from Kyle's head and put it on, modeling it for him. She tilted her head this way and that, then spun around in a circle. She looked adorable. Kyle eventually took his hat back, then Wren hugged him again and took off at a fast walk toward Main Street.

Sophie rolled up her drawing and returned it to its tube. When Ellie passed her, she laid a comforting hand briefly on her shoulder before moving on. A few minutes after Wren had gone, Sophie said goodbye to Ellie and left the restaurant. Kyle saw her across the street and waved his cap at her cheerfully. She waved, forcing a smile, thinking about how agreeable he was and how different he would be if he knew she had spent a deliriously passionate night with his wife.

She was disturbed and saddened by her new knowledge. Despite everything she'd been telling herself, she'd been secretly hoping for some happy turn of events, a little magic or just a quirk of circumstance that would defy everyday life and deliver her a dream. She was disappointed in herself. By now she should have known better.

CHAPTER EIGHTEEN

Ah me! for aught that I could ever read,
Could ever hear by tale or history,
The course of true love never did run smooth.

—*A Midsummer Night's Dream*, Act I, Scene I

Wren was able to get two great seats for the Friday evening performance of *Private Lives*. She hoped Raven was okay with her not coming to see him yet again. He couldn't really expect that, she was sure. Almost sure. She'd go once more before she left Ashland and hoped that would prove her enthusiasm. Kyle, too, was glad for the chance to see something different, but hadn't been bold enough to suggest it. "Just wait," she'd told him. "After three years together, he'll have to bribe you to go to his plays even once."

She tucked the tickets into her bag, then walked downhill to Main Street where she strolled along the sidewalk, window-shopping. There was an endless number of interesting gift shops here, not just the usual T-shirt and tacky souvenir places, though those were also available. But there were lots of shops with unique crafts and art objects. She stopped to peer into the window of an antique store at some old toys, some of them she remembered from her own childhood, some older, like the adjustable metal roller skates. There was a Care Bear that reminded her of her own and one of the original My Little Ponies, a pink one that looked identical to the one Raven had had. Of course, as had always happened, people gave such toys to Wren and then she swapped them with whatever Raven had gotten, like Transformers. She momentarily considered buying that pony for him, but it would probably seem like a gag gift and she didn't mean it that way at all.

She turned from the window to continue down the sidewalk. Up ahead, through the crowd, she saw a woman walking away from her who had a familiar and heart-stopping swing to her hips. Wren caught her breath and stared. The woman pulled a Styrofoam cooler on a wheeled cart and was wearing jeans and a blue and white striped blouse. It had to be Sophie, she realized, then started walking rapidly toward her.

Sophie stopped at the corner and waited for the light. Now that she'd turned to cross, Wren could see her face in profile and her identity was confirmed. The sidewalk was crowded. By the time she made it to the corner, Sophie was across the street and the light was red again. Cars passed between them.

"Sophie!" Wren called loudly, jumping up and waving. "Sophie!"

Sophie turned and looked, and her eyes seemed to lock directly on Wren's for a split second as Wren continued waving, but then she walked off down the street. She seemed to be walking even faster than before. Frustrated, Wren decided she hadn't actually seen her, or at least she hadn't recognized her if she did. The line of cars finally stopped and Wren raced across the street and headed after Sophie, who was already a block ahead of her.

She dodged through the strolling tourists, feeling like a fish working its way upstream. Then suddenly she caught sight of someone who brought her to a dead stop. Only fifty feet ahead was Ellie's sister Cassandra. She wore her long brown cape and was moving slowly in Wren's direction, though she didn't appear to have seen her yet. *Holy Crap!* Wren said to herself.

She ducked through the door of the nearest shop, moving around to the front window so she could keep an eye on Cassandra. Standing a few feet back, she watched, resting her hand on top of a tall, inflated plastic toy. Cassandra came into view and turned to look at the display in the window. She seemed to be looking straight at Wren, who froze. Cassandra's icy eyes were vacant, her expression neutral. For once, she didn't look threatening and Wren realized she hadn't seen her. She was looking at something in the window. She apparently couldn't see past the window display. Wren let out her breath and relaxed. Finally, Cassandra moved on.

It was then that Wren glanced around to see she was standing next to a wall of DVDs. She read some titles: *Saturday Night Beaver, Rambone, Star Whores.* Confused for a second, she suddenly realized these were porn movies. She then took a better look at the plastic balloon beside her. At first she'd assumed it was a kid's punching bag. But now she saw that her hand rested atop a three-foot inflatable pink penis with realistic looking red arteries, ridges and a tip she had mistaken, in her distraction, for a clown head.

She jerked her hand away, wiping her palm on her jeans. What would anybody do with a three-foot inflatable phallus? Maybe it was a punching bag, after all. She looked at the base, wondering if it was weighted like her mother's oft-remembered Bozo the Clown. Her mother had loved that toy, the way she could punch it and punch it with all her might, knock it all the way to the floor and it would pop right back up, still smiling with that garish mouth and signature orange hair. Wren hauled off and punched the thing, smack, right in the middle and watched, horrified, as it sailed into the arms of a person who had been quietly watching her. There stood a freakishly tall Goth-styled girl, her black hair shaved on the left side of her head and hanging down about five inches on the right. She had four silver rings in her nose and a diamond stud in her cheek. The hardware in her ears was too much to count. The expression on her face was inscrutably passive.

"Can I help you?" the young woman asked in a calm, measured voice hinging on irritation. She set the penis balloon aside.

"No thank you," Wren said, disconcerted. "Just looking."

The girl nodded very slowly, once, as Wren caught sight of a shelf of vibrators.

"Oh," she said, "on second thought, I could use some batteries. But I'll have to come back. I've got to run."

She dashed out of the store and took off in the direction she'd last seen Sophie, scanning the sidewalks on both sides of the street. She waited for a while, leaning against a building at a busy intersection. This sucks, she thought, then wondered what she'd been intending to do when she caught up with her. She'd had nothing in mind. She just wanted to... Yeah, that was the problem. Even if Olivia had another lover, Sophie was still married. A potentially very messy situation there.

Wren gave up and walked up Second Street to Kyle's makeshift studio. She fell into his customer chair, feeling discouraged.

"Hey, don't sit there," he said, "people will think I'm not available."

Wren frowned. "Or maybe they'll think you're popular and start forming a long line around the block."

"Why so sullen? Couldn't you get tickets for tonight?"

"No, I got them. Then I saw Sophie and I lost her. Didn't even get to say hi."

"Sophie?" Kyle said, clearly not knowing who she was talking about. He looked suddenly enlightened. "Oh, right, the girl you...the goat farmer."

She gave him a brief, sarcastic grin.

"That's funny," he said, wiping his hands on a white rag, trying to get the graphite off. "I had a customer named Sophie earlier today. It's gotten to be a popular name, hasn't it? I know a guy who just had a baby and they named her Sophie. Of course, the Sophie here earlier was around thirty, so not part of the current trend, after all."

Wren stared at him in disbelief. "Sophie was here this morning?" she asked.

"A woman named Sophie was here this morning. I drew her."

"What did she look like?" Wren leaned forward in the chair.

"A few inches taller than you, blonde with hair down to about here." He held his hand at the base of his neck. "Blue eyes."

"Blue? Or more like gray? Sort of gray-blue?"

"Maybe gray-blue. I don't worry much about color with the black-and-white drawing. Just light or dark." He picked up a pencil and began drawing with short, rapid movements. "I remember she had a little cart with her."

Wren leapt out of her chair. "That was her! She's delivering her cheese. Every Friday she comes into town to deliver it."

Kyle looked up from his easel. "I had no idea she was your Sophie. The thought never entered my mind. She seemed nice. I liked her. Sit down. I'm drawing you."

Wren sank into the chair. "Did she tell you anything of interest?"

"Like what?"

"Like she's getting a divorce."

Kyle pursed his lips and gazed at her silently for several seconds, then returned to his sketch.

"Anything at all then?" Wren asked hopefully.

"The only thing she said that was even a tiny bit personal was that she liked to garden."

"Garden? That's it?"

He nodded without looking at her. "Is that bad?"

"No, it isn't bad. It's actually good, but it isn't very useful. You had her sitting here captive for twenty minutes and didn't find out anything more than she likes to garden?"

"Fifteen minutes," he corrected. "Maybe if you'd given me a script or we'd had more rehearsals, I could have done a better job. Or maybe if she'd told me she was the Sophie who slept with you, I would have had an opening to ask all these personal questions you think I should have asked." He continued drawing as he spoke. "In my defense, I'd also like to point out that you yourself talked to her for several hours and never found out she was married or even that she likes to garden."

"Okay, okay," Wren relented, frowning at his smug expression.

"Getting involved with a married woman is an invitation to disaster, in my opinion."

Wren nodded. "I know. That's why I'm staying away. If I'd known about Olivia in the beginning, I never would have batted my eyelashes at her. So, yes, I'm done with Sophie. I'm going to purge her completely from my mind."

"And heart?" Kyle asked.

Wren didn't answer. She watched Kyle's rapid hand movements as he focused on his drawing.

"Let me see," she said after a few minutes, moving around behind him and looking over his shoulder. She was startled to see a recognizable but cartoonish likeness of her head, in profile, attached to a tiny bird's body, flying. Her nose was thrust forward like a beak. She laughed. "That's different! I like it. I'll leave now so you can attract some paying customers."

"You mean you aren't going to pay me for this?" he joked.

"I'll cook you dinner. How's that?"

"Fair enough. You heading home?"

"Yes. But first I need to stop by this little store I found a while ago and pick up a couple things."

"What kind of store?"

"Toy store."

He looked at her quizzically, but didn't ask any more questions. She wouldn't have answered him anyway.

CHAPTER NINETEEN

Your tale, sir, would cure deafness.

—*The Tempest*, Act I, Scene 2

Saturday morning Wren slept in. When she finally rolled out of bed, she found herself alone in the house. Raven and Kyle had left her a note that they'd gone to the Farmers' Market. She was sorry they hadn't wakened her for that, as she liked to check out the Farmers' Markets wherever she went. Maybe after some coffee, she thought, she'd run over there on her own.

She took her first cup to the den and logged into her computer to read her email. The den in this house wasn't large. It was detailed in dark wood and finished off with intricate crown molding like the other rooms. The modern desk with Wren's laptop open on it looked out of place amid the old-fashioned surroundings. The room occupied the southwest corner of the house, with a window facing the side yard and another facing the street, both of them covered with yellowed lace sheers and pull-down blinds, the kind that always snap up screaming in cartoons, frequently trapping some lumpy animal inside. Every time she opened these blinds, like this morning, in her mind she saw a comical blue mouse rolled up inside with his head sticking out one end.

The wall art in this room no doubt contributed to her predisposition to think of cartoons. Some of Kyle's caricatures adorned the walls, including a framed pair depicting himself and Raven in pirate attire—big black hats, wooden legs, parrots, long black mustaches, the works. These reminded her of the drawing he'd made of her yesterday.

After opening the blinds, she unlatched the window to the side yard and opened it, letting the outside air flow in. It was already warm out. It was going to be a hot day.

She sat at the desk and logged into Eno Threlkeld's email account. She made her way through yesterday's, then today's messages, eventually arriving at one with the subject, "Your Review of Sprouts." As she clicked it open, she saw the name on the From line: Sophie Ward. For a second, she forgot she was reading Eno's mail and thought Sophie had written to her. Her heart lurched before she saw the salutation: *Dear Mr. Threlkeld.*

This note wasn't for her at all. At least not in Sophie's mind. She prepared herself for the type of objection Eno received on a regular basis. Sophie would suggest that her mediocre cheese had not been given a fair shake, that maybe she could have a do-over. What she didn't know was that Eno could have been even harder on her. A cheese pretentiously described as "hand-crafted" should be significantly better than what you can buy in a grocery store. Hers wasn't. Wren read through Sophie's very formal note, imagining that if she replied at all, it would be a more polite version of "that's the way the cookie crumbles" than she'd given to Bâtarde. She didn't need to make any more enemies for Eno.

Dear Mr. Threlkeld:

We are the faces behind the Tallulah Rose Creamery mentioned in your recent review of Sprouts. Although your opinion of the chêvre you were served is no doubt accurate, you should know that it was an imposter. That was not our cheese. Against the wishes and knowledge of the restaurant owner, you were served a common variety of store-bought chèvre instead.

Tallulah Rose is a tiny family farm run by just my mother and me...

Wren stopped reading. A chill ran down her spine.

"Her mother!" she said aloud. "Olivia is her mother?"

She leapt from her chair and impulsively picked up the phone receiver and yelled, "Olivia is her mother!" at the dial tone.

Wren was beside herself and so excited she couldn't stand still. She ran to the window and stuck her head out, looking at the sky and the sparrows in the crepe myrtle trees. She closed her eyes and breathed deeply. Then she returned to the computer to finish reading Sophie's note.

Tallulah Rose is a tiny family farm run by just my mother and me. We're working hard to get this business off the ground and negative comments like yours could be devastating to our reputation. I've no doubt you would like our cheese if you actually tried it. I hope you'll at least consider publishing a retraction. The owner of Sprouts will vouch for these facts.

Sincerely,

Sophie & Olivia Ward

Wren leaned back in her chair, staring at the screen, overjoyed. What incredibly wonderful news! Not the part about the cheese mix-up, though she was grateful to hear that because it meant Sophie's cheese at least still had the potential to be excellent. No, that wasn't the real news. The real news was something much more momentous, something that changed everything. She dashed off a reply, anxious to leave the computer and act on her new knowledge.

Dear Sophie and Olivia,

I'm sincerely sorry for the mix-up and the possible damage done to your reputation. Although I'm most willing to print a retraction, they rarely do much good. People don't read them. But I may be able to find another way to help amend the situation and will make this a top priority.

Best Wishes,

Eno Threlkeld

She hit Send, then raced to her room to get dressed.

Just as she grabbed her keys from the kitchen counter, the doorbell rang. She peeked out the window and saw Max standing there, kicking at the wooden planks under his feet. He wore jeans and a T-shirt with a black leather vest over it. No tie this time. His motorcycle was parked at the curb. Wren reluctantly went to the door.

Max held a small terra-cotta pot with a hardy mint plant in it. "Hi," he said, thrusting the plant toward her. "Raven said you were complaining you haven't seen a fresh mint leaf since you've been here, so I brought you this from the nursery."

Wren took the pot. "Thank you. But I'll have to take it home with me. If I plant it here, they'll let it die."

"You can have mint in your tea while you're here, anyway."

Wren chuckled. "Is this why you came over?"

"No. Raven said I could come by today and practice some lines."

"He's not back yet from the Farmers' Market, but shouldn't be long."

"I'll wait."

Wren shut the front door, realizing she wasn't going anywhere until Raven returned. She would have to keep Max company until then.

"It's not your lines you're going to practice, I'm guessing," she said.

"No. I've only got two lines and one of them's 'Signior.' Don't really need to practice that." Max grinned that wide, full-faced grin Wren was beginning to think of as his signature expression. "It's Beatrice he's going to help me with."

Wren led the way back to the kitchen where she offered him a chair at the table. "How about some iced tea? We have fresh mint to put in it."

Max nodded. "Nice house."

Wren poured tea over two glasses of ice, bruised a couple of mint leaves for them, then sat down across from Max. He took a long drink from the glass, during which she examined his youthful features, surprised all over again that he was nearly her age. She watched his neck as he chugged the tea. No evidence of an Adam's apple. Sitting this close in the bright light of day, she could see there wasn't a hint of stubble on his smooth, freckled face, just some fine downy hairs like her own. Twenty-six and no facial hair?

"I don't think Raven's inclined to give you a chance to play Beatrice," she confided.

Max put the glass down. "You never know. Gotta be prepared, just in case. The history of theater is full of unexpected opportunities for the understudy. When your break comes, you'd better be the best you can."

"That's the right attitude."

"Raven's phenomenal, don't you think?" Max smiled, revealing all his upper teeth.

Wren was amused at his enthusiastic admiration of Raven. It was no wonder he had invited him over to rehearse. "Yes, he's doing a fine job. Really great."

She noticed Max's hand where it lay beside the drinking glass. He had thin, delicate fingers. His hands were almost dainty. She glanced up to his chest, obscured by the vest.

"Have you been with the company long?" she asked.

"Just a couple months. I know you gotta start at the bottom, work your way up and prove yourself with bit parts. That's okay. I'll be patient, learn the ropes from guys like Raven. A few years from now, I'll be playing the leads."

"If you keep at it, I'm sure you will." Wren held his eyes for a moment, trying to read past the eager optimism, the buoyant, good-natured conviviality, but she saw no deeper layer of meaning. "Max, what's your background? Where do you come from?"

He shrugged, then dropped his hands to his lap. "You mean my family?"

"Your family, sure."

"I'm from New Jersey. Small town called Verona. Not a great neighborhood. Kind of rough. There was this family from another house we didn't get along with. Always fighting."

"Like a gang war?"

"No. Just a couple families fighting over some old screw-over. We were supposed to steer clear of them, but my older brother fell in love with this girl from the other family. Her name was Julie. Mom and Dad would have hit the roof if they'd known. So my brother and Julie had a secret wedding." Max leaned toward Wren as if confiding a secret himself. "Not really legal, since they were underage. She was only fourteen. They wanted to run away together, so they cooked up this whacked plan." Max shook his head. "Man, that was a crappy plan!"

"What happened?"

"Everything went wrong. Everything! Like if it was a play, it'd be nothing but miscues. The end result was a double suicide, Julie and my brother. It was really messed up."

Wren straightened in her chair, appalled. "Oh, my God! How horrible for you. For your whole family. How tragic!"

Max nodded sadly.

"How old were you when this happened?"

"Just five. I don't remember much. But you couldn't be in my family and not know this story really well."

"No, of course not. What happened then?"

"My dad made up with the other family. Feud was over."

"Their shared tragedy buried their strife."

"Uh-huh."

"What a sad story."

"Yeah. It sucks." Max gulped down the rest of his tea. "My dad never really got over it. His son, you know."

Wren peered into Max's eyes. "But you were his son too, right?"

Max looked startled. "Yeah, sure. I just meant it was like his son, a son he lost. A big deal."

"No girls in your family?" Wren was more suspicious than ever.

Max shook his head. "Just me and my brother. Then just me."

Wren stood and picked up the empty glass. "Teen suicide is always so tragic." She laid a comforting hand on his shoulder, then walked to the sink and rinsed the glass. "Such a waste."

A clamor outside drew her attention to the driveway where Raven and Kyle were unloading their bounty—bags of fruits and vegetables ripened in the sunshine of southern Oregon.

"Your Beatrice has arrived!" Wren announced.

Max bounced up from his chair and ran to greet Kyle and Raven, helping them carry in the produce. When everything was put away, Raven ran himself a glass of water from the kitchen tap while Max waited for him in the living room where they would rehearse.

"How well do you know that boy?" Wren asked.

After gulping down his drink, Raven said, "Not well. Just met him when I started this play. Why?"

"I'm suspicious."

Raven put the glass on the counter and faced her. "About what?"

"Are you sure Max is a boy?"

Raven looked confused, then smiled. "Is this a joke?"

"No. I'm serious. How do you know he's a male?"

"I don't know for certain, of course, but what reason would he have, or she have, to lie about it? Besides, Cleo was adamant that both Beatrice and Benedick would be played by male actors. The fact that Max was chosen as my understudy proves he's a he."

"Does it? How do you know Cleo knows more about it than you do?"

Raven started to speak, then stopped, looking thoughtful.

"Would you say Beatrice is the lead role in this play?" Wren asked.

"Absolutely! I mean, she's part of a subplot, I suppose, if you want to be technical about it, but as far as stealing the show, she's got huge potential for being the star. Sharing the spotlight with Benedick, anyway. Their relationship is the most entertaining thing about this play."

"So one or the other is the star and both have to be played by men."

Raven gazed levelly at her for a moment, before saying, "I see your point. You think Max is a girl pretending to be a boy so he, I mean, she, could try out for a lead role. But he didn't get the part, either part. So there'd be no reason now to keep up the pretense."

"He thinks he's still going to have the chance. He believes

in miracles. In this case, the miracle would be you getting sick or dying."

Raven looked indignant. "Of all the nerve!"

"It's not personal. Just a kid looking for a chance to prove herself. I'm sure she doesn't want any harm to come to you. She's a worshipper at your feet."

"So you think Max is a girl?"

"I do. I'd be willing to bet on it."

"As tempting as that wager is, I know better than to oppose a lesbian's intuition on this subject. So let's pull down his pants and take a look!"

Raven stepped toward the doorway. Wren grabbed him by the arm. "Try something a little less offensive, why don't you? Like asking. While you're divining the mystery of Max's gender, I'm taking off for a while."

"Where are you going?"

"Tallulah Rose Farm." Wren's earlier excitement was returning now that she was free to leave. "Sophie's not married after all."

"They're divorced?"

"No. Olivia is her mother."

Raven stared, wide-eyed, then burst into a happy smile and hugged Wren tightly. "Congratulations!"

"Thank you. I'll see you later." She moved toward the door. "And while you're questioning Max about her gender, ask about her family tragedy too."

Raven looked intrigued.

"Thereby hangs a tale," Wren quipped.

CHAPTER TWENTY

I would I were thy bird.

—*Romeo and Juliet*, Act II, Scene 2

Tallulah Rose Creamery was easy to find with the directions Wren had from the Internet. A sign on a narrow country road marked a long, unpaved driveway that disappeared over a rise. There was no gate across the driveway, just an opening in the fence. She turned into the drive and continued amid gently rolling hills punctuated by an occasional oak tree. The countryside was beautiful and tranquil. She'd encountered no cars after turning off the highway. In the distance, a cloud of dust signaled a piece of farm equipment at work in a field.

She crested a hill to get her first glimpse of a modest white house, single-story with wood siding, sheltered within a cluster of well-established trees. Near the house were several small outbuildings of varying sizes, all weathered gray wood. An old green tractor sat beside one of the sheds. A detached garage stood next to the house and a pickup was parked in front of that.

She came to a stop in front of the house as the front door opened and Sophie stepped out onto the wide front porch. She wore a T-shirt and shorts, casual at-home clothes.

I should have brought flowers, Wren thought, but she had made this decision so quickly, she had planned nothing. She jumped out of her car and moved toward Sophie. "Hi," she called, waving.

Sophie looked stunned, not in a happy way. "What are you doing here?" she asked, as if she were making an accusation.

Wren stopped where she was, abandoning her plan to rush into Sophie's arms. They stood about eight feet apart.

"I wanted to see you," Wren said tentatively. "I've been wanting to see you again ever since..." She was now feeling uncomfortable. "You're not happy to see me?"

"No. I'm not."

"Oh." Wren hesitated, not knowing what to say. "We had such a good time. I thought we did anyway."

"Yes." Sophie's voice was ripe with sarcasm. "Great fun, wasn't it?"

She was like another person, not at all the woman Wren had met before. She was cold, even angry. *Thy cloudy brow stings like daggers.*

"I thought it was fun, yes," Wren said quietly. "Maybe even more than that. I've been thinking about you a lot since then. I thought—"

"I'm not interested." Sophie's statement was flat, her voice terse.

"Are you mad at me for some reason?"

"No, not mad. I'm just not interested, that's all." The look in Sophie's eyes was complicated, a mixture of sorrow and anger. "What happened between us," she said in a softer tone, "was a mistake. Please…just go."

"Go?" Wren couldn't understand. She tried to think of a way to stall. "Can I at least see your place? Take a look at those Nubian goats and taste some cheese?"

"I don't see any point in—" Sophie began.

Her answer was interrupted by the squeaking of the screen door behind her as Olivia appeared on the porch and came down the steps toward them. Why couldn't I see she was Sophie's mother? Wren thought, observing the now obvious resemblance between them.

"Hi," Olivia called, approaching her daughter. "Wren, that's your name, right? Like the bird. You decided to come out for a visit after all?"

Sophie looked confused. "Do you two know each other?"

"We met," Wren said, "the other day."

There was a message of caution on Olivia's face, which Wren understood was to remind her not to say anything about Dr. Connor.

"Nice to see you again, Olivia," Wren said.

"Are you staying for lunch?" she asked.

"She's just leaving," Sophie interjected.

Wren looked into her eyes, detecting ambivalence, but didn't want to press her in front of her mother. "Yes," she said, reluctantly. "I was hoping for a look around at the cheese-making operation, but Sophie's busy today. Maybe some other time."

"I'll show you around," Olivia offered.

Sophie looked frustrated. "Mom, I—"

"No problem," Olivia said, waving Sophie off. "You go do whatever it is you're so busy with that you can't take out a few minutes for a friend who comes to visit." Olivia was clearly disapproving of Sophie's manner. "I'll show her around."

Sophie's shoulders slumped, then she turned and strode into the house.

"Sophie seems to be in a bad mood," Wren said, following Olivia around the side of the house.

"Is she? She was in a good mood just a while ago. We got an email from that big city food critic about the— Oh, you don't need to know about that. Come on, I'll introduce you to Tallulah and Rose. They were the originals, what we named the place after. We've got seven of them now, including one young one, born right here. That's Poppy and she's Rose's daughter. Such a little sweetheart. I just love her to death!"

144   Robbi McCoy

Wren took her camera out of her bag. "You don't mind if I take some pictures, do you?"

"Go ahead if you want. The goats won't mind."

Wren met the goats, each one introduced by name. In addition to Tallulah and Rose and her kid Poppy, there was Twopenny, Maribelle, Tater and Niblets. All of them had the long ears and convex noses typical of Nubians. Rose and Tater were both tan-colored. Tallulah was white with a gray patch on her shoulder. Niblets and Poppy were black and white. Twopenny was caramel brown with white markings on her face and underbelly. Maribelle, the largest, and according to Olivia, the most bad-tempered, was almost entirely black except for her ears and tail, which were white.

"Don't turn your back on that one," Olivia warned. "She'll send you into the next county."

Tater was the dumb one, Wren learned, and Niblets the spitter.

"You gotta watch her," Olivia said. "She'll take a big ol' drink of water, then hold it, looking all innocent. The next thing you know, she's spraying it all over you. Then she'll just laugh like a son of a gun. Not so bad in the summer, but in the dead of winter, ooh, that's a real nasty shock, let me tell you." Olivia wrinkled up her face with the thought.

"It sounds like they all have distinct personalities."

"Oh, they do! No different than people."

Wren took photos of the animals and of Olivia hugging Tallulah around the neck. She took careful notes too as Olivia explained their process.

"You ever milked a goat?" Olivia asked.

"I have, actually. Do you milk them by hand?"

"Yeah. If we both do it, we can usually get it done in a half hour, forty minutes. But if she gets any more of these critters, I'm gonna insist on a machine."

As Olivia led her to the potting shed where Sophie dried her herbs, Wren glanced at one of the windows of the house and thought she saw Sophie watching them. If so, she withdrew immediately. Wren didn't have an explanation for Sophie's behavior other than the obvious one. She didn't want to see Wren

Two On The Aisle   145

again and she resented her turning up here. It was supposed to have been an anonymous encounter. It wasn't supposed to spill over into real life, even if Olivia was not her wife. By showing up here, Wren had broken the rules and invaded Sophie's territory.

No matter how much she had insisted to the boys, she had never really believed it was like that. Maybe it had started out that way, two strangers who found one another irresistibly appealing, who let themselves have one hell of a joy ride. But during the course of that ride, they had made a few detours that were equally memorable. They had talked. They had laughed. They had touched one another, not just with their bodies.

How could the woman who had threaded their fingers together and kissed her palm tenderly in the middle of the night be the same one who had just faced her with such cool detachment? If there had been nothing between them but sex, why had Sophie talked to her about her childhood and laughed so much during the cooler moments of that night as they lay side by side in the dark getting to know one another? Why, in fact, had they been getting to know one another?

But there was nothing open to interpretation in Sophie's behavior today. She was completely clear she didn't want anything more to do with Wren.

She stood in the shed beside Olivia, smelling lavender and sage. Bundles of both were tied to hooks on the ceiling. "You grow these herbs here?"

Olivia nodded. "The lavender grows wild on the property, but Sophie planted the sage. She's got a big garden with vegetables and herbs. You'll see."

They continued to the back of the house where a broad swath of ground was cleanly planted with neat rows of tomatoes, bush beans, peppers and clumps of herbs. Cooking herbs like basil and oregano, not herbs for chèvre. On one side of the plot was a raised bed containing nasturtiums and some tender lettuces. This was most definitely a kitchen garden, a cook's garden, something Wren longed to have in her life again. She knelt and took up a handful of soil next to a zucchini vine loaded with long, slender squashes and bright yellow flowers. She wanted to pick them, but resisted the urge.

"Sophie's garden has been a big help in my new healthy eating regimen," Olivia said.

"You make it sound like you're not involved in any of this," Wren observed, standing. "The cheese making and gardening. You always say Sophie's this and Sophie's that."

"It's mostly her thing. I help out, but she's the mastermind. I never was much of a farmer. I mean, wasn't interested in serious farming or even gardening. I worked full time, you know, and raised a couple of girls."

"Now you're retired?"

"Yes. More time now, but it still isn't really my thing."

"What is your thing? Kayaking?"

Olivia laughed. "It's fun. But that may be more Warren's thing than mine. That's a question I've been asking myself a lot lately, what's my thing. Maybe should have asked it sooner. But life has a way of slipping by."

Wren observed Olivia silently while they both smiled distantly at one another.

"Can I ask you a personal question?" Wren proposed.

"If I can ask you one."

"That's only fair."

"I'll go first," Olivia announced. "I sensed something between you and Sophie."

"Like hostility, you mean?" Wren laughed nervously.

"Under that. Something more intense."

"Intense hostility?"

Olivia didn't smile. Instead, she waited for Wren's serious answer.

"I don't think it's my place to say anything about that," Wren said.

Olivia gave a slow nod. "That more or less answers my question. Now your turn."

"Why don't you want Sophie to know about you and Dr. Connor?"

Olivia's gaze was shrewd and piercing. "Two years ago, I had a stroke and was partially paralyzed. Sophie moved back here to take care of me. I needed taking care of then and I was so thankful for her. But I don't need caring for any more."

"Clearly you don't."

"She gave up her career, her home, her friends and the entire life she'd made for herself for me." Olivia seemed pained.

Wren began to understand the situation. "You're worried you'll leave her with nothing if you strike out on your own, try to figure out what your thing is?"

Olivia nodded, her expression sober. "How can I do that after what she's done for me? She imagines she's the focal point of my life."

Wren smiled sympathetically, but didn't know what to say. She didn't know either of these women well enough to express an opinion.

"That's why I was asking," Olivia clarified, "about you and Sophie. She never talks. About her feelings, I mean. Keeps everything to herself. She's always been like that. I was wondering if the two of you were…something, if she's found someone."

Wren nodded. "Yeah, I get it. But, you know, I only met her a couple weeks ago. I like her…a lot. But judging by her behavior just now, I'd say, no, I'm not something. In fact, I'd say she can't wait to see my taillights."

Olivia frowned and turned to squint in the direction of the house, then sighed with resignation and asked, "You want to see where we make the cheese?"

Sophie watched her mother lead Wren around the farm. Standing firm against her had been close to impossible. Sophie had tried not to look at her mouth, those luscious lips she remembered kissing so eagerly. How could a woman look so innocent and be so full of deception? Shakespeare, as usual, sprang to mind. *Look like the innocent flower, but be the serpent under it.* That guy has a quotation for everything, she thought with a combination of admiration and resentment.

She'd tried not to hear the pleading sincerity in Wren's voice. She knew from experience how earnest a woman could sound in the midst of deception. She knew too how vulnerable she was to a woman's tears, and Wren had looked like she wanted to cry. A

148   Robbi McCoy

woman's tears could turn everything inside out for Sophie. Jan had been a master at that particular ploy, probably because it worked. She could be standing there guilty as hell, turn on the tears, and in just minutes have Sophie apologizing for accusing her of any wrongdoing.

But Wren wasn't Jan. Wren was nobody to Sophie, and she reminded herself of that several times. She belonged to someone else. Sophie hoped, for his sake, that Wren wasn't deceiving him, that they had some agreement, as Ellie had suggested.

As the tour continued, especially as it progressed into the house, she was sorry she hadn't been more firm and just made Wren leave. This was hard, hard to keep herself from running out there just to look at her. No matter how steadfastly she denied it to Wren's face, she wanted that woman. She had wanted her from the moment she first saw her. Having had her, she still wanted her, more than ever. But she didn't just want her body. She wanted all of her. Better to have nothing, she reasoned, than the meager scrap she was being offered, regardless of whether or not her husband minded.

Sophie leaned weakly against the wall, listening to the sound of Wren's melodious laughter from the kitchen.

Finally, she left. Sophie watched her car rolling down the driveway. She waited until it was out of sight, then went to the kitchen where she found her mother spreading mustard and mayonnaise on slices of sandwich bread.

"She's a nice girl," Olivia said.

"She seemed nice, didn't she," Sophie said with a tinge of bitterness.

Olivia turned to give Sophie a puzzled look.

"Let me make the sandwiches, Mom. Why don't you go relax."

"All right. Klaus is coming in for lunch today. I invited him because he's been working on the section of fence that fell down. So you'll need to make him a couple."

Olivia left the kitchen and Sophie took over lunch preparations. She couldn't get her mind off Wren. She felt agitated. Maybe she should have confronted her, she thought, and asked her point-blank if her husband knew about her lesbian lovers. *Lovers*, yes, because it was obvious she was experienced with women. She knew exactly how to…where to… Sophie stood with a slice of turkey in hand, suddenly paralyzed as she caught her breath and closed her eyes, carried back to that night in the hotel.

She had never tired of kissing Wren's mouth. It was a whole-body experience that just got better as the night went on. Everything had gotten better as the night went on, as they learned one another. The hot, frantic lovemaking, the cool, calm conversation, the soft, seductive stroking, the learning…trusting. And Wren's gentle breathing against the skin of Sophie's shoulder as she fell asleep mid-sentence when Sophie, continuing their conversation, asked her if she liked rain. "I do," she had answered softly, "when it falls gently down without malice, like…"

Wren's voice had trailed off. Sophie had finished her sentence with, "mercy." Then she had touched Wren's cool cheek lightly before falling asleep herself.

"Hey there, Sophie!"

She spun around, flinging the turkey from her hand smack into Klaus's broad chin. He caught it before it fell to the floor, then looked at her, amazed.

"Why'd you sneak up on me like that?" she accused.

"Sorry. I left my boots outside because they were muddy." He lifted one size twelve stockinged foot to illustrate.

Sophie snatched the turkey from his hand, tossing it in the sink.

"Is lunch ready?" he asked cautiously, peering around her at the cutting board where several sandwiches were lined up waiting for lettuce and tomato.

"Almost."

Klaus helped himself to a soda from the refrigerator and sat down at the kitchen table while Sophie finished the sandwiches, slicing a brilliant red beefsteak tomato from her garden.

"I'm just about finished," he said cheerfully.

She turned to face him, completely blank about what he was talking about.

"The fence," he said. "All the posts are in. Just one more section of barbed wire to attach."

"Oh, right. Good."

"Sophie, are you okay?"

"Yes. Why do you ask?" She turned back to the counter and put the top slices of bread on all the sandwiches. She handed him one on a paper napkin.

"You seem kind of jumpy," he said. He put the sandwich down on the table and lifted the bread to see what was inside. "Uh," he started, "there's no meat in here. Lettuce, tomato, mustard, mayo. That's it." He laughed heartily. "You putting me on a vegetarian diet?"

Sophie grabbed the sandwich from the table and put it back on the counter. "Oh, you want meat? Well, why didn't you say so? Do you think I can read your mind? You want turkey or ham?"

Klaus stood and came up behind her, putting his giant, soothing hands on her shoulders. She wanted to cry.

"You want to tell me what's wrong?" he asked gently.

"Nothing's wrong," she said, forcing herself to sound calm. "Turkey or ham?"

"I know you, Sophie, and I know something's wrong."

She turned around to look him in the eye. "You know me? No, Klaus, you don't know me."

He took a step back, looking alarmed, as if he expected a knife in the sternum. She looked down at her hand and saw she was holding the knife she'd been using to slice the tomato. She put it on the cutting board and faced him again.

"You don't know me as well as you think," she said. "Sit down. We need to have a chat."

CHAPTER TWENTY-ONE

You thief of love! What! have you come by night,
And stol'n my love's heart from him?

—*A Midsummer Night's Dream*, Act III, Scene 2

The after-party for *Much Ado About Nothing* was well underway backstage by the time Cleo Keggermeister, the artistic director, strode assertively in wearing black velveteen pants and a black chiffon blouse under a glittery black jacket. Wren had been told it was typical of Cleo to dress all in black, as if she were in perpetual mourning. Not for something as mundane as a person who had died, but for everything she felt should have been hers and was denied her. That was Raven's interpretation, but Wren thought maybe she just knew she looked good in black. Like certain merry widows, Cleo's mourning clothes were chic and expensive and gave her an air of drama rather than tragedy. Her thin smile looked a tiny bit lopsided as she took in the room. Under indoor lighting, the white streak through her black hair stood out even more prominently than the first time Wren had seen her, that day outside the theater when she'd chased Cassandra away.

"Fantastic show, everybody!" she boomed at the cast as she swept into the room. "Beatrice, loved the fan action!" She nodded toward Raven, who beamed his pleasure at the compliment. "Dogberry, stay stiff, arms straight at your sides. You're always at attention. The chuckle was perfect! Got a laugh every time."

Wren searched the room to locate Tammy, aka Dogberry, the officious, ineffectual constable, who was nodding emphatically. Tammy was their designated driver. She was a friendly, hefty young woman with short blonde hair and a pink face. She played Dogberry as he should be played, as a clown. Wren laughed whenever she walked on stage. She didn't need to say a word. She did it all with her face and body. Brilliant.

"I know what you're thinking," Cleo said, holding a palm up to Tammy like a stop signal. "That review that said you went too far, over the top. Forget it!" Someone placed a glass of champagne in her hand as she turned to address the entire room. "Don't read reviews, people! Critics don't know shit. They think they have to slam somebody to make it look like they know what they're talking about. I mean, look what he said about our deliciously campy John the Bastard." She waved toward the play's villain, who bowed his head. "Critics! Worthless wannabes!"

Hearing these familiar insults, Wren stiffened. Raven gave her a sympathetic pout.

Cleo drained half the glass of champagne without pause, then said, "Listen to the audience. They loved our Dogberry. They wanted to take her home, for Christ's sake! Did you hear the applause when she took her bow? Am I right? Am I right?"

Everyone clapped and hooted their agreement. Tammy blushed.

"Boy!" Cleo called. "Boy, where are you?"

What could she possibly have to say to Max? Wren wondered. She had only two lines and she had delivered them without mishap. Max popped up like a prairie dog and faced Cleo, her orange eyebrows slanted in a worried question.

"I could see you," Cleo accused, "waiting to come on in the wings. Stay back a bit."

Max nodded her understanding and ducked out of sight behind her fellow actors.

"We can continue this tomorrow," Cleo said. "Conclusion is, it was wonderful and I'm proud of you all. Well done! Party on!"

Cleo proceeded to mingle and join into spirited conversation with the cast and crew. She was a riveting presence, Wren noted, made more interesting by one of the few things Wren knew about her, that she'd banned Cassandra from the theater for life. When Raven brought her over for an introduction, Wren decided to simply ask her about it.

"That's a story I'd like to forget," she said before taking a swallow of champagne.

"Oh, come on," Raven urged. "Tell it."

Cleo smiled at him and shrugged. "All right. I was playing Ophelia. Cassandra thought the role should be hers. It had been hers, but she was abominable at it. I had to take over. We were midway through the season but I had no choice. Her father, Anthony Marcus, was a great actor." She thrust her free hand into the air and pronounced the name as someone might introduce a king, her eyes looking off into the distance. Lowering her hand, she said, "But the daughter, a pale imitation."

"I heard she was actually very good," Wren interjected, recalling Sophie's remarks.

Cleo shrugged. "I didn't fire her. I let her stay on and help with props and set changes and such. She was good with a paintbrush, I'll give her that."

Wren glanced at her brother, wondering if he was as skeptical of Cleo's motives as she was.

"I'm sure you know that Ophelia carries a bouquet of flowers in her final scene." Cleo scanned their faces and they nodded to reassure her that they were following the story. "In this tender, somber scene, I walked across the stage parsing out herbs from my bouquet. I'm saying the lines, thusly: 'There's rosemary; that's for remembrance.'" Cleo made a plucking motion above her champagne glass. "As I'm returning to my bouquet for pansies, I'm assaulted by a stream of water that comes shooting out of it and squirts me full in the face." She jerked her head back, opening her eyes wide in an expression of terror, reliving the moment. "Like a goddamned clown's prop. I scream. The audience bursts into uproarious laughter and you could hear Cassandra cackling in the wings from any seat in the theater."

Raven and Wren began to snicker, but they both cut it short at the sight of Cleo's stern look.

"If I were you," she said quietly, "I'd reconsider guffaws of delight as an appropriate response to my humiliation."

"Sorry," Raven said, barely controlling his urge to giggle. "I'm sure it was a horrible shock."

"That woman was completely off her rocker even then," Cleo said, as if in defense of her actions, as if, Wren decided, she were answering to someone's accusation that she had driven Cassandra mad.

When Cleo had moved on, Raven whispered, "That isn't the whole story. I asked around."

He led Wren to a nearby hallway containing several posters from past productions. They stood in front of one advertising *Macbeth*, starring Anthony Marcus in the lead and Cleo Keggermeister as Lady Macbeth. It wasn't an Ashland production, but one from a theater on the East Coast. The image was of the two of them, heads only, facing away from one another, set against a stormy sky above a forest of spooky black trees, both of them looking positively menacing. Marcus was dramatically handsome, his eyes penetrating, one eyebrow raised strategically. Cleo was young, exotically beautiful, her hair jet black with no sign of a white streak, her thin nose pointed sharply frontward, her eyes dark and intense. They captured the chilling, horrific spirit of the play precisely with that pose.

"Cassandra's father and Cleo," Wren said. "They worked together."

"They did more than work together. They were lovers."

"When was this?"

"Twenty-five years ago, more or less. Marcus gave her up and returned to his wife, then the family moved here. The girls,

Cassandra and Ellie, were still little kids then. Years later, Cleo turned up here and got hired into the company."

"She followed him?"

"Right. The whole mess started all over again. This time, Marcus's wife divorced him. As a result, Ellie became very angry and wanted nothing more to do with her father. Cassandra went the opposite direction, doing everything she could to get his love and attention."

"So she became an actor."

Raven nodded. "After a few years, their mother got sick. Marcus, driven by guilt, left Cleo to take care of her. Cleo was absolutely furious."

Wren regarded the harsh eyes of the man in the poster, trying to imagine the husband and father behind the character. "What happened to Ellie's mother?"

"She died. It devastated them, the girls and their father. He felt he had ruined them all, that it was his fault. He took off. Ran away, basically, and hasn't been seen since. That was several years ago."

"That explains a lot, doesn't it? Ellie's resentment. Cleo's bitterness."

"And her revenge against Cassandra, his daughter. Not fair or even logical, but Marcus was beyond her reach. Cassandra was easy prey once Cleo became artistic director here."

"Is that story about Ophelia's flowers true?"

"Yes. But that was just a small episode. That was Cassandra fighting back, getting in a last dig before she got tossed out."

"That's a sad story, especially seeing what's become of Cassandra."

"She's not the only victim. They say Cleo never got over Marcus. One of those grand passions, I guess." Raven sighed at the poster. "Ready to go home?"

A few minutes later, they were buckled into the backseat of Tammy's SUV. Behind the wheel of her car, Tammy looked ordinary in jeans and a T-shirt, no longer wearing Dogberry's oversized navy blue coat with gold buttons, but even now when Wren caught sight of her round pink face in the rearview mirror, she felt like laughing.

156   Robbi McCoy

Wren had drunk a fair amount of wine, enough to insure that she would be asleep within seconds of hitting her pillow, which she impatiently longed for. She was still smarting over Sophie's harsh rebuke from earlier in the day. Raven had decided the party would be just the thing to cheer her up, and he'd been right. She did feel better. Easy come, easy go, she told herself. Sophie had never been hers to lose, so she had lost nothing.

Tammy was quite a chatterer, it turned out, and talked continuously from the moment they left the party. Fortunately, the drive was a short one.

"My husband won't come to see the play," she was saying. "Not his cup of tea, he says. He'd rather get harpooned in the eye than sit through a Shakespeare play. Or any play, for that matter. Just getting him off his boat takes a major act of God. Or me threatening to leave him. That's what I did too. I told him he didn't have to go to any of the plays, but he does have to be my date at the Gala next Saturday. I'll be damned if I'm going without a date to the biggest event of the summer. I'm a married woman. My husband has to be there."

"So he's coming?" Raven asked.

"He damn well better be! But getting him on dry land is tough. He's lived on boats all his life. We live in Westport, Washington. You know where that is? Not exactly in Westport. In the bay off Westport."

"You live in the water?" Wren asked drowsily.

"Right. We've got a fifty foot sportfishing boat with all the comforts of home. When we're not out on a cruise, we're berthed there in the harbor. For this summer, though, we're docked over in Rogue River. Not far."

Raven sat up, suddenly alert. "How'd you get this far inland on a boat that big?"

"Oh, don't ask!" Tammy threw up her hands. "Anyway, he'll come to the party or he's fish bait. But he'll have to take some Dramamine to manage it. He gets queasy when he gets on dry land. Can't tolerate it for too long. He's always been like that. He belongs to the sea, he does, just like his daddy."

"What costume are you wearing to the Gala?" Raven asked.

"Why not Dogberry?"

"Because Dogberry isn't a character in *A Midsummer Night's Dream*."

Tammy considered it for a moment, then said, "Seeing as how Dogberry is an ass, maybe I'll come as Bottom, since he was turned into an ass."

Wren sat up straight to peer into the rearview mirror at Tammy's face. "That's logical...and consistent."

"What about you?" Tammy asked Raven.

"I'm coming as Titania."

"The queen of the fairies!" Wren squawked. "How appropriate."

Raven nodded, looking pleased with himself. "And Kyle—"

"Oberon, of course," Wren interjected. "King of the fairies."

Tammy chuckled. They turned down their street and the car slowed.

"It's the Victorian there on the left," Raven said, pointing to his house. "Thanks for the ride. You were better tonight than I've ever seen you. I wanted to lie down laughing right there on stage."

"You too," Tammy said, looking at them in the rearview mirror. "That one time when you turned and flung your skirt over Benedick's head, that was genius. The audience was rolling in the aisles. He was stumbling around blind, while you just carried on, walking across the stage, pulling him behind you, as if nothing had happened. How did you keep from cracking up?"

Raven shrugged with mock modesty.

"This is the third time I've seen the play," Wren said, "and I could definitely see the improvement. So many little comedic gestures and expressions. Your characters are coming into their own. The entire company is so talented."

Tammy grinned at her in the mirror as she pulled the car to the curb in front of the house. "Here we are. 'Good night, good night! Parting is such sweet sorrow.'"

Raven stole the next line from her. "'That I shall say good night till it be morrow.'"

"Good night!" Wren said, hopping out of the car.

Raven joined her at the curb, then Tammy made a U-turn

and drove away. Raven yawned deeply and stretched his arms above his head. "'To sleep—perchance to dream.'"

Wren's own yawn was cut short by the sound of a loud thud at the side of the house. They both turned their attention to the den window where the dark figure of a man hung through the open casement, his lower half dangling outside, legs banging against the wooden siding. This scene was in deep shadows, as the streetlight didn't hit that side of the house, so they could see no details as the man dropped from the window to the side yard, then dashed into the bushes, crashing straight through them in his rush to escape. Raven took off running after him, yelling, "Stop or I'll shoot!" He too disappeared into the bushes.

Wren stood on the sidewalk, momentarily stunned. She gathered her wits and ran up the front walkway of the house, letting herself in just as Kyle came bounding downstairs in his bathrobe, looking sleepy and alarmed. But still, she marveled, not a hair out of place.

"What's going on?" he asked.

"Call the police. There was a man in the house. He just escaped out the study window."

Kyle's eyes widened. "I didn't hear a thing!" He darted to the hall phone. "Where's Raven?"

"He went after him."

"What?" Kyle let the phone receiver drop to the floor. "He'll get himself killed!"

"You make the call. I'll go after him."

"Why should *you* go after him? I should go after him." Kyle seemed worried out of his wits.

"No, I'll do it," Wren said calmly and firmly. "I know where he went."

"Oh!" He threw up his hands in exasperation. "It's one of those special bond of twins things. You can smell his trail or sense his presence with your extrasensory perception."

"No. I saw where he went." She pointed at her eyes in case he was still thinking ESP. "Now make the call, please, Kyle."

She dashed back outside and followed the path the other two had taken through the bushes. She emerged on the other side of the shrubbery on an open expanse of lawn in the neighbor's yard. The sprinklers were on and Raven was lying face down and motionless under a shower of water on the lawn. Wren ran into the spray and knelt beside him, her heart pounding in her throat with terror. Just as she laid her hand on his shoulder, he rolled over, screamed in a high-pitched voice, then said, more deeply, "Unhand me, villain!"

He began swatting at her wildly, his eyes squeezed shut.

"Raven!" she yelled. "Stop! It's me!"

He opened his eyes and looked up more calmly, then she helped him up and they moved out of range of the sprinklers. They stood dripping, looking around at the quiet night. There was no sign of anything amiss other than a dog barking in the distance.

"I tripped over one of those damned sprinklers," Raven explained. "The scoundrel got away."

"Did you get a better look at him?"

"No. His back was to me the whole time. If I hadn't tripped, I'd have had him. He wasn't much of a runner."

They walked to the road and back to the house where Kyle was waiting, frantic. He wrapped his arms around Raven for a split second before leaping back, declaring, "You're all wet!" He turned to Wren. "So are you."

While Raven explained the sprinklers, they heard a siren approaching. Within moments, a female police officer was at the door to take the report. In her tipsy state of mind, Wren was reminded of Tammy's portrayal of Dogberry. The officer had the same stocky build and fleshy lips. And, of course, the most obvious similarity was that she was wearing a uniform. It made it a little hard to take her seriously, having just come from a play where the most memorable moment of Dogberry's performance was when she said with a great sense of righteousness, "But masters, remember that I am an ass: though it be not written down, yet forget not that I am an ass." The performance had wedged itself so tightly in Wren's mind that whenever this officer spoke to her, the refrain "Thou art an ass" repeated continually in her head. Which, she knew, was completely uncalled for. Officer Whiteley did nothing to deserve it, but Wren was unable to stop herself from thinking it.

160   Robbi McCoy

They could give almost no description of the intruder, other than he looked like a man, a sort of bulky man in dark clothing.

"Have you been drinking?" Officer Whiteley asked Raven as they all stood by the open window in the den.

"Yes," he answered, his hair plastered flat on his head. "But I know what I saw and my sister will back it up."

Wren nodded. Officer Whiteley walked to the window and looked over the latch and casement.

"Was this window locked earlier this evening?" she asked.

They turned to Kyle, who shrugged. "I didn't check it before I went to bed. It's possible it wasn't locked."

"No sign of forced entry," observed Whiteley.

After a cursory inspection of the room where Wren's state-of-the-art laptop still sat on the desk running its screen saver of random flying fruits, and the valuable pieces of art, not Kyle's caricatures, still hung on the walls, they could find nothing missing.

"Either you scared him away before he had a chance to take anything," Officer Whiteley concluded, "or he wasn't a burglar in the first place."

She then peered at Kyle suspiciously. He stiffened and narrowed his eyes defiantly.

"If you come across anything missing," Officer Whiteley said, "give us a call."

Wren walked her to the front door, where she said, "You weren't implying something back there, were you?"

Officer Whiteley regarded Wren impassively. "No. Just that you all want to report a burglary, but nothing's missing. A burglar takes stuff. This appears to be something else."

"He just didn't have time to take anything. We came home unexpectedly early. We thought we'd be home around one. We got here just after midnight."

The officer curled her upper lip. "How would a burglar know when you were coming home?"

"Uh, good point."

"Besides, this guy, whatever he was after, wasn't concerned about the house being empty. Your brother's boyfriend was here, wasn't he?"

"Asleep upstairs."

"So he says." Officer Whiteley looked noncommittal.

"Just why are you trying to cast suspicion on him?" Wren demanded.

"It was you that said you and your brother came home earlier than planned, wasn't it? There's a rule in this business. The most likely explanation is usually the right one. I'll be on my way now. Good night."

No sooner had Wren shut the door than she heard raised voices from the living room. She hurried through, arriving just as Raven threw a purple pillow in Kyle's direction. It missed. Raven squatted on the sofa, his fists knotted up, his face covered with tears. Kyle stood nearby. As Wren entered the room, he looked at her and shrugged.

"Thou liest, villain!" Raven shouted at Kyle.

"What's going on?" Wren demanded.

"This man has broken my heart," Raven cried. "Get out! I never want to see you again!"

Kyle looked helpless. "He's talking nonsense."

Raven bounced on the couch cushion impatiently. "Get out!"

"Wait a minute," Wren said. "Is this about the man in the window?"

"What else? Even that policewoman doesn't believe he was a burglar. You saw the look she gave him." Raven pointed and glared at Kyle. "He says he knows nothing. He says he was asleep."

"Is it a crime to be asleep after midnight?" Kyle asked.

"It is when my boyfriend is having a sex-ez-vous."

Kyle stared. "This is ridiculous. I'm completely innocent."

"There was a man in this house tonight, a *bulky* man, who tried to sneak away when I came home. What does that tell you?"

"That a burglar broke into the house," Kyle said emphatically, "and was scared away by your arrival. Very simple."

"Do you think I'm an idiot?" Raven asked, then turned to plead his case to Wren. "I'm slaving away at the theater night after night and this, this...deceiver is reveling in the company of bulky men! You cad! Why don't you just take a pound of flesh while you're at it." Raven ripped his shirt open to bare his hairless chest.

"Maybe we should—" Wren started.

Raven bolted off the couch and pointed again at Kyle. "'What man was he talk'd with you tonight at your window betwixt twelve and one?'"

Wren recognized the line from *Much Ado About Nothing*. After seeing it three times in two weeks, she had nearly memorized the play. No doubt Kyle was equally familiar with the accusation. False accusation, as it turned out in the play. Raven was apparently not thinking of that.

Kyle stared, unbelieving. "I've had enough of this," he declared, then marched toward the door.

"Where are you going?" Raven demanded.

"I'm going to a hotel." He slammed the door behind him.

Raven slumped back into the sofa and started sobbing in earnest. Wren came over and sat beside him, cradling him in her arms, feeling chilled from their damp clothing. When he had gained control of himself, he spoke melodramatically. "'Speak of me as one that loved not wisely but too well.'"

"Maybe you're being a little theatrical," she suggested. "It's hard to imagine he would do that. I mean, if he were going to cheat on you, you'd think he'd do it more cleverly than having a man over here right before you came home."

Raven spoke calmly. "It was never his brains that attracted me to him."

Wren clunked his head gently with her fist. "Don't play that game with me. I know you love him. And he loves you too. You really should try to be less impetuous."

When Raven left to change into dry clothes, Wren went to the study and examined the window, which was still open to the cool night air. She slid it shut, then looked around the room, trying again to find something amiss, anything at all that would give a clue to the reason behind the break-in. An antique cuckoo clock on the wall, ticking audibly as its wooden pendulum swung back and forth, may have been the most valuable thing in the room, though a run-of-the-mill thug wouldn't necessarily know that. A run-of-the-mill thug would go for electronics.

She inspected the desk where her laptop resided. Beside it was a plate of aebleskiver. She noticed a light dusting of powdered sugar on the desk. She ran her fingers over home row of her keyboard, feeling a slight stickiness. She distinctly recalled wiping down the keyboard this morning when she was done working. Was it possible, she wondered, that the intruder had been looking for information rather than valuables? She doubted anyone would be able to get past her password, at least not quickly, so it wasn't likely he had gotten into her computer. She did a rapid check of the desk drawers and papers on the desk to make sure nothing there would connect her with her alter ego—no printed emails, no restaurant notes or half-written reviews. She tried to be careful, but she didn't stay on guard at all times against the remote possibility of someone breaking into the house.

If he wasn't a thief and he wasn't Kyle's lover, which seemed unlikely, at least to Wren, who was this bulky intruder with a sweet tooth? She felt a shiver run up her spine as she considered the answer.

CHAPTER TWENTY-TWO

In complete glory she reveal'd herself.

—*Henry IV, Part I*, Act I, Scene 2

Sophie came around the side of the house to a chaotic scene. Her mother was in the front yard bent over Twopenny, wrestling with her. Maribelle, the largest of the goats, reared up on her hind legs, preparing to make a head-butt dive at Olivia's backside. Completely unaware of the hit that was coming, Olivia had Twopenny's head clamped in one arm and her other hand wrapped around the wad of paper disappearing between the goat's rubbery lips.

Sophie shouted and dove toward Maribelle like a linebacker, hitting her from the side and taking her down. Both of them rolled over on the lawn. Maribelle bleated angrily and was back on her feet with a flick of her white tail. Olivia was still tussling with Twopenny.

Sophie hauled herself up. "What's going on?"

"She's eating my newspaper!" Olivia whined. "Pry open her mouth."

While Olivia held Twopenny, Sophie coaxed her mouth open until Olivia could grab the soggy paper. She then stamped up the steps of the porch and collapsed in her rocker.

"It wouldn't have hurt her," Sophie said, releasing Twopenny, who complained noisily at the indignity of having her snack stolen. "At least not enough to kill yourself over."

"It wasn't her I was worried about."

"Then what?"

"It's this." Olivia waved the paper toward Sophie. "My picture's in here."

"Your picture? Why are you in the paper?"

"It's a big write-up of the farm. It's that Eno Threlkeld. He said he'd fix it and damned if he didn't." She unwadded the paper. "I hope that goat didn't eat my picture. She's just jealous because it's Tallulah, not her, that got her picture in there with me." Olivia looked up, her face contorting into a sudden look of alarm. "Sophie!" she warned.

But it was too late. Maribelle's head collided solidly with Sophie's left butt cheek, sending her flying forward. She stumbled and hit the ground, landing on her stomach, face first in the grass. As she rolled over and spit, Maribelle galloped away toward the goat pen. Like all of the goats, she considered it the safe zone. Bad assumption, Sophie thought, gritting her teeth.

"Are you okay?" her mother asked, suddenly standing beside her.

Sophie got to her feet shakily, then rubbed her butt. "I'll be okay. I'm not sure that goat will be able to say as much when I'm through with her."

"Before you kill her, read this."

Sophie sat on the steps and took the paper from her mother, flattening it out to find a substantial feature article on Tallulah Rose Creamery. There was indeed a photo of Olivia with her arms around Tallulah's neck, both of them smiling at the camera.

"He says our cheese is divine," Olivia crooned, sitting beside Sophie. "Divine, that's what he said."

166   Robbi McCoy

Sophie read the article carefully. It was very flattering as it accurately described their small herd of Nubian goats and their kitchen process of making small-batch, French-style chèvre. He mentioned the mother-daughter team of Olivia and Sophie, two "charming, capable women who took their product seriously and had made excellent decisions in their short tenure as cheese crafters." It described in detail the texture and flavor of their three varieties. He did use the word "divine." He also said the cheese was "smooth, rich and creamy, a perfect balance of tang and sweetness with a clean, satisfying finish." The herb cheeses were "subtly flavored and delightfully vibrant." All in all, he said, "Tallulah Rose Creamery is producing chèvre as fine as anything from Provence."

When Sophie had finished, she looked at her mother incredulously. Olivia was grinning, her eyes bright with happiness.

"What did I tell you?" she said. "Passable, indeed! Not on your life! Divine, that's what it is." Olivia cocked her head upward with an air of smugness. "A perfect balance of tang and sweetness."

This was better than anything Sophie could have imagined, tremendously superior to a retraction.

"Charming," Olivia persisted. "That's what we are. That's what he said."

"Yes, so he did." Sophie stared out across the hills for a moment. "But I'm confused."

"Why? Don't you think I'm charming?"

She looked at her mother and laughed. "I'm not confused about that. You're definitely charming. No, that isn't it. Where did this photo come from? When was he here? Did he come when I was out? You must have talked to him and given him all this information. You must have seen him because he took your picture."

Olivia's grin faded. "I didn't think about that. No, nobody's been here." Olivia squinted, obviously aware that didn't make sense. "Except that girl," she said at last. "Wren."

Sophie nodded, having already come to the same startling conclusion.

Her mother looked suddenly enlightened. "Yes! She's the one who took that picture. I remember. She asked me to pose with Tallulah. So he must have gotten his information from her. Maybe she's his assistant."

Sophie remembered the phony real estate agent story Wren had given her. Then she recalled Wren's surprisingly detailed knowledge about food that she had downplayed when questioned.

"I think maybe she's more than just his assistant," she said thoughtfully.

"Is this making sense to you?" Olivia asked.

"A lot of things are beginning to make sense to me."

"I get the feeling there's something you're not telling me."

"A girl's got to have a few secrets, Mom. Haven't you always said so?"

Sophie sat on the porch watching Twopenny jumping joyfully on pieces of stacked plywood. Niblets arrived to join in the game.

Wren had to know I would figure this out, Sophie thought, that she'd blown her cover by writing this article. She smiled to think Wren had handed her this gift and trusted her with it, revealing her true identity. Although this gesture went some distance toward softening Sophie's opinion of Wren, it did nothing to take away the brutal reality that Wren was married to a man and was therefore only interested in Sophie as sport.

She remembered back to the day Wren had shown up here at the farm, the day she'd done the research for the article, how coldly Sophie had greeted her, how thoroughly she'd rejected her. Yet she had still written this glowing article, had called Sophie "charming." That was big of her. She was apparently capable of separating her personal and professional selves. Maybe that was easier to do when they each had their own name. Sophie ran her finger over the byline, "Eno Threlkeld." That name suddenly conjured up a completely different set of images and feelings for her than it had minutes ago.

"You can put that on our website," Olivia said, pointing to the newspaper article. "How's that coming along anyway? Are we online yet?"

"No, but I—" Sophie was about to tell her mother she'd found an artist to design their logo, but remembered that he was Wren's husband, so no longer an option. "No, but maybe I'll be more motivated to get it done with an endorsement like this."

"That paper's all soggy," Olivia said. "Why don't you go to the store to get a couple good copies?"

"Good idea."

"While you're doing that, I'll make lunch."

"You don't need to. There are a couple pieces of chicken left from last night. Why don't we just have those?"

"What about Klaus?"

"He isn't coming in for lunch today."

Olivia looked puzzled. "He didn't come in yesterday either. Why not?"

"I don't think he has much reason to hang around the kitchen now."

Sophie recalled Klaus's sadness from the other day when she'd finally told him she was gay. Apparently the idea took him completely by surprise. He was embarrassed too because of his displays of affection toward her, which he now assumed she had found ridiculous. She hadn't. She'd been touched, even if she couldn't respond the way he wanted. He could barely look at her now. She shouldn't have waited so long to tell him, she knew that. Now things were just plain awkward between them.

"Things have changed between me and Klaus," Sophie said.

"You told him you weren't interested, didn't you?" Olivia surmised.

Sophie folded the newspaper into a log. "I had to."

Olivia nodded solemnly. "That was the right thing to do. He's a good boy, but he's not for you, is he? No point leading him on."

Sophie shook her head.

"Sophie," her mother said in her maternal voice, "I think we need to have a talk."

"About?" Sophie asked.

"About your future. What you want to do with the rest of your life. Where you're headed."

Sophie was taken aback. "Things are fine the way they are now. I mean, I like living here with you."

"But you aren't planning on living like this permanently, are you?" Olivia stared at her purposefully, her blue eyes peering hard.

"I don't know. I haven't given it much thought."

"Maybe you should. I'm very grateful you decided to come home and help me out. You gave up your career and put your life on hold. But I'm okay now. I want you to feel free to make your own way again."

"You want me to leave?"

"No, no, that's not what I'm saying. You can stay as long as you want to or need to. I'm just saying I could be okay on my own now, if you felt like moving on."

Sophie shook her head. "I don't. I'm happy here. I don't want to go back to what I was doing before."

Olivia pursed her lips, looking thoughtful. Sophie was unable to read her intention.

"What about romance?" Olivia asked. "Don't you think you'll want to find someone, eventually?"

Sophie shrugged. "Sure, I suppose. This isn't about Klaus, is it? There's no way he—"

"No, no, it isn't about Klaus. I knew you were never interested in him. But I was wondering if there was anyone you *were* interested in."

Sophie thought of Wren, the only person she'd found interesting since she'd left Jan. "No, not particularly."

"I see." Olivia rocked forward on the step, then back, gazing at the goats as they continued their game on the stack of plywood. "What if I was gone?"

"Oh, Mom, that's not going to happen! You're so healthy now. Dr. Connor said you're like a thirty year old. He said you're going to outlive us all."

Olivia nodded indulgently. "Yes, but just for the sake of discussion, what if I wasn't here? Maybe just gone, not necessarily dead? You're a young woman and you aren't like me,

Sophie. You aren't the sort to live alone. You're such a nurturing person. You need someone to nurture. I worry about what you would do if I...was out of the picture."

"I don't understand where this is coming from, Mom. Everything's fine. I'm happy with the way things are. You're not going anywhere."

Olivia gazed silently at Sophie, then smiled reassuringly. "I'm glad you're happy, Sophie. Happy to be living here with your mother. Such a contrast from ten years ago when you couldn't wait to get away."

Sophie smiled. "Kids rebel. That's all over, thank God, and I'm sorry I gave you so much grief."

Olivia sputtered dismissively. "Water under the bridge."

Sophie waited to see if her mother wanted to continue this conversation, but she turned her attention back to the goats, clearly done talking. Sophie was still unsure of the point of this discussion. Was Olivia worried Sophie was neglecting her own needs to care for her mother? That seemed the most likely explanation with her assurances that she could manage on her own. Sophie hoped she had persuaded her that wasn't the case. Sophie had no longings she was neglecting. Other than her desire for Wren, but that had nothing to do with Olivia. Wren's unavailability wasn't something her mother could do anything about.

"We should celebrate this," Sophie said, waving the newspaper. "Would you like to go out to dinner tonight?"

"Naw, not tonight. But maybe when you go to the store for the paper, you can get us something special."

"Okay. Do you have anything in mind?"

"When she was here the other day, that Wren told me about a salad they have at Sprouts with beets, sugar-glazed walnuts and goat cheese. I'd like to try that, if you could make it."

"So you want to have goat cheese to celebrate?"

"Sure, why not? I hear it's divine." Olivia smiled complacently.

CHAPTER TWENTY-THREE

There's nothing in this world can make me joy:
Life is as tedious as a twice-told tale
Vexing the dull ear of a drowsy man...

—*King John*, Act III, Scene 4

Raven wore a silky navy blue bathrobe and lay on the sofa in the sunroom. He had been there all morning. Wren came in from the backyard, disappointed to see him still there just as before, doing nothing. She pulled off her gardening gloves and stood a few feet away from him, waiting to be acknowledged. His eyes were open, but he was immobile and staring at the ceiling.

"Are you going to stay there all day?" she finally asked.

"Yes," he said without looking at her.

"What about the play? There's a performance tonight, isn't there?"

"I've called Max. Or should I say Maxine?"

172   Robbi McCoy

"You mean you're not going on?" Wren sat in the chair next to the sofa.

"I'm too depressed."

"Raven, you need to buck up. This is ridiculous. You can't throw away your big break over a fight with your boyfriend."

He turned his head abruptly to look at her. "To lose one's love is to lose one's life. What else is there after that?"

"He'll be back. You haven't lost him. I know he'll be back."

"You know no such thing."

As Wren was about to object, the doorbell rang.

"Will you get that?" Raven asked, as if he had a broken leg. "That'll be Max."

She walked through the house to the front door where she greeted Max, who seemed more timid than ever, even a little reluctant to come in. Now that she knew Max was a girl, Wren could see it even more clearly than before, the feminine mouth, the small hands. She wore the same black leather vest as the other day and a pair of killer black boots. In Wren's mind, she'd gone from being a goofy, juvenile-looking boy to being a sexy-cute, twenty-something butch woman. A decided improvement.

She led Max to the sunroom where Raven remained prone.

"Your hour has come, Max," he announced dramatically. "Tonight you will be Beatrice. I am not going on."

"What?" Max looked stricken. "Why not? What's wrong with you?"

"I am murdered by the slings and arrows of outrageous fortune."

Wren rolled her eyes at them both as Max fell to her knees beside the sofa.

"He had a fight with Kyle," she explained. "He should go on tonight. Otherwise, he'll just lie here like that being worthless and feeling sorry for himself."

"Yes," Max agreed, grabbing Raven's arm. "You must go on!"

"I won't," Raven said. "I can't. You'll go on and you'll be brilliant."

"Brilliant? No. I'm not ready. It's only been two weeks."

Raven gripped Max's hand. "You're ready. You can do it."

His gaze was grim and stern. "'Well, niece,'" he said in his stage voice, "'I hope to see you one day fitted with a husband.'"

Max gawked, then adopted a similarly unnatural voice and said, "'Not till God make men of some other metal than earth.'"

Raven released her hand, saying, "You see! You know all the lines. You're ready."

Max fell backward, then picked herself up and was on her feet, eyes wide with terror. "I have to go rehearse," she said, then tore out of the sunroom and out of the house.

Next they heard the sound of the motorcycle blasting down the street.

"Is she really ready?" Wren asked.

"Who knows?" Raven turned over, facing the back of the couch. If he really didn't care about the show, Wren surmised, maybe he wasn't exaggerating his despair after all.

"Why don't you call Kyle and apologize?" she suggested.

He flipped over to face her. "I've tried. I've called three times. I left messages. He hasn't returned my calls."

"Do you know where he's staying? You could go there."

"No. He might be staying with his friend Henry. I hope not. Henry's had a thing for Kyle since they met. I can't bear to think what they're doing!" He buried his face in a pillow.

"You should work on your jealousy issues. Isn't that what caused him to walk out in the first place? Really, Raven, you're your own worst enemy."

"You're right. Jealousy is the one thing Kyle can't abide." He sat up, hugging a pillow to his chest. "That was what destroyed his family, you know. Jealousy, the green-eyed monster."

"Really?" She sat on the arm of a chair.

He nodded fatalistically. "He carries a photo of his parents in his wallet. His mother Mona was very beautiful. His father so-so. They hadn't been married long and were very much in love. Kyle was just a newborn infant when his father was tricked by a black-hearted villain into thinking his wife was unfaithful. False evidence was planted. Mona was completely blameless, but 'trifles light as air are to the jealous confirmations strong as proofs of holy writ.'"

"What happened?" Wren asked in a whisper.

"Kyle's father let suspicion drive him crazy. He confronted his wife. Of course she denied any wrongdoing. He wasn't able to believe her. He ended up strangling her to death in a jealous rage."

Wren gasped.

"Then," Raven continued, "when he found out the truth, that she was innocent, he killed himself out of remorse."

"That's horrible!"

"Yes, it is. It's a deep wound for Kyle. He carries the pain of it in his heart forever, poor thing. Best not to bring it up."

"I won't. But thanks for telling me." She shook her head. "Knowing that, you'd think you would think twice before accusing him of infidelity."

"You'd think, yeah." Raven flung himself against the back of the couch. "If he ever comes back, I'll never for an instant doubt him again. I miss him so much!"

They sighed simultaneously.

"Aren't we a pair?" Wren observed. "Two lovesick fools."

Raven turned his bleary eyes to face her and gave her a sympathetic smile. "What were you doing out in the yard?"

"Weeding the garden."

"Garden? You mean those tomato plants that sprung up on their own?"

"Yep. They're blossoming. They might give you a few tomatoes if you water them now and then."

He frowned. "That's what the Farmers' Market's for."

"If I thought you'd take care of them, I'd plant some beets and carrots for the fall."

"No point putting down roots now," Raven muttered, smiling weakly at his own joke. "I can't afford the rent on this place by myself." He sat up and hugged his knees to his chest. "I was beginning to imagine staying here. Maybe not in this house, but in Ashland. I like it here. I'm sure they'd keep me on at the theater. But without mine own true love, I can't imagine it."

"He'll be back. But even without him, I think it's a good plan to stay here. It's time you did put down some roots. Since it's just the two of us tonight, how about we get a pizza delivered and watch some old movie on TV? Something silly in black and white."

"As cozy as that sounds, you aren't free tonight."

"I'm not?"

"No. You have to go to the theater and watch Max perform."

"What?" Wren objected. "Why don't you go?"

"Because Cleo thinks I'm sick. Besides, I can't bear it. Please, dear sister, be mine eyes, mine ears tonight."

Wren frowned in exasperation as Raven trained his puppy dog eyes on her.

"It's not like you have anything better to do," he pointed out.

She stuck her tongue out at him.

CHAPTER TWENTY-FOUR

Eye of newt, and toe of frog,
Wool of bat, and tongue of dog,
Adder's fork, and blind-worm's sting.
Lizard's leg, and howlet's wing,
For a charm of powerful trouble,
Like a hell-broth boil and bubble.

—*Macbeth*, Act IV, Scene 1

"Thanks for meeting me," Wren said, fingering the stem of her wineglass.

She sat across from Kyle at a round café table on the sidewalk outside an Italian restaurant.

"Sure," he said. "I'm glad you called. I miss our escapades."

He had a sketchpad open on the table and was rapidly drawing. His hair, as usual, was perfect. He wore a short-sleeved mesh shirt over relaxed tan pants, his feet in Teva sandals. He seemed calm and collected. Such a contrast to Raven.

She tasted her wine, a full-bodied old vine zinfandel. "What are you working on?" she asked.

"A label for a local winery. They hired me to come up with a design to announce their newest shiraz. But I can talk while I'm doing this. I'm using a different part of my brain."

"What winery is it?"

"Newt's Eye."

Wren balked. "Newt's Eye? Never heard of it."

"That's what I'm drinking here." Kyle tapped his glass with the end of his pencil. "You want to taste this one? It's pinot noir."

She took a sip from his glass, letting the wine splay itself across the surface of her tongue before swallowing. She shook her head. "It's one of those doctored up pinots."

"What do you mean?"

"It's a new trend, to let the grapes get overripe so the wine is sweeter with a higher alcohol content, to appeal to a wider audience. Then they mix in some syrah or some other beefier red to make it darker and more full-bodied. Not a true pinot at all. Pinot should be light, delicate with spices, herbs and flowers, not just sweet fruit."

Kyle took another sip, looking thoughtful. "Well, I like it."

"Then you should drink it and enjoy it. I'll stick to my zin."

Kyle looked amused. "That's sort of a drawback to your business, isn't it?"

"What's that?"

"Not being able to just enjoy a tasty glass of wine or a plate of pasta. It's got to be measured against everything you know, to meet such high standards. Not just a simple pleasure."

"You're right. It's not just a simple pleasure. On the other hand, when it's really good, when it meets or exceeds the standards, it's a truly satisfying pleasure. That's the upside. When I taste a really good pinot noir or plate of pasta, I'm going to know it and I'm going to appreciate it more than you ever will."

"So which is better, do you think? Simple pleasures enjoyed on a regular basis or mind-blowing pleasure enjoyed once in a blue moon?"

She smiled, her mind wandering to things other than wine and food. "Hard to answer."

"Did you want to order something to eat?" he asked. "I'm not hungry, but go ahead if you want."

"No, thanks. I had a big lunch."

"Don't want to review this place? Seems kind of nice."

"I'm taking a break. No more reviews here. This town is so small it's hard to go unnoticed and stay off the grid." Wren was thinking of the intruder who had left powdered sugar on her keyboard. "San Francisco has more restaurants per capita than any other city in the country. At least thirty-five hundred total. I'm guessing this town has less than a hundred. I'm going to lie low for the rest of my visit."

"Do you really think anyone could figure it out just by knowing you're in Ashland?"

"I think someone may already be a lot closer than I gave him credit for."

"Oh? Who's that?"

"A certain bulky Frenchman."

Kyle lifted his pencil from his drawing and bolted to attention. "Did you say 'bulky'?"

She nodded. "I'm almost certain I know who broke into the house."

"Who? He's not my lover, right?"

She laughed. "Kyle, you would know that better than I do."

"No, I mean, you can prove he isn't."

"Enough to satisfy Raven, yes. I believe it's my nemesis, John Bâtarde."

"You have a nemesis?" he asked with interest. "I've always wanted a nemesis. How do you get one?"

"It's easy if you're a critic. Nobody's really okay with criticism, despite what they say. Tell me what you think, they say. Tell me the truth. I want the truth. But they don't! They never do. Most of them sulk. But some of them take it further and want revenge. I'm in the business of doling out an honest opinion. That makes me a target."

"So this Bâtarde, he broke into the house because of you?"

She nodded. "Looking for proof, I'm guessing. He must have me on his short list."

"If that's true," Kyle said, "if he's close to identifying you, what's with the ginormous spread on Tallulah Rose Creamery in today's paper?"

Wren shrugged. "I had to do that. The mediocre goat cheese we had at Sprouts was an imposter. I had to make it right."

"So it was just professional integrity? Not a lesbian foodie seduction thing?"

"Right, just professional. She doesn't want to see me again."

"I'm sorry." Kyle looked sympathetically distressed before returning to his drawing.

Wren didn't know if Sophie had seen the article. She hoped so. She knew Sophie would be happy with it. Who wouldn't? She also knew she had revealed her identity to Sophie. She thought she could trust her. She just had a feeling she could. And maybe it would help, somehow, although Wren still didn't know why Sophie wanted nothing to do with her, wouldn't even talk to her. Maybe she'd done something wrong, though she didn't know what. Now she'd done something right, so maybe it would even out. Even if it didn't, the article was good and it was true. No harm done to anyone with that except, as Kyle pointed out, it offered one more set of footprints for someone to follow.

He put his pencil down, observing his drawing before turning it around to show her. "What do you think?"

The label he'd drawn was impressionistic, some swirls and curls suggesting a wineglass shape, an artistic style that reminded Wren vaguely of psychedelic patterns of the sixties. In the center of the design was a round eye with a dark band running across it horizontally. In whimsical letters above and below were the words "Newt's Eye Shiraz, Rogue Valley, Oregon."

"Do you want an honest opinion?" she asked.

He looked puzzled, glanced at his drawing, then laughed. "Oh, I see! You're joking. Yes, I do want an honest opinion, but only if it's positive."

"I like it! I really do. It's eye-catching."

He nodded appreciatively at her wordplay and closed his sketchpad. They sat silently then, watching passersby and drinking wine until the time seemed right to bring up the main reason for this meeting.

180   Robbi McCoy

"How have you been since you stormed out of the house?" she asked.

He waggled his head and frowned. "I miss him. How is he?"

"There's no doubt he misses you. He's been moping around ever since you left, not bothering to get dressed, lying on the couch all day. He's not even going to the theater tonight."

Kyle looked surprised. "That's serious."

"That's what I thought. You can't always tell with Raven, you know, what's put on and what's real feeling, but in this case, I'd go with real feeling. You're so special to him, so critically important."

Kyle looked skeptical. "So he says."

Wren shook her head. "No. He didn't say. I just know. I know his heart. I guarantee you, he loves you madly. I want you two to reconcile. What would it take?"

"I don't know. It hurts that he thinks I would do that, right under his nose. Why does he have to assume I have a lover? Why is that the explanation he latches onto?"

"Sweet Kyle," Wren said, laying her hand on his arm, "'you are wronged, you are slandered, you are undone!'"

"Oh, please!" Kyle rolled his eyes. "I don't want to hear any more lines from that play. You do realize I had to rehearse with him for weeks before you arrived on the scene. Do you have any idea what that's like?"

"I do, actually. Who do you think rehearsed with him in high school? He does get very caught up in his roles."

"I'm sick to death of Hero and Claudio and Beatrice and Benedick and all their non-problems. I'm especially fed up with Beatrice."

"You have to admit he does her well. He's wonderful in that role."

Kyle chuckled. "It's hard not to admire a man who can pull off sixteenth-century drag."

"If he apologizes, will you come back?"

"In a flash. If it's a sincere apology, not some soliloquy from *Hamlet* or something."

"I'm sure he's prepared to apologize. Just make an appearance and he'll prostrate himself."

Kyle raised his eyebrows. "Oh, now you're talking."

Wren laughed. "What if I arrange a little meeting for you two?"

"I'm game."

"Preferably before Saturday night," Wren said, remembering the Gala.

"Yes. I was looking forward to going with him to the annual fairy fête."

"Fairy fête? I like that."

"Thank you." Kyle looked pleased with himself, then turned thoughtful. "I really love that jerk." He shook his head and took another sip of wine.

Just then, Wren caught sight of Cassandra walking along the sidewalk in their direction, pulling an antique red Radio Flyer wagon. Her dog Spot sat in it, his tongue hanging out one side of his mouth. Wren gasped and grabbed hold of Kyle's arm, causing him to slosh his wine. A single drop of purple splashed onto the table. He spun around.

"Oh, God!" she cried, ducking. "Hide me."

"Hide you?" He turned back to her, his face a helpless question.

But it was too late. Cassandra had spotted her. She plodded toward them, pulling her wagon behind her. Resigned to her fate, Wren swallowed and steeled herself.

Cassandra stopped within three feet of their table, then narrowed her eyes at Wren and spat out her warning. "Fie! coward woman and soft-hearted wretch! Hast thou not spirit to curse thine enemy?"

"Coward?" Wren repeated, sitting up straighter and releasing Kyle's arm. "What enemy are you talking about?"

"He who even now is knocking at thy gate and plotting thy destruction."

"Huh?" Kyle said, wrinkling his brow. "Is that even Shakespeare?"

"What difference does it make?" Wren said through gritted teeth. "Since when did crazy require consistency?"

"Can you clarify that?" Kyle asked Cassandra, obviously toying with her.

"Nay! Mock not, mock not," Cassandra warned, scowling at

182   Robbi McCoy

Kyle. "All things I see come to pass, in this world or the next."
She pointed threateningly at Wren. "Thy fate will be sealed by
the midsummer moon."

"I don't think you should make fun of her," Wren whispered
close to his ear.

"You don't think she's for real, do you? I think she's putting
it on for the tourists. Okay, I'll be nice." He turned back to
Cassandra. "Thank you, lady prognosticator." He handed her a
couple of dollars, which she took, stuffing them into her jacket
and grinning, the first time Wren had seen anything approaching
a friendly expression on her face. But her grin was as off-putting
as her scowl and hardly endeared her to Wren.

Cassandra started off down the sidewalk, pulling her wagon
behind her.

"What did I tell you?" Kyle said. "Just another kook trying
to make a few bucks."

"Maybe you're right. I don't know why I let her scare me."

"Never mind her," Kyle said. "After all, we can't have you
believing that bit about your fate being sealed by the midsummer
moon. Midsummer's only a few days away and the full moon is
due on Saturday. Ah! The night of the gala!"

Kyle's obvious delight at that realization gave her no comfort.
She was sure Cassandra was a kook, as he said, or just putting on
a show. Either way, nothing she said was of any consequence. But
the way she said it, so menacingly, left a cloud of apprehension
over Wren. If she had wanted to put any store in what Cassandra
said, that part about her enemy closing in on her would be eerily
credible.

She heard her BlackBerry buzz and slipped it out of her bag
to see a new message. "An email from Sophie," she breathed.

"Oh? What's she say?"

"It's to Eno, not me. She says, 'Dear Ms. Threlkeld, I want to
thank you so much for the incredibly generous article about our
farm. It more than makes up for the earlier slight and I appreciate
your taking the time to do it. Don't worry. Your secret is safe
with me. Sophie'."

Kyle frowned. "Not even 'Love, Sophie.' She does know it's
you, right?"

Wren put the device back in her bag. "She does. She obviously doesn't want to see me again, even after that flattering article."

Kyle patted her hand sympathetically. "Sorry."

Feeling the wave of disappointment descending upon her, Wren realized she'd allowed herself to hope again. "It was stupid, thinking anything I said about her cheese would make any difference, one way or another."

"Ungrateful bitch!" Kyle looked comically indignant. Seeing she wasn't able to muster up a smile, his face fell. "Poor thing. I wish there was something I could do."

Wren shrugged. "'Oh, I am fortune's fool.'"

"When we're done here, I'd like to stop by Sprouts."

"Are you hungry after all?"

"No. I want to ask Ellie where I can get one of those No Shakespeare signs."

CHAPTER TWENTY-FIVE

You have witchcraft in your lips, Kate.

—*Henry V,* Act V, Scene 2

As she and her mother were finishing dinner, Sophie got a curious call from Ellie, begging her to go to the theater.

"What play is it?" she asked.

"Much Ado About Nothing."

"What?" Sophie was stunned. "Shakespeare? Are you kidding? Why in the world—"

"I know! I'll explain everything when I see you. Will you come?"

"All right," Sophie relented. "I'll come. I'll meet you outside the theater at seven thirty."

She hung up, puzzling over this odd request. As far as she knew, Ellie had never actually been to a live production of a Shakespeare play, unless you could count her father's living room rehearsals. So what had persuaded her to go tonight?

When Sophie arrived at the theater, Ellie was waiting for her out front. She wore black dress pants and a shimmery turquoise blouse, cut low with a ruffled open V-neck, revealing a significant amount of cleavage. When she caught sight of Sophie, she hurried over to greet her with a hug.

"Thank you so much for coming!" she said. "I know you've already seen this play, but it's going to be different tonight."

"How?"

"Max is the star!" Ellie smiled joyfully, looking beside herself with excitement. "He's playing Beatrice."

"What happened to Raven?"

"He's sick. Max says nothing serious. Maybe only for this one performance, so of course Max is ecstatic, terrified, out of his mind. He begged me to come. He said he may never have another shot at a big part like this. I had to come, he said. So here I am."

Sophie felt her mouth fall open. "You must be really serious about that guy."

"I admit I can't stop thinking about him. I've never felt like this…about anyone."

"He still hasn't asked you out?"

"No. Unless this counts."

"Not really. You're out with me, not him."

Max had given Ellie his guest tickets, so they were excellent seats, similar to the ones Sophie had originally gotten from Raven, two on the aisle in the center orchestra section. Ellie took the inside seat and Sophie took the aisle. Though this was her second time seeing this production, Sophie had to admit to some curiosity about the upcoming performance. For one thing, she couldn't picture Max in the role of Beatrice. Raven's style was all over it now. She was worried, for Ellie's sake, that Max, the soft-spoken moppet, would stink as Beatrice. But with no experience of live Shakespeare, Ellie might not recognize a stinker when she saw one. All the better for Max. Sophie continued to puzzle over how Ellie had fallen so suddenly and completely under his spell. She had never been romantically interested in a man before. Why this one? What was it about this small, effeminate, hyperactive boy that attracted her so?

"This is exciting," Ellie said, glancing around the theater. "Is that the sky, the real sky up there?"

Sophie looked up and laughed. "Yes. It's an open-air theater. Does it look painted on to you?"

"No. I was going to say, it's very realistic."

"Later when the stars are out, it creates a special ambience."

Moments before the curtain went up, as the ushers were taking their seats and the lights started to dim, a woman rushed in and slid silently into an aisle seat ahead, across the aisle. She wore light-colored pants, sandals and a long-sleeved blouse. Her dark brown hair was short and cut close to her head. From the back, she looked remarkably like Wren Landry. Though the curtain was rising, Sophie remained transfixed by the late-comer. Just someone who looks like her, she told herself. There was no reason for Wren to be here, especially not tonight. Raven wasn't performing. It was only when she heard Ellie gasp that she gave off looking at the Wren-like woman.

Ellie gripped Sophie's arm with one hand and covered her mouth with the other, staring wide-eyed at the stage, her expression one of astonishment.

Sophie looked to the stage to see Hero, Beatrice and Leonato speaking to a messenger. Beatrice looked surprisingly similar to the first time she'd seen this play. With the same wig, costume and makeup, little redheaded Max looked a lot like little brown-headed Raven. Sophie recalled the first time she'd seen Raven in that costume, mistaking him for a woman. A grotesque woman. The guise played more naturally on Max with his more feminine features. So much so that the audience might not realize Beatrice was being played by a man, and the playfulness of that device would be lost on them.

"I pray you," Beatrice spoke, loud and clear in a convincing female voice, "is Signior Mountanto returned from the wars or no?"

Sophie pried Ellie's fingers off her arm. Ellie glanced apologetically at Sophie before settling into her seat.

Max didn't stink after all. He was competent. He used some of Raven's gestures and mannerisms for comic effect, especially the fan, which he used as a pointer and flipped open with attitude just as Raven had done. He spoke his lines accurately in a much more natural voice than Raven's, whose voice was deep and had to be artificially raised for the part. Max wasn't as funny or flamboyant as Raven, but Sophie attributed that in part to nerves and lack of practice. He was slightly stilted. With nothing to compare it to, the audience seemed satisfied, laughing in the right places. Ellie was completely rapt. Even when Max was offstage, she seemed caught up in the action.

At the end of the third act, the lights came up for intermission amid enthusiastic audience applause. Sophie glanced at the woman ahead on the aisle. She caught her breath, certain it was Wren even before she stood and turned to reveal herself.

"Oh, God!" she whispered, then grabbed her program and opened it in front of her face.

"What's wrong?" Ellie asked.

"Shhh!" warned Sophie, wrapping the program around her head so close she couldn't possibly have read it.

After Wren had passed by, she lowered the program and breathed deeply. "Sorry. Wren's here. I didn't want her to see me."

"Why not?"

"Uh, just awkward. You know, the whole thing has gotten so weird."

"Is she here with her husband?"

"No. She's alone." Certain Wren was out of the theater, Sophie relaxed and said, "What do you think of the play?"

"I think it's wonderful!"

"You mean, *he's* wonderful?"

"No. I mean, it's wonderful. Very funny. I thought Shakespeare was incomprehensible. When I was a kid, I couldn't understand three-quarters of it. But it's making sense to me tonight."

Ellie was flushed and excited. Sophie was speechless to hear her enthusiasm for Shakespeare, so she just smiled.

"Max is rockin' it!" Ellie continued. "He's so cute in that

costume. I just want to run up there and give him a big old kiss."

"Maybe afterward," suggested Sophie.

"He did ask me if I wanted to go somewhere after. I wasn't sure about that because I didn't want to say anything about hating the play, you know. I thought for sure I would. But now I can tell him the truth, that I love it!"

"You don't know how glad I am to hear that. I always did think you were giving Shakespeare short shrift."

"I don't know what I'd think about all the others, but this one's funny. And this theater is gorgeous." Ellie craned her neck to look straight up. "The stars are out now, just like you said. What a beautiful night!" She looked back at Sophie, then seemed to look past her. "Wren's coming back in."

Sophie grabbed her jacket from the back of her seat and flung it over the top of her head like a hood, hunching over her knees so there was no way anyone could have seen her face.

"This seems kind of silly," Ellie whispered.

"Is she gone?" asked Sophie from her cloth cave.

"She's in her seat, yes."

Sophie removed her jacket. "It may seem silly to you, Ellie, but you don't know what that woman does to me. I don't trust myself with her. I need to stay away from her. I'm afraid I'll go all wobbly if I hear her say my name or she looks me in the eye."

"I know what you mean," Ellie said, shaking her head. "I've felt it myself these last few days. Heart palpitations, giddiness. I never know what kind of stupidity's coming out of my mouth next. The only thing that's saved me from running and hiding is that Max is equally affected. We've barely had a conversation of more than two sentences. We both stand there looking at one another, dumbfounded and blushing."

Sophie smiled at Ellie's incredulous expression. A trumpet announced the beginning of the fourth act as the lights dimmed. The next time Beatrice appeared on stage it was to parley wits with Benedick again. The scenes between the two reluctant lovers were among the best in the play. Beatrice wielded her fan as a sort of weapon as usual. Benedick reclined on a bench, trying to convey nonchalance.

"But for which of my good parts did you first suffer love for me?" Beatrice asked.

"Suffer love!" spurted Benedick. "A good epithet! I do suffer love indeed, for I love thee against my will."

"In spite of your heart, I think." Beatrice laughed and snapped her fan shut. "Alas, poor heart!" She spun on her heel toward the audience. The momentum of her twirl wrenched the fan from her hand and lofted it over the first several rows of seats. All eyes in the theater followed its arc up nearly to the bank of lights above and then downward as it began its descent. Sophie stiffened, planting her feet firmly on the floor, realizing the fan was headed directly for her. She reached out and snatched it before it made contact.

Both Beatrice and Benedick heaved a sigh of relief. The audience clapped at Sophie's catch. She realized everyone was looking at her. Including Wren. Their eyes rested on one another. Wren's look of surprise faded into a mild expression of melancholy.

I'm responsible for that sadness, Sophie thought, her heart melting.

"Allow me!" Benedick called, leaping from his bench and off the stage, bounding up the aisle to Sophie's seat. He bowed and took the fan from her, then took her hand and kissed it gallantly. "Thank you, milady. A most excellent catch!"

He was then back down the aisle and on the stage in a flash, snapping the fan open Raven-style and handing it back to its owner to warm applause from the audience. The action resumed.

Sophie found it hard to laugh at the rest of the show, thinking about how sincerely hurt Wren appeared. Ellie, on the other hand, laughed so hard she had tears on her cheeks. When the final bows came, Ellie jumped in place and whistled shrilly.

"Meet you out front," whispered Sophie.

She rushed out before the rest of the audience had finished clapping, wanting to get out ahead of Wren, to make sure they didn't have an awkward moment. She recalled the other time they'd both tried so hard to connect here after the play, desperately wanting to keep one another in view. What a contrast!

When Ellie came out, they walked to the curb together. The night was calm and cool. Ellie glowed with excitement and evident joy. She looked almost like a different woman tonight.

"Max said he'll pick me up here," Ellie said. "Oh, that was such a wonderful show! I really liked it."

Sophie laughed. "Imagine that! You're a Shakespeare convert."

The sound of a motorcycle drew their attention. Max came riding around from behind the theater and drove up to the curb. He'd changed into street clothes, but still had makeup on his face, including the remnants of red lipstick, apparently in too much of a hurry to make a full divestiture of Beatrice. As he saw Ellie, he beamed blissfully at her.

"Max!" she hollered, running up to him and flinging her arms around him. "You were wonderful!"

She held his face in her hands and kissed him hard. Then he kissed her, softer. She climbed on the bike behind him, wrapping her arms around his waist. Max glanced at Sophie and winked. She waved as they sped off looking for all the world like a couple of girls. Sophie smiled to herself, then glanced around at the thinning crowd, wondering if Wren had looked for her. Noticing it had gotten chilly, she pulled on her jacket, then walked down the hill toward the parking lot with her hands in her front pockets, fingering her car keys.

A few feet from the car, she pressed a button and the car responded with a flash of its lights as the doors unlocked. She opened the driver's side door and was about to get in when she heard her name, spoken softly. She turned to see Wren standing beside her. Her eyes sparkled like black pools in the dim parking lot light. The expression on her face was earnest, full of feeling. She couldn't have looked more lovely or more fragile with the tinge of sadness around her mouth.

Sophie reached for her and Wren responded by coming close and lifting her face, her open, welcoming face. Sophie wrapped her arms around her and kissed her long and deep, pressing their bodies tightly together. She felt so good. She tasted so good. Her mouth was warm and eager, merging into Sophie's, spreading happiness and desire throughout her body.

Suddenly realizing what she was doing, Sophie reeled back, dismayed with her inability to manage her emotions. "I didn't mean to do that," she whispered. "I've got to go."

"Sophie," Wren pleaded, "can't you stay awhile? Can we talk?"

Sophie shook her head, feeling desperate. "No, I can't." She knew if she stayed another minute, she'd never be able to pull herself away. She escaped into the car and started it, then rolled down the window. "'Bye," she said to Wren, then backed out of the parking space. She tried not to look back as she drove out of the lot, but the image of that sweet woman standing there looking helpless and forlorn haunted her all the way home.

CHAPTER TWENTY-SIX

You're much deceived:
In nothing am I changed
But in my garments.

—*King Lear*, Act IV, Scene 6

When Wren arrived back at the house, she saw Max's motorcycle parked at the curb. She was momentarily disappointed to see they had company. It had been her intention to slink off to bed. She wasn't in the mood for socializing. She was still bummed and confused by Sophie's behavior. The woman was obviously attracted to her. The memory of her kiss lingered vividly. Why, then, did she keep running away? It had made sense when it appeared she was married. But now... Wren shook herself as she walked up the steps to the porch, preparing to be cheerful for Max. Maybe she could just stick her head in and say hi and leave Max and Raven to their conversation, a deconstruction, no doubt, of the night's performance.

When she passed through to the living room, she saw Max standing and gesturing in front of Raven, who was half-sitting, half-lying on the sofa, listening with interest. Ellie stood to the side with a goofy smile. Her normally surprised-looking expression looked even more surprised tonight. Wren had been startled to see Ellie at the theater, knowing she was not a fan of Shakespeare. Seeing her here, Wren decided it was Max, not Shakespeare, who had lured her there.

"Wren," Max greeted her with enthusiasm, "what did you think?"

She walked over and hugged Max. "I thought you were wonderful. Nobody would ever guess you hadn't been doing it for weeks."

"Really?"

"Really. Except for the fan incident, maybe."

"Fan incident?" Raven asked.

Max blushed.

"Just a tiny bobble," Wren said, approaching Ellie. She gave her a hug as well.

"I was just telling Raven how exciting it was," Max said. "Such a rush. I'm wide awake and full of energy. Ellie and I are going out for a late dinner. Maybe we'll go dancing. What do you say, Ellie? Do you dance?"

She nodded vigorously. "It's been a while, but I'll give it a try."

"It'll be hours before you come down," Raven said. "Dancing sounds like a good idea. Burn off some of that energy."

"Does anybody want anything to drink?" offered Wren.

"No, thanks," Max answered. "We won't be staying."

"I could use a glass of water," Ellie said, "if you point me at the kitchen."

"Come on," Wren said, "I'll take you."

They went to the kitchen where Wren took a glass from the cupboard. "You and Max are a thing now, I guess."

"This will be our first date, actually. It'll be nice to be out with him on such an important night. He's so happy!"

Wren filled the glass from a pitcher in the refrigerator, noting Ellie's use of male pronouns. Apparently she didn't know they were in on the ruse.

194   Robbi McCoy

Ellie took the glass and swallowed a gulp of water before saying, "Max is just so fascinating, so unlike any man I've ever met before. To be honest, men have never appealed to me much...that way. I dated boys in high school, but none of them ever seemed very interesting. As I got older, I figured someday I'd meet a guy who could blow my gaskets, you know. But it never happened. Until now." She laughed nervously.

Okay, thought Wren, annoyed, that's taking it a little too far. "You do know I'm gay, right?" Wren asked. "And Raven too?"

"Yes, I know." Ellie looked startled. "I mean, I wasn't really sure about you." She narrowed her eyes and looked momentarily bewildered. "I don't have anything against gays. Really. I'm not the least bit prejudiced. One of my dearest friends is a lesbian. Oh! Of course you know Sophie!" Ellie blushed a bright shade of pink and looked positively horrified.

Confused, Wren stared at her as she took another guzzle of water. "No, I didn't think you were prejudiced," she said. "I just meant, you don't have to pretend around us. We know about Max. We've assumed, given the pretty obvious signs, that Max is also gay."

Ellie choked on her water and started coughing. When she recovered, she said, "Oh! You're confused about me and Max because you think he's gay. I can see why you might think that. I wondered too at first. He's not a very macho man, is he? And he's in the theater. So many actors are gay, aren't they? But I know his interest in me is more than platonic. Yes, I'm sure of that. There's a powerful sexual element between us. I've felt it since the day we met. He kissed me a while ago, just in front of the house. Oh, Sweet Sally Sue! Definitely a sexual attraction. Looks can be deceiving. I have nothing against homosexuals, truly, but Max, I'm sure, is *not* a gay man." Ellie sucked in a deep, calming breath, then smiled benignly. Then, as if she were speaking in confidence, she lowered her voice and said, "I believe tonight will be definite proof of that."

She giggled as she handed the glass to Wren, who stood flabbergasted, at a total loss for words.

A few minutes later, Ellie and Max walked out hand in hand

and were on their way for a night on the town that promised to be deliciously interesting.

Raven stood barefoot in the living room, yawning. "So how was she, really?" he asked. "Did Beatrice bomb?"

"She was good. She was no you, but she did well."

"Well, who is me?" He grinned. He seemed to be in a better mood than earlier in the day.

"Even if Max can handle it, I hope you'll be going on tomorrow."

"I'll try. I guess I don't want her to get used to this. She did seem thrilled."

"Why wouldn't she be? She got to play the lead in a classic and has a new girlfriend who's expecting fireworks tonight. Ellie's about to burst."

Raven nodded, smiling crookedly. "Oh, yeah. Max is excited about that too."

"Is she? She's not a little nervous?"

Raven shrugged. "Everybody's a little nervous the first time. But, you know, nature takes over and everything's fine."

"I'm not so sure nature is going to know what to do with this pair."

Raven wrinkled his nose. "What? I'm surprised to hear you say that. You of all people should know that nature works as well with two girls as with anybody."

"That's not what I mean. Ellie thinks Max is a dude."

Raven stared, incredulous, then said, "You're not serious?"

"I am. After the conversation I just had with her, I'm certain she doesn't know she's on a date with a woman."

"How's that possible?"

"She's a little green when it comes to dating. I wouldn't be surprised if she's never even..."

"Oh, my God!" Raven rushed to the front door and flung it open, looking out into the silent night. "Max!"

When he came back inside, Wren was waiting in the hallway, leaning casually against a doorframe. "She must have a plan," she said calmly. "This is their first date. Max will know how to handle it. Over drinks, she'll gently explain. She'll let it sink in, see how Ellie—"

Raven was shaking his head. "While you two were in the kitchen, Max went on and on about Ellie and how perfect they are for one another. She thinks Ellie's a lesbian. And she figures she's been with other women. She said the first time they met, in the restaurant, she knew right then and there this woman was for her. And it seemed Ellie felt the same. Max thinks Ellie has always known she was a woman. Like you knew."

"Those two should talk more! If Ellie *was* a lesbian, an experienced lesbian, she probably would know." Wren shook her head. "Apparently, they're both in for a surprise tonight."

"What should we do?" Raven asked, clearly distraught.

"I vote for letting nature take its course."

"But you just said—"

"I know, but maybe I was underestimating nature. It seems they're really in love with one another."

Raven sighed. "'Love looks not with the eyes, but with the mind; and therefore is wing'd Cupid painted blind.'"

"Here's one for you," Wren replied. "'Cupid is a knavish lad, thus to make poor females mad.'"

Raven laughed. "I hope they work it out."

CHAPTER TWENTY-SEVEN

Fetch me that flower, the herb I showed thee once:
The juice of it on sleeping eyelids laid
Will make or man or woman madly dote
Upon the next live creature that it sees.

—*A Midsummer Night's Dream*, Act II, Scene 1

Sophie stepped into the back porch and lifted off her sun hat, having just finished planting some lemon thyme, an herb she thought would complement chêvre. Her mother met her in the kitchen in a state of spirited anxiety.

"Sophie, we're getting calls from people wanting cheese," Olivia reported breathlessly. "A man from all the way up in Portland just called. And that fancy produce market in Medford wants to stock us."

"It's exciting, isn't it?"

"What do I tell them?"

"Tell them we're sorry, but we can't take any new customers right now. If it's somebody local, take their name and number and tell them we'll see what we can do."

"Okay. What *can* we do?"

"Get a couple more goats. I don't know. Maybe we could think about something a little more professional than this." Sophie nodded toward the cheese hanging over the kitchen counter. "If we want to get serious, we could always hire somebody to help. For now, let's just go easy. The hoopla from the article will die down soon enough." Sophie slipped an arm around her mother's shoulders. "We don't want to get carried away and outpace ourselves."

A car horn sounded from the direction of the front yard.

"Are we expecting someone?" Olivia asked.

Sophie shook her head and walked through the house as the horn sounded again. She went out the front door to see a taxi in the driveway and a woman standing beside it. The taxi driver hauled an enormous suitcase out of the trunk. The woman, who was wearing a lime green pantsuit, waved cheerfully in their direction. As soon as she saw that color, Sophie knew it was her sister Dena. Lime green was her favorite color, her signature color, and she almost always wore it.

Olivia took off at a trot to greet her and the two of them embraced warmly while Sophie stood on the porch wondering what had induced Dena to make the trip from Tucson with no advance warning.

"Why didn't you tell me you were coming?" Olivia was saying as Sophie approached.

"I just took off," Dena said. "Just threw some stuff in a suitcase and took off this morning without a thought in my head."

Dena was shorter and wider than Sophie. Plumpish, but not fat. Girlishly rounded and soft with curly hair and an unblemished, rosy complexion. Her eyes were more of a true blue than Sophie's, round and glamorous. She was pretty, feminine and flouncy. She wasn't the sort of woman you'd expect to put oil in her own car. Though she was two years older than Sophie, she looked like the younger sister. Sophie knew she had more of a gaunt look to her, a lived-in look.

Two On The Aisle   199

"Hi, Sophie!" Dena squealed, flinging herself at her sister.

Sophie hugged her, then said, "Hank didn't come with you?"

Dena rolled her eyes dramatically. "I've left him! I just took off, took off without a thought in my head. I've had enough!"

She seemed awfully proud of taking off without a thought in her head, as this was the second time she'd said it in five minutes. It was all Sophie could manage this time not to laugh.

"It wasn't until I got to the airport I decided to come here." Dena looked from one to the other of them gleefully. "Just went up to the counter and bought a ticket."

She paid the taxi driver, then stood beside her suitcase, waiting for somebody to offer to move it for her, her long, painted fingernails resting on the top of her stylish leather purse. Sophie glanced at her shoes—taupe, three-inch heels.

"Come on in," Olivia said, taking hold of Dena's arm and leading her toward the house.

Sophie stood beside the suitcase for a moment, considering leaving it there, then relented, snapped up the handle and rolled it over to the house, lifting it up the stairs to the porch. It was heavy and big and Sophie was certain there was no outfit in there suitable for milking goats.

By late afternoon, the three women were sitting on the front porch with a pitcher of lemonade, watching the sun set. Poppy was asleep in Olivia's lap. Dena had talked herself out and was now silent. She had been telling them about the last straw that had sent her packing. Hank had invited his deadbeat brother to move in with them. Two deadbeats in one house, yeah, that would be hard to take, Sophie sympathized. But that wasn't even the worst of it. What had really torqued Dena off was how Hank had started insulting and demeaning her in front of his brother. It was one thing to call her dumb with just the two of them there, but to do it in front of "company" was apparently unforgivable.

Yesterday while the two fun-loving brothers sat in the front room watching TV, Dena had been taking throw rugs out to the backyard to shake them out. She had left the back door open to make it easier to carry out the rugs and a bird, a sparrow, had flown into the house. Dena had panicked and started screaming and had instinctively shut the door. The bird flew around the room looking for a way out while their cat chased it, knocking lamps over. During this fracas, Hank stood in the middle of the room trying to catch the bird with his bare hands whenever it passed by, while fruitlessly yelling, "Open the door!" at Dena. His brother ran after the frenzied cat, trying to prevent any more damage. Finally, the bird flew into the glass of the closed door, knocking itself senseless. It fell on Dena's feet, which were in sandals, sending her into greater hysterics. She screamed at the top of her lungs and kicked her feet into the air wildly while Hank yelled at her to shut up. As the bird flopped on the carpet where it had been kicked by Dena, the cat snatched it. Hank opened the door and the cat fled outside with her prize.

It was then that Dena had stopped screaming and Hank had turned to his brother and said, "See what I mean?"

The telling of this tale took two hours because Dena took side trips to give other examples of Hank belittling her, building her case so they'd understand why this was the last straw. By the time she was done with her story, Sophie actually felt sorry for her. She also felt sorry for the sparrow.

That was why Dena was here. She had nowhere else to go and she needed the comfort of her mother's roost. Nobody was talking now. They were just drinking their lemonade and enjoying the warm summer evening, the low bleating of goats and the chirping of crickets. There was an occasional small sigh from one or the other of them, sighs of regret, contentment or weariness, all sounding the same.

"Gonna be a warm night," Olivia said, reaching behind herself to adjust the smiling school bus pillow higher on her back. Poppy opened her eyes briefly, then curled into a tighter ball and went back to sleep.

"Uh-huh," Dena replied lazily.

Sophie tried to remember the last time all three of them had spent a night here together. It had to be over fifteen years ago, before Dena left home. When Olivia had her stroke, Dena had stayed here two nights with Sophie, but their mother had been in the hospital. There had been nothing relaxing or congenial about the two of them occupying this house together then. They weren't used to the house anymore and they weren't used to one another. Without their mother as axis, they bumped awkwardly into one another and took out their anxiety over Olivia on each other. This was different. Sophie felt peaceful. She felt a sense of belonging too. This was her home now and it felt like it. Having Dena here was beginning to feel right. Their little family was complete.

A pickup appeared at the top of the hill and headed up the driveway. All three of them came to attention.

"It's Klaus," Olivia said.

"Who's Klaus?" Dena asked.

"A friend. He helps out around here from time to time." Sophie stood.

Klaus got out of his truck, carrying a cardboard box up to the porch. Sophie was glad to see him making a friendly call. After their talk, she'd been afraid he would turn their relationship into strictly business.

"Hi," he said, grinning brightly. "Guess what? I'm a bake-off finalist!"

"Wonderful!" Sophie exclaimed.

"Sorry to interrupt," he said, glancing at Dena. "I won't stay. I brought you ladies a sample of my last practice batch of cupcakes. This is it, for better or worse. I've got all three flavors here. Enough for your guest to try them too."

He smiled at Dena, who stood, taking a step toward him, a brilliant, toothy smile on her face.

"This is my daughter, Dena," Olivia announced. "She's just arrived for a visit."

Klaus thrust his box at Sophie. Then he took Dena's hand and said, "Nice to meet you. I'm Klaus. How long are you here for?"

"I don't really know," Dena said. "I thought I'd just play it by ear and see what develops."

Sophie was certain she saw Dena's chest expand, and there was no doubt the two of them had locked eyes on each other with some sort of fascination. Olivia grabbed one of the cupcakes from the box.

"I'll put these inside," Sophie said. "Thank you, Klaus. They look like winners to me."

She went in the house and set the box on the kitchen table, wondering if it was possible for a man to fall for two women as different as she was from Dena.

When she returned to the porch, Klaus and Dena were standing in the driveway talking. Sophie sat back in her chair, watching the two of them while sucking on an ice cube from her empty lemonade glass.

"What do you suppose is going on there?" she asked her mother.

"The oldest story in the book." Olivia chuckled and bit into her cupcake.

Sophie watched her sister and Klaus with a mixture of interest and bewilderment.

Dena swatted playfully at Klaus's arm, pivoting back and forth on the toe of one foot like a defective wind-up ballerina, stuck in a thirty-degree angle of motion.

Klaus waved toward the porch, then drove away as Dena walked back in the twilight. She dropped into her chair and leaned toward Sophie. "Tell me everything," she commanded.

"About what?"

"About Klaus, silly. Is he single? Is he nice? What are his aspirations? What's his family like?"

"Hold on, Dena. Don't you think you're getting ahead of yourself?" Sophie doubted Klaus had any ability to protect himself against the wiles of a woman like Dena. He wasn't stupid, but he also wasn't worldly. "You just met the man."

Dena frowned. "So what? Oh, I know what happened with you two. He told me he used to like you."

"Used to?" Sophie asked.

"And that you weren't interested."

"That was like three days ago."

"Don't tell me you were just playing hard to get. Because that really isn't nice. He's a sweet guy."

"I know he's a sweet guy," Sophie said indignantly. "I've

known him for two years. And, no, I wasn't playing hard to get. I'm not interested in him that way. Just as a friend."

"Good. So he's available." Dena grinned with satisfaction, then her expression gradually turned suspicious. "Why aren't you interested? Is there something weird about him?"

"No. He's a real sweetheart. He's bighearted, gentle and honest."

Dena turned her questioning face to Olivia, who was licking frosting from the corner of her mouth.

"Yep," she said, affirming Sophie's description. "And he makes a hell of a cupcake. He's a great guy. Just not Sophie's type."

"That's what he said."

"He said he wasn't my type?" Sophie asked.

"Right."

How discreet of him, she thought.

"I don't really get that," Dena said. "I'd guess he *was* your type. Another Norwegian."

"Klaus isn't Norwegian. He's Danish."

"Practically the same thing."

Sophie laughed. "Dena, wars have been fought over—"

Dena pulled herself up stiffly. "Don't start, Sophie."

"What?"

"Showing off your college education."

Sophie stuttered, starting to lose her composure. As usual, Dena was pitting them against each other based on a completely fabricated disagreement arising out of her own insecurities.

"It doesn't matter," Dena insisted. "Danish, Norwegian. Whatever. He's a big, handsome blond Nordic hunk. And you've already had yours. Mom told me all about your Norwegian. He was Norwegian, right? Not Danish or Swedish? Jan what's-his-name."

Dena pronounced Jan's name as Olivia did, as "Yahn."

"Or was he Finnish?" asked Dena defiantly. "Or maybe he was from Iceland. See, I know a little bit about geography too."

"No," Olivia asserted, "he wasn't from Iceland. He was Norwegian. Isn't that right, Sophie, your Jan was Norwegian?"

Sophie stood, clenching her fist in frustration. "No!" she blurted. "He wasn't Norwegian. It was *Jan*, Mom, Jan like Jan Donleavy over at the Save-Mart."

Olivia's eyes snapped open in an expression of wonder. "Ah! Well, then—" She nodded, looking totally delighted, and popped the last of her cupcake into her mouth. "I really like this lemon flavor. Really lemony, especially that glob of whatever that stuff is in the middle." She put Poppy down gently on the porch. "I'm gonna try the others."

Olivia rose from her chair and went into the house, leaving Sophie bewildered.

Dena frowned. "Why would your Jan pronounce his name like that and have everybody think he was a girl?"

"Because he *was* a girl!"

"He was a girl?" Dena looked irritated, as she always did when she didn't understand something.

Sophie shook her head. "No, *she* was a girl. Jan was a girl. She was always a girl. She's still a girl. Her name is Janet and she isn't Norwegian."

"Is she Danish?" Dena asked.

Sophie scowled at her sister, disapprovingly.

Their mother returned with a lavender cupcake and sat back in her rocker, seeming unconcerned about the conversation between her daughters.

"She isn't Danish," Sophie stated bluntly, "she's from New England. But that's completely beside the point."

Dena narrowed her eyes defensively.

"I don't think you understand what I'm saying," Sophie added in exasperation.

Olivia peeled the paper off the sides of her cupcake. "What Sophie's trying to tell you, in her own bungling way, is that she's a lesbian."

Both Sophie and Dena turned abruptly to face their mother, then Dena looked wide-eyed at Sophie, who confirmed Olivia's statement with a nod.

"I never did know what you were doing with that Norwegian man," Olivia said. "It was obvious to me you were a lesbian by sixth grade. Frankly, I'm glad to have that cleared up."

Sophie gawked for a moment at her mother, who was intent on her cupcake, then she moved toward the door.

"If you're going in, Sophie," Olivia said, "can you bring me a glass of milk?"

Sophie pulled open the screen door and went into the house, pausing on the other side of the door, her heart pounding furiously.

That was nothing like the coming out speech she'd been rehearsing in her mind. She wasn't much of a talker, generally speaking, but when she got agitated, things came gushing ungoverned out of her mouth and didn't always make sense. Apparently, it didn't matter. It never had. Her mother already knew.

On her way back to the porch with the milk, she heard a car door slam. Another visitor? she wondered, annoyed that the farm was so popular today. Coming out of the house, she was surprised to see Ellie running toward them, waving her arms frantically. Sophie handed the milk to her mother, trying to imagine what disaster had occurred. Ellie never came to visit and she looked completely hysterical.

"Sophie! Sophie!" she hollered, bounding up the steps and flinging herself at Sophie, grabbing her in an insistent hug.

"What's happened?" Sophie asked, gently holding Ellie at arm's length.

"I'm a lesbian!" Ellie shouted emphatically. "I'm a lesbian!" She threw both arms up to emphasize her announcement, like an actor prompting an audience for applause. She was beaming, smiling like a lunatic. "Max is a lesbian too!"

"Is this National Coming Out Day?" Dena asked.

"Everything makes sense now!" Ellie declared, oblivious to Dena and Olivia.

"Maybe to you," muttered Dena.

"Last night," Ellie continued, breathlessly, "when she took off her, you know, and I was expecting a...you know." She held her hand near her belly and pointed out with her index finger. "But, oh, my God! Instead, she was this gorgeous girl!"

"Come inside," Sophie suggested, taking Ellie by the arm. "You can tell me all about it."

As she escorted Ellie into the living room, she heard Dena say, "This place is a lot more exciting than I remember. I can't wait to see what's going to happen tomorrow."

CHAPTER TWENTY-EIGHT

O, it is excellent
To have a giant's strength; but it is tyrannous
To use it like a giant.

—*Measure for Measure*, Act II, Scene 2

The next morning the three of them had cupcakes and coffee for breakfast and nobody mentioned Sophie's big revelation or Ellie's dramatic transformation. But Dena was extra sweet to Sophie, giving her an affectionate good-morning squeeze and saying, "How's my baby sister today?" She actually seemed happier with her. The only conclusion Sophie could draw was that Dena was thankful that in this one area at least, they were not in competition. Sophie never had felt she was in competition with Dena, but she had always had an inferiority complex and had overreacted whenever Sophie was praised for anything, for being smart, for being pretty, for knowing how to handle a horse or spell some obscure word. No matter what Sophie did, Dena always saw it as a reflection, a poor reflection, on herself.

If nothing else, she could now be the best straight daughter at everything and maybe that was enough for her. After breakfast, Dena and Sophie sat in the kitchen finishing their coffee while Olivia took Gambit out for a morning ride.

"Do you think he has a chance?" Dena asked, nodding toward the three half-eaten cupcakes on her plate, one yellow, one lavender and one pink. She looked more comfortable today, wearing tan pants and a lime green and white striped shirt, sneakers and no lipstick.

"I do," Sophie said. "I think these are excellent. Of course, I haven't seen the others. And the competition includes a display, a big construction that holds a thousand of these. That's how they'll be served at the party."

"I hope he wins." Dena sighed. "You know, you never told me about his family."

"He only has his mother. There was a boating accident when he was just a baby. His father and brother were drowned."

"That's so sad."

"Yes, it is. But his mother lives in town and they're close. A really nice woman."

Would it be so bad, Sophie asked herself, if Dena and Klaus got together? For either of them? They might actually make each other happy. And it would make Sophie feel better if he moved on from his crush on her. Things would definitely be less awkward and she couldn't imagine a finer choice for a brother-in-law.

After the breakfast dishes were done and the goats were milked, Sophie started a batch of cheese, reflecting on Ellie's confession from the night before. She was completely beside herself with the discovery that she was a lesbian and had understandably wanted to share it with her lesbian friend. Sophie had never suspected it. It was funny to hear Ellie tell how it had come about. It had been touch and go there for a while, apparently, when Ellie realized she was making out with a woman and then when Max realized that was news to Ellie. But after a serious discussion, they concluded they were in love and that's what mattered. By morning, Ellie had further concluded that her heart had taken her where her mind never could and this was what she was destined for. She was happy, Max was happy, and Sophie was happy for them.

Upon returning from her ride, Olivia came in through the kitchen where Sophie had just finished hanging new curds to drain. "Somebody's coming up the drive," she announced.

Sophie went out to meet a black four door sedan in the driveway. A stout, middle-aged man with a ginger mustache and a perfectly round face stepped out of the car. He was partly bald with wisps of straight dark hair straggling across the top of his head. His mouth was set in a self-satisfied expression that turned into a practiced smile as he leaned in to shake her hand. He wore a sports jacket and neatly-pressed slacks.

"Hello, Miss Ward, is that right? I'm John Bâtarde."

She shook his hand. "Hello."

He seemed to expect her to recognize his name. His smile, which was emphatic but hinted at insincerity, persisted. There was a slight accent in his speech, which she guessed was French.

"You haven't heard of me?" he asked.

"No, sorry."

"No matter. I'm in the restaurant business." He had a folded newspaper in his left hand, which he waved between them. "I'm here because of this. Threlkeld's article. Wonderful, isn't it?"

"Yes, it is wonderful," agreed Sophie. "We're thrilled with it."

"And you should be. A feature like this, well, that's unusual for Threlkeld. He...*or she* must have been very impressed." He tilted his head and peered expectantly at her before continuing. "If Threlkeld was impressed, then I'm sure I will be also. I own several restaurants, well-known, celebrated restaurants. My flagship is Josephine in San Francisco. Do you know it?"

"No. I haven't spent much time in San Francisco."

"Believe me, it's top-notch. I'd love to find a reliable, high-quality source of chêvre suitable for my menu." Bâtarde's forced smile persisted. "Do you have a few minutes to show me around?"

"I suppose, but you must know, if you read that article, that this is a tiny operation. We can't do much more than we do already."

"But you're going to expand, aren't you? You must. Besides, as far as I'm concerned, the more exclusive the product, the better for us. I'd like to taste your cheese and then we can talk more about bigger dreams for you."

This guy is full of himself, Sophie thought.

"Okay, I'll give you a tour. This will be only the second tour we've ever given."

Sophie walked toward the goat corral with her visitor following.

"The first would be Threlkeld, right?" he asked.

"Right."

"What'd you think of Threlkeld?"

Sophie started to answer, then remembered that Wren's identity was a secret. Eno Threlkeld was a faceless mystery to most people. She didn't know what this man knew, if he knew her at all. One thing she did know was that he gave her the creeps.

"I don't think I'm at liberty to talk about Threlkeld," she said as they arrived at the fence surrounding the goat pen.

"Oh, right. But that's for the amateurs. Threlkeld's reviewed all my California restaurants and we've had a professional relationship for years. For instance—" He lowered his voice in confidence, though nobody but the goats could possibly hear them. "Everyone assumes he's a man. But we know better, don't we?"

Sophie put on her most neutral smile, wondering if he was fishing. "Do we? I'm not even sure I met Threlkeld. It's very possible he sent a proxy."

"You're going to play coy with me. Okay, okay." He looked amused. "Let's continue."

Sophie introduced him to all the goats. Little Poppy came up to the fence and pushed her head through the boards, nuzzling Bâtarde's fingers. He jerked away and took a handkerchief from his pocket, wiping his hand.

"Poppy's my mother's pride and joy," Sophie said. "The beginning of our second generation."

They walked over to the shed where she showed him her herb drying operation.

"Just lavender and sage so far," she said. "I grow those myself here on the farm. I've just planted some lemon thyme. I thought I'd give that a try next."

"Good choices. I'd stay away from tarragon if I were you. And please no oregano. Too overpowering."

In the house, she showed him bags of curds dripping milky whey into a bowl in the sink. "I just started this batch this morning."

"Yes, this *is* a small operation," he said, clucking joyfully. "You're using your kitchen sink."

"That's what I was trying to tell you. All of this publicity may have been premature."

"Still, if you could supply just two restaurants, that could be worth it to me to begin with." He fingered the edge of the plate containing Klaus's cupcakes. "What's this?"

"Those were made by a friend. He's a finalist in the cupcake bake-off tomorrow."

"Really? Then you'd better get them out of my sight. I'm judging that contest."

"Oh!" Sophie snatched up the plate.

Bâtarde stood with his nose hovering over the cupcakes. "They look scrumptious. I guess it wouldn't be ethical to taste them now, would it?"

"No, it wouldn't." Sophie whisked the plate off to the back porch.

"I've got a relentless sweet tooth," Bâtarde said when she returned to the kitchen. "You haven't considered making any sweet cheese, have you?"

"I've considered it. Adding honey. Something for the future."

Bâtarde's eyes lit up with the thought. "Excellent! Do you have any finished cheese around that I could taste?"

She gave him a chair at the kitchen table and laid out the three types of cheese, a cheese knife, and a glass of water.

She watched him taste, methodically, wordlessly, without expression. She couldn't tell if he was enjoying himself or if it was simply work. She didn't want it to ever just be work for herself. So far it was fun. It should stay fun. Otherwise, why do it?

This laborious tasting process took long enough that Sophie was getting impatient when at last he put down the knife and drank his last swallow of water.

"Very fine," he said. "Surprisingly fine, considering what a short time you've been at it."

"I work very hard at getting it right."

"Threlkeld was right on the money. This is first-rate. Well done." He wiped his mouth on a napkin and stood. "I've made some inquiries around town. I know what you charge your current customers. I can pay you twice that plus the cost of shipping. And I can take everything you produce. No more peddling door to door for you."

He opened his wallet and took out a card, which he handed to her. He sounded very authoritative and most likely thought he was intimidating and impressing her. She was a simple farm girl, after all. She at least must look like one with her worn jeans and dirty boots. He couldn't know that two years ago she had spent her days schmoozing guys like him, bigger than him, as she moved their millions around like bubbles in bathwater.

"I don't know," she said. "I like dealing locally. It's got a warm and friendly feeling to it. That's the whole point of an organic microfarm, isn't it? Eco-friendly, small footprint, connecting our simpler roots to a safer future?"

"You're very sly, aren't you?" He grinned, showing his rabbity front teeth. "Two and a half times what you currently charge. That's as high as I go. You consider my offer and call me. I can tell you're a smart woman. I don't have to tell you all the ways this makes good business sense."

Now he was trying another old tactic, making the farm girl think they were intellectually equal. Flattery. She realized she did not like this man. He reminded her too much of her old colleagues.

"I'm going to level with you, Sophie," he said. "I need to figure out who Threlkeld is and you can help me. I'll zero in eventually on my own, but with your help, I can get there a lot faster. I'm going to show you my short list. All you have to do is point to Threlkeld. You don't have to say a word."

He opened his portfolio to a laminated page of small photos.

Two On The Aisle   213

There were six of them, four men and two women. Sophie quickly noted Wren's face among them, but didn't linger on it, worried that she'd give her away. Obviously, this was the only reason he was here, to get her to finger Wren.

"Sorry," she said. "I can't help you."

He bit his lower lip and closed the portfolio. "What I can't figure out is why you're being so protective of someone you've just met, why you'd give up my generous offer for something this trivial."

"Because I'm not interested in your offer," Sophie said matter-of-factly. "Besides, if identifying Threlkeld is so trivial, why are you going to so much trouble to do it?"

He stared at her steadily for a moment, a hint of anger in his eyes, then shook his head in dismay. "It doesn't matter. I'm closing in. With or without your help. You're a fool to reject my offer. I could have put this little backwater farm on the map."

Sophie felt like spitting as she watched John Bâtarde drive away. She was left with a feeling of anxiety. His parting words about Threlkeld had sounded threatening. What would he do when he was certain he had the right person? And why was he so intent on finding her?

CHAPTER TWENTY-NINE

What a damned Epicurean rascal is this!

—*The Merry Wives of Windsor*, Act II, Scene 2

Coming into the house from a long walk Saturday afternoon, Wren turned on her phone to call Kyle and saw she had voice mail. It was from Raven a couple hours earlier.

"Your friend Sophie's trying to get hold of you," he said. "See you this evening."

Sophie wants me! thought Wren, her pulse quickening. She didn't care what the reason was for her change of heart, only that she'd had one.

She rushed to the garage to get her car, heading quickly out of town. Remembering Kyle, she called him as she hit the interstate.

"What's up?" he answered.

"I've set it up with Raven for five o'clock at the Stratford Inn."

"Great. I'll be there. You too, right?"

"I was planning on it, but something else's come up. You don't really need me there, do you?"

"You were going to be the arbiter."

"I might still make it. If not, just accept his apology, then kiss and make up."

"You make it sound so businesslike," Kyle complained.

"Sorry, but I've got something on my mind."

"Is anything wrong?"

"No. At least…I don't actually know."

She realized she had no idea why Sophie wanted to see her. She had leapt to the unlikely conclusion that she wanted a date and was now driving out there to throw herself into her lover's arms. She eased up on the accelerator as she reevaluated her plan. It made more sense to call Sophie and ask her what she wanted. Remembering the last time she'd shown up at the farm uninvited dampened her enthusiasm considerably.

Although she had been clever enough to program the phone number into her phone, she saw the battery light flash just before the phone turned itself off. *Oh, well*, she thought, *I'll stick with the original plan.* Even if Sophie turned her away again, the chance to see her, even for a minute, was worth it.

When at last she pulled into the gravel driveway in front of Sophie's house, she was out of the car nearly before the engine was off. She raced to the front porch just as the door of the farmhouse flew open. Olivia came rushing blindly out of the house and crashed into her. Wren observed her frantic face, contorted in fear and hysteria. In her hand was a piece of yellow paper.

"Is something wrong?" Wren asked. "Is Sophie here?"

"Sophie!" Olivia cried, reeling back. "She's not here." She waved the piece of paper between them. "Oh, my little one, my little one! She's been kidnapped!"

"Kidnapped?" Wren grabbed the paper from her hand and quickly read the handwritten note.

I've got your kid. If you ever want to see her alive again, you'll tell me what I want to know. Call me at exactly seven o'clock tonight and give me Threlkeld's real name. If you don't, your kid's stewed. If you call the police, you'll never see her again. J. B.

There was a phone number at the bottom of the page.

Wren gasped. "J. B.? John Bâtarde! Oh, my God! Has Bâtarde been here?"

"That was the guy who was here yesterday, the restaurant guy."

"The bastard!" Wren cried. "I can't believe it! He wouldn't..."

"What are we going to do?" Olivia looked like she would burst into tears at any moment.

"This is all my fault." Wren put her hand on Olivia's shoulder. "Don't worry. I'll find her. I'll make sure nothing happens to her."

Wren was astonished that Bâtarde was so desperate and ruthless he would resort to something as despicable as kidnapping Sophie. Would she talk? Would she tell him who Eno Threlkeld was? At this point, Wren realized, there may be no way to avoid that. Her career was not worth the life of a woman, any woman, much less the woman she loved. She would tell him herself if it would save Sophie's life.

Wren raced to her car and was back on the deserted country road in seconds. On the main road, heading toward town, she spotted a line of animals up ahead on the side of the road. She passed them without slowing down, but got a good enough look to determine they were Sophie's goats, running single file with Rose in the lead. She knew the goats weren't kept in their pen all the time, but this seemed strange. But there were more important things to worry about. At least the little one, Poppy, wasn't with them and was likely home safe with Olivia.

Wren gradually began to realize she didn't know where she was racing to. She glanced at the yellow note on the seat beside her. She had no idea where Bâtarde was holed up or where he might have taken Sophie. All she knew was that he was expecting a phone call at seven o'clock. She slowed her pace, recognizing she had several hours of waiting ahead.

After picking some blooming lavender branches near the east fence, Sophie walked back up the hill with her fragrant bundle and plunked it on the workbench in the potting shed. She checked her cell phone for messages, even though she knew it hadn't rung. Why wasn't Wren returning her call so she could warn her about Bâtarde?

She'd managed to catch Raven at the theater and he'd promised to leave a message for Wren. He seemed to know who she was, which surprised her, even naming her "my sister's lovely goatherd," and inviting her to join the two of them for drinks later at the Stratford Inn, saying, "I know Wren would be thrilled to see you." She wondered what Wren had told her brother about them, surprised she had said anything at all. Wasn't she worried her husband would find out? At least Raven was friendly, suggesting that whatever Wren had said, he thought they were on good terms, not that they weren't even speaking to one another. Barely speaking. Not speaking, but... Sophie rolled her eyes at herself, remembering how she had impulsively kissed Wren the other night. As nice as it had felt, it had been a stupid thing to do and must have confused poor Wren considerably. No, I mustn't think of her as "poor Wren," Sophie warned herself, conjuring up an image of a small bird with a broken wing. There was no way to resist her with that kind of sympathetic vision.

While she cut the stems short and tied the flower heads into small bundles, she thought about Bâtarde and his menacing glare, like some two-bit hoodlum. His visit yesterday had left her shaken. There was probably nothing to his threats. He was just blowing hot air. Even if he did discover Threlkeld's true identity, what would he do about it? It wasn't as if he'd kill her. She was a food critic, not an international spy.

Sophie realized she'd been more threatened by his bluster than she should have been. Her frantic call to Raven this morning had been sheer panic. By the time she got to talk to Wren herself, she'd be more reasonable. She smiled at herself as she finished hanging the flowers to dry, then she pulled off her gloves and left the shed, taking a can of goat chow with her.

The gate to the goat pen stood wide open. She poured the feed into the pan, expecting to hear the excited calls of the herd as they came gamboling in to crowd around their food dish. But there was no sound other than a meadowlark on a fence post and the distant hum of a tractor working a field. Confused, Sophie returned the can to the shed, then walked around the perimeter of the house, expecting to find the herd munching grass in the front yard. She started calling their names loudly, cupping her hands in front of her mouth. Normally, she could at least count on Tater to come when called. Unless she had her head stuck in something or was trapped somewhere, and then she'd be sure to make her whereabouts known to anyone within two miles.

Sophie stood in the front yard, scanning the surrounding fields for any sign of movement and was about to head around back when her mother came flying out of the house, yelling, "Sophie! Where have you been? I've been hollering for you for the last half hour!" Olivia stumbled toward her out of breath.

"What's wrong?" Sophie asked, catching her mother in a steadying embrace.

"He's got Poppy!"

"Who? What are you talking about?"

"The restaurant guy kidnapped Poppy. He left a note. He's going to kill her!"

"Kill her?" Sophie was aghast. "I don't understand, Mom. Calm down and tell me what happened."

Olivia took a deliberate deep breath. "A while ago, I heard an uproar from the goat pen, so I went out to see what was wrong and found a note on the gate. Said he took her and sure enough, she was gone. Tallulah was chattering to beat the band and Rose was bleating like somebody'd cut off her leg. The whole lot of them were riled up. He said he'd kill her if we didn't call by seven and tell him who Eno Threlkeld was."

Sophie was stunned.

"Poor little one," Olivia said, shaking her head. "She's got to be terrified."

"Where are the rest of them?" Sophie asked.

Her mother shook her head. "What do you mean?"

"They're not here. They're not in the pen. They're not anywhere around here."

Olivia looked around, confused. "I don't know. They were all there when I came out and found Poppy missing. I guess I left the gate open, but they should be around here somewhere."

They stood staring at each other for a moment, at a loss.

"Where's the note?" Sophie finally asked.

Olivia wrinkled her forehead, then seemed to remember. "Wren took it."

"Wren? Wren Landry?"

"She came by. I told her about Poppy. She took the note and said she'd try to help. She seemed very upset about it and said it was all her fault." Tears appeared in Olivia's eyes. "I shouldn't have let her take the note, should I? Now we don't have the number to call. If we don't call at seven o'clock, he's going to kill Poppy!"

"It's okay," Sophie said gently. "I have his business card. We can call." She jogged into her room and found Bâtarde's card on her dresser. She showed her mother the numbers on the card. "Do either of these look familiar?"

"No. It started with a 5-4-1. I noticed that because that's our area code. It was a local number."

"I was afraid of that. He's not going to use his regular line for blackmail, is he?"

"Oh, poor Poppy!" Olivia cried, putting her face in her hands.

"Don't panic," Sophie said. "I'll find Wren in plenty of time. I know where she'll be at five. But I have to get going. Take Gambit out and see if you can find the rest of them."

Olivia nodded. As Sophie turned to go in the house, her mother grabbed hold of her arm and stared in her face with a fierce determination. "Do whatever you have to do, Sophie, to save our Poppy."

CHAPTER THIRTY

How shall I be revenged on him?
For revenged I will be, as sure as his guts are made of puddings.

—*The Merry Wives of Windsor*, Act II, Scene 1

Wren folded the yellow ransom note and shoved it in her jeans pocket, then walked rapidly down Main Street to the Stratford Inn where she saw Kyle and Raven sitting at a sidewalk table. They were sitting close together, talking and holding hands. Apparently they had reconciled without her help. She was relieved to see it. It would be good to be a threesome again.

"Hi," Kyle said cheerfully. "Sit down and join us for a wheat beer."

She sat while Raven waved over a waiter and ordered her a beer. Raven and Kyle both seemed to be in a wonderful mood, smiling at one another with the ecstasy of new love or, in this case, renewed love.

Wren glanced at her watch. It was just a few minutes after five. Two hours to go until Bâtarde's deadline.

"You'll be happy to know," Kyle reported, "that we've made up and all's well. I'm so looking forward to the gala tonight. It'll be a blast. Although—" He craned his neck to look up at the cloudy sky. "I'm a little worried about the weather."

The waiter put a beer down in front of Wren and she sipped without tasting it as Raven and Kyle spoke excitedly about their costumes and the revelries planned for the evening. Wren barely heard them, preoccupied as she was with her own problem.

"Wren," Raven said, drawing her back to the present by clamping his hand over hers, "I can sense you're troubled. What's bothering you?"

She sighed. "I hate to spoil your reunion, boys, but I've got a problem."

"Batteries ran down again?" Kyle asked sympathetically.

Wren frowned. "This is very serious. Deadly serious."

Kyle opened his eyes wide. "Tell us."

"My nemesis, John Bâtarde, has kidnapped Sophie and is holding her in return for Threlkeld's true identity."

Raven gasped. "The bastard!"

"I have no idea where she is," Wren continued. "But at seven o'clock, he's expecting a phone call from her mother giving him my name. If he doesn't get it, he says she'll never see Sophie again."

"Oh, my God!" Kyle cried. "This is serious. What're we going to do?"

"What choice is there? I'm going to call him at seven o'clock and reveal myself."

"How do you know he'll let her go?" Raven asked, gripping her hand tighter.

"I just have to believe he will. I have no leverage."

"The police?"

Wren shook her head. "He said he'll kill her if we call the police."

Raven looked horrified. "All this over a dry Dobos torte?"

Wren shook her head and swallowed a gulp of her beer. "I can't believe I've done this to her. She was an innocent bystander. She could die because of my precious sense of self-importance."

Raven hugged her. "Don't blame yourself. He's a maniac."

"Isn't there some way to get to him before seven o'clock?" Kyle asked. "Get the jump on him somehow?"

She shook her head morosely. "I don't know. All I know is the woman I love is in mortal danger and I'm sitting here doing nothing about it."

As she fought against the upwelling of emotion in her throat, she caught sight of Ellie's weird sister Cassandra plodding along the sidewalk, her cape dragging on the ground, her hair completely wild, heading toward them.

"No!" she screamed, jumping out of her chair and knocking over her beer.

Kyle snatched the glass and set it upright, then the boys both turned to look as the woman locked her gaze on Wren and continued her slow, steady gait, making a direct line toward her.

"Here thou still sits 'mongst idle gossiping whores?" Cassandra accused, snarling.

Raven's mouth fell open in indignation. "Whores?"

Cassandra came within two feet of Wren, who held her ground. "Like a misbehaved and sullen wench, thou pout'st upon thy fortune and thy love: Take heed, take heed, for such die miserable. Go! Get thee to thy love."

"What?" Wren asked.

"I think she wants you to go somewhere," Raven suggested.

Cassandra nodded. "Away, I say!" She raised her arm to the sky. "Stay'st thou to vex me here?"

"Sorry, I just don't understand. If I knew where my love was, I'd go to her, believe me."

Kyle thrust a five-dollar bill toward Cassandra, who shoved his hand away. "It worked before," he said apologetically.

Cassandra heaved a heavy sigh, then reached into her voluminous clothing and retrieved a tight roll of paper. She unrolled it excruciatingly slowly, then held it up to Wren. It was a flyer for the cupcake bake-off. On it was a photo of Bâtarde, the celebrity judge.

"Okay," Wren said, exasperated. "I know he's the guy. I know all about it. If I knew where he'd taken her, I'd be there in a heartbeat. Don't you think I'm sick to death worrying about this? Don't you think I'd strangle him with my bare hands if I could get hold of him?"

Cassandra looked impatient, then sighed again. "Does anybody have a highlighter?" she asked in a perfectly ordinary voice.

Wren stared, unbelieving.

"I do," Raven said. He opened his messenger bag and dug down to the bottom, producing a neon yellow highlighter.

Cassandra took it and ran it over a small line on the bottom of the flyer, then held it up to Wren again. She had highlighted the date and time of the bake-off finals. It was today from one to six at the Ashland Convention Center. Wren took the flyer from her, focusing on the time and place with a sudden understanding.

"Oh, my God!" she said. "What an idiot I am!"

Cassandra nodded, handing the highlighter back to Raven. "Lord, what fools these mortals be!" She snatched the five-dollar bill from Kyle's hand, then trundled off down the sidewalk.

"What was that all about?" Raven asked.

"I know exactly where to find Bâtarde!" She put the flyer on the table. "He's judging the cupcake bake-off right now. I can keep an eye on him and maybe he'll lead me to Sophie."

She took the scrap of yellow paper from her pocket.

"What can we do?" Raven asked.

She handed him the ransom note. "If you haven't heard from me before seven o'clock, you have to call this number. Give him my name. Then let's hope he lets her go."

"I should go with you," Raven offered.

"No. I'll need to do this stealthily. The fewer people, the better. Besides, you have a very big event tonight. You can't miss that. You're practically the belle of the ball."

Raven smiled. "My brave-hearted sister. 'Cowards die many times before their deaths. The valiant never taste of death but once.'"

"Stop talking about death!" Kyle protested. "Be careful, Wren. If it looks like trouble, call the police."

She nodded. "Don't worry. There's going to be a big crowd there. It's a public event. I won't do anything foolish."

Raven gave her a warm hug, then Kyle did the same.

"Don't forget to call that number," she cautioned. "Sophie's life may depend on it."

"We won't," Kyle assured her.

CHAPTER THIRTY-ONE

Come: The croaking raven doth bellow for revenge.

—*Hamlet*, Act III, Scene 2

It was impossible for Sophie to erase the image of poor little frightened Poppy from her mind as she drove into town, berating herself for not taking that pompous Bâtarde more seriously. Was he really depraved enough to turn Poppy into a stew? At the thought, she nearly started crying, but reined in her emotions.

She parked downtown at twenty after five, hoping she wasn't too late to catch Wren, and rushed toward the Stratford Inn. Raven was sitting in front of the pub with another man, just the two of them, Raven facing her and the other man with his back to her. They were sitting close, their hands knit together on top of the table. His boyfriend, no doubt, Sophie thought. Her guess was confirmed when Raven leaned into the other man and kissed him on the lips.

As she walked rapidly toward them, Raven's companion

turned to look in her direction and she froze in midstride. It was Wren's husband Kyle! Wren's brother was kissing Wren's husband, Mr. Not Straight and Narrow! At that instant, Raven saw her and stood, looking shocked. As well he might! She felt her knees buckle. She thought for sure she was going down, but she wrapped herself around a lamppost and held herself up through sheer determination. If my legs weren't jelly, I'd run away this instant, she thought.

Raven was watching her, looking concerned, and then he was bounding toward her. He reached an arm around her waist and pulled her up against him, supporting her.

"Are you hurt?" he asked breathlessly. "How did you escape?"

Sophie's head was spinning. "Escape?"

She forced her legs squarely under her and was finally able to stand under her own power. She noticed Kyle was here too.

"I'm okay," she assured them, observing the concern on both their faces, which seemed all out of proportion to her momentary faintness.

"Come on over and sit down," Raven said, taking her arm and leading her gently to their table where she slid into a chair. "Tell us what happened?" he urged, sitting beside her. "How did you escape that murderous villain Bâtarde?"

"What are you talking about?"

"The kidnapping. Wren told us all about it."

"You must have misunderstood her, then. It was Poppy who was kidnapped."

"Poppy?" Kyle asked, his eyebrows arching. "Who's Poppy?"

"Our kid goat."

Kyle and Raven looked at one another, then at a piece of yellow paper on the table.

"Your kid," Kyle said thoughtfully, then his face lit up with understanding. "Oh! Your kid!"

Kyle and Raven looked at one another with their mouths open.

"We've got to tell Wren!" declared Raven. He pulled out his phone. A few seconds later, he said, "Damn! Went right to voice mail."

"Can't you just send her one of those telepathic messages?"

Kyle asked. "You know, the special bond of twins thing you're always talking about."

Raven glowered at Kyle.

"What's going on?" Sophie asked, thoroughly lost.

"Wren thought Bâtarde kidnapped you," Kyle explained. "She's gone to rescue you."

"You're kidding?"

Kyle shook his head.

"That guy could be dangerous," Sophie said, worried now about both Poppy and Wren.

"As Wren pointed out," Raven said, "it's a public event. She's just shadowing him, so not likely to be in danger."

"Good," Sophie said, uncertainly. "Even though I don't need rescuing, Poppy still does, and I'm beginning to worry she's in real trouble. If anything happens to Poppy, it'll break my mother's heart."

Despite her efforts to steel herself, tears fell from Sophie's eyes as she imagined Poppy's lifeless body. Raven leapt to his feet.

"O villain, villain!" he cried, pointing at the photo of Bâtarde on the bake-off flyer. "'Thou shalt be whipped with wire, and stewed in brine, smarting in lingering pickle!'" He slammed a fist on the table. "I'll rip out his liver with my bare hands and feed it to my dogs."

Kyle tossed a cautionary glower at Raven. "Meanwhile," he said cheerfully, putting a comforting hand over Sophie's, "don't worry. I'm sure he won't hurt your goat. We'll give him what he wants. We're supposed to call this number at seven and tell him Wren's name." He tapped on the yellow paper. "Then he'll let Poppy go. That's all there is to it."

Sophie snatched up the ransom note and read it quickly. "Thank God you've got the phone number. What time is it?"

Raven sat down and consulted his phone. "Nearly six. Another hour to go."

All three of them calmed down considerably, realizing there was little to do for the next hour but wait.

"In all the excitement," Raven said, "I forgot to introduce you to Kyle."

"Sophie and I've already met," Kyle said. "I did a drawing

for her last weekend. At the time, I didn't know she was Wren's Sophie. So, in a way, we're meeting today for the first time." Kyle shook her hand. "Glad to meet you, Sophie. Wren has spoken so fondly of you."

"She has?" Sophie thought for sure she was going to faint. Wren had told her husband about them? So they did have an open marriage. Not only open, but incredibly complicated, she decided, remembering Raven and Kyle kissing.

"Oh, yes," Kyle said, smiling amiably. "You girls seemed to have really hit it off."

"Would you like a beer?" Raven asked.

Sophie swallowed hard, feeling completely beside herself. "Several, please."

Raven laughed. "We'll start with one, how's that?"

He ducked into the building. Realizing she was alone with the husband of her lover, Sophie started to panic again.

"I was sorry to hear it," Kyle said, "when Wren told me you didn't want to see her again."

Sophie peered into his face, trying to see some evidence of sarcasm, but if it was there, it was well hidden. He appeared completely sincere, charming and suffused with suave self-confidence.

"She's really into you," he continued. "I hope she wouldn't mind my saying that. But I'm sure you know it already. She wouldn't reveal her identity to just anybody. It would have to be someone very special to be trusted with that."

"I don't mean to sound like a prude or anything," Sophie said, "but I'm really not comfortable with the whole open relationship type of thing. I'm a one-woman woman. And I want my woman to be the same."

"Sure." Kyle shrugged. "I'd be surprised if Wren didn't agree. She's a sophisticated woman, but when it comes to love, she strikes me as a traditionalist."

Sophie was at a loss for words. Raven returned with her beer. She immediately took a long swallow. The two men sat close together, clearly doting on one another.

"I wish there were some way to get in touch with Wren," Sophie said.

"Chances are she'll be at the gala tonight," Kyle said. "Everybody's going to end up there."

"Which reminds me," Raven announced, "we need to change into our costumes." He bounced to his feet. "'Give me my robe, put on my crown; I have immortal longings in me!'"

"Why don't you finish your beer, Sophie," Kyle said, "while we run over to the theater to change? We'll come back here before we go to the party, in plenty of time to make the phone call."

Sophie nodded. "Okay."

"Do you want a costume?" Raven asked.

"No, I think I'm good."

"We can turn you into Hermia or Helena with a lovely ball gown." Raven raised one eyebrow. "Or a swashbuckling courtier, perhaps?"

"I don't think so."

He let his eyes wander over her jeans and cotton shirt with undisguised disapproval. "We could do you up as one of the little fairies. Maybe Cobweb."

Sophie gave him a discouraging look.

Kyle stood, grinning. "See you in a bit," he said to Sophie as he led Raven away.

"Mustardseed?" Raven called over his shoulder.

Sophie took another gulp of her beer, then remembered she didn't like wheat beer.

She phoned her mother to give her an update.

"I've got the phone number," she told her. "I'll call at seven."

"What about Wren?" Olivia asked. "You'll blow her cover."

"I don't think I have much choice. Any sign of the rest of the goats?"

"Not yet. Warren stopped by to help. I've got him driving up and down the roads. I'm just back from a ride down to Berry Creek and back. I don't understand where they could be. They've never run off before."

"I'll call you again later. Don't worry. We'll get Poppy back safe. And the rest of them are bound to turn up somewhere."

She hung up, then picked up the flyer from the table, fixing on the image of John Bâtarde with his overbearing air of conceit. *Bastard!* she thought. Then her thoughts turned to Wren, her sweet little bird. Sophie was ashamed to think how badly she'd behaved toward Wren. I've treated her horribly, she realized, from the very first morning, leaving that perfunctory, breezy note that must have seemed like a dismissal, an almost literal slam, bam, thank you, ma'am. She had been trying to seem cool and sophisticated, but her cavalier attitude must have hurt Wren's feelings. How could it not have? At every turn since then, she'd done nothing but tromp on her heart. But after all the abuse, that adorable, lovely woman was risking her reputation, her career, perhaps even her life for Sophie's sake. I can't let her sacrifice herself, Sophie decided.

CHAPTER THIRTY-TWO

Good name in man and woman, dear my lord,
Is the immediate jewel of their souls:
Who steals my purse steals trash; 'tis something, nothing;
'Twas mine, 'tis his, and has been slave to thousands;
But he that filches from me my good name
Robs me of that which not enriches him.
And makes me poor indeed.

—*Othello*, Act III, Scene 3

The problem with confronting Bâtarde had become obvious to Wren as soon as she got in the car to drive to the convention center. She had to be smarter than he was. There was no way he'd kill Sophie, she decided. He couldn't be that nuts. By threatening to do so, he probably thought he could flush Eno into the open. She had almost played right into his hands by storming in there as herself. Obviously, he was watching her, suspected her. Otherwise, he wouldn't have broken into their house. So if Wren Landry showed up tonight at the convention center, his suspicions would be confirmed. Yeah, it was a smart move and she had nearly fallen for it.

Maybe there was still a chance to save both her anonymity and Sophie, she had decided. After a detour home to get a disguise, she now stood outside the men's room in the convention center, staring at the door with its blue triangle. She swallowed hard, then went in. There was a man standing at a urinal. She went past him into the stall and shut the door. When she heard him leave, she came out and examined her appearance in the mirror. She'd gelled her hair, parted it on the side and slicked it back. She had stuck on a tiny sable-colored mustache and goatee she'd found in Raven's makeup kit. She wore one of his nicer suits, a navy blue sports jacket with a silk handkerchief in the pocket, a pair of his black shoes, a button-down shirt open at the neck, no tie. The sleeves of the jacket were a little long, but otherwise everything was a good fit. She looked so much like her brother, it was startling. An effeminate young man, that's what she looked like, and that was good enough. All she really cared about was not looking like herself.

Satisfied with her appearance, she turned to leave. The door opened and a brawny sandy-haired man walked in. He wore a gray suit and was over twice as broad as Wren in the shoulders. He raked a thick-fingered hand through his shaggy hair, looking distraught, and caught Wren's eye. He cast her a small, unconvincing smile, marring the pleasantness of his hunky good looks. He looked familiar, but she couldn't think how she knew him. Just a familiar type, she decided, a blond, blue-eyed Nordic fellow who belonged on a ski slope somewhere wearing a cable-knit sweater.

"Something wrong?" she asked, adopting a deeper than normal tone of voice.

"The competition," he said, approaching a sink. "Driving me crazy. So much stress."

"You're competing? Sorry, I've only just arrived."

"I'm one of the three finalists. I'm Klaus Olafssen." He looked earnest and pained. "This is my chance, you know? If I win this, I'm on my way to being a serious baker. I want to make my mama proud."

"Your mama?"

"My mama, Katrina Olafssen. You must be from out of town. Everybody knows her. She's famous for her aebleskiver."

"Oh! Yes, I do know her." Wren realized her voice had gone up, close to normal. Klaus eyed her warily. She lowered her voice again to say, "I mean, I know her pastries. I haven't met her. How are you doing, then, in the judging?"

He shook his head. "They're about to give the decision. We're on a break. Then they'll announce it. Mine is one of those with the fairies." He frowned. "The theme is A Midsummer Night's Dream. What would you do with that theme?"

"Fairies?" Wren guessed.

"That's what I figured. But that guy they brought in from San Francisco, that Bâtarde, he says, 'Fairies? Not especially original, is it?'" Klaus threw up his hands in exasperation. "No, not original, but neither is the whole idea of the gala, is it? It's based on a play that's over three hundred fifty years old. How *original* is the whole thing?"

Wren nodded sympathetically, hearing the tension in his voice.

"That Drew Lippincott," he complained, "she did fairies too, but hers is totally brainless. When you see it, you'll agree. And what's with the pumpkin cupcakes? It's not Halloween. It's not even fall."

Wren tried hard to suppress a smile, thinking about herself in disguise, thinking about her brother in his Titania costume and all the others who would be masquerading tonight. In some ways, it was like Halloween.

"Alison White," continued Klaus, peering at himself in the mirror, "the other finalist, did toadstools." He turned abruptly to face Wren. "Toadstools? Hello? Alice in Wonderland calling Alison White. You took the wrong damned pill!"

Klaus leaned over the sink and moaned. Wren's head began to spin from Klaus's panic attack. Again she had the feeling she knew him.

"Do you have an aspirin?" he asked morosely.

"No, sorry. Look, everything will be over soon. Either way, you'll be fine. Try to calm down. I'm going out to find a good spot. Good luck."

"Thanks," Klaus said weakly.

Wren left the restroom thinking she had at least passed the test of Klaus Olafssen, though he was extremely preoccupied with his own concerns. She proceeded into the main hall where a crowd milled around the floor where the three finalists' productions were staged for judging. As Klaus had described them, there were two with fairy themes and one shaped like a giant mushroom, one of those classic cartoon types, white with red circles painted on it, its flanks spread wide and curling slightly upward at the edges so it could serve as a platform for hundreds of dainty cupcakes. Beneath the umbrella of its main body, clustered around the stem, were a dozen small mushrooms with brightly colored caps—red, yellow, green, blue and purple with white polka-dots. The cupcakes arranged on top were frosted with similar colors—bright, perhaps even gaudy primary colors. The mushroom idea wasn't so far afield as Klaus implied, Wren mused, since the display would be located in a forest, like most of the action of the gala's namesake play.

She approached one of the fairy-themed displays. It was done in pastel colors: lavender, pink and light yellow. Two garish figures, apparently the king and queen of the fairies, Oberon and Titania, sat on top of an oversized leaf, a veined expanse of green that served as the cupcake platform so the little desserts were spread out at the fairies' feet. The two figures were posed in a chaste kiss. Extending from a pole behind the fairies were pastel-colored cloth streamers, a filmy, transparent material that sparkled, giving the impression of a rainbow of fairy dust. As a whole, Wren thought it beautiful and tranquil.

The third display, that of Klaus Olafssen, was designed as a gigantic open flower, painted brilliant scarlet. Its flattened petals served as trays for the multitude of cupcakes. A brilliant gold six-foot long stamen protruded from its center in an alarmingly erect and suggestive fashion. Wren couldn't help thinking that was a calculated move, designed to appeal to a man with a very large...ego. The only natural flower Wren could liken it to was a hibiscus. Strategically placed around the display were delicate fairy figures with dragonfly-like wings, mounted on flexible supports. They swayed about as if hovering above the cupcakes.

The cupcakes themselves were of three varieties, frosted in yellow, pink and lavender. The pink ones sported a miniature version of the floral phallus as a garnish. The idea of putting that in her mouth made Wren a tad uncomfortable.

The three finalist entries were all elaborate and fascinating. She knew the entrants would also be judged on the quality of their cakes, but she had arrived too late to taste them or even hear them described, and was feeling tremendously sorry about that before remembering why she was here.

She quickly searched the floor for Bâtarde and saw him standing near the overgrown mushroom with a clipboard, making notes. At the sight of him, she became enraged. The last time she'd seen him, she was now certain, was climbing out of the den window at Raven and Kyle's house. Today, he was formally dressed in a three-piece suit and striped silk tie. He had a look of serious concentration on his face, his brows knit together, his mouth shut tightly under his carefully-trimmed ginger mustache. What's the plan? Wren asked herself as she stepped toward him.

By the time she stood directly beside him, she still had no answer. All she could think of was strangling him, possibly not the best way to proceed. He looked up from his clipboard and seemed momentarily startled by her presence, then smiled congenially.

"Quite bold, isn't it?" she asked in her lowered voice.

Bâtarde looked her up and down slowly, before saying, "Sorry. I can't comment. Not yet, anyway."

"Understood. You've got a tough decision."

"Are you here with one of the finalists?"

"No. Just a foodie. My name's Rick."

Bâtarde nodded politely, then seemed to get lost in Wren's face. Does he see something amiss, she worried. Maybe her mustache was askew. Under the bright lights, she wasn't sure her disguise would hold up.

"You look familiar," he said. "Have we met?"

Wren laughed, trying not to sound as nervous as she was. "That's a very old line. How quaint."

Bâtarde looked momentarily flustered, then he relaxed into

a knowing smile and let his eyes wander down the length of Wren's body. Ah, thought Wren, a new possibility has opened up. Rick might have some advantage here Wren did not.

"You'll be sticking around for the results?" Bâtarde asked.

"Wouldn't miss it. It's a special kind of thrill seeing you in action."

"Why don't you come sit over by the judge's booth, Rick?" he suggested in an unmistakably flirty voice. "You get the best view from there. And I'll have a better view of you too."

Wren summoned up one of her brother's leering come-on looks, the kind frequently sent over an uplifted shoulder, then followed Bâtarde to a seat just to the right of the judge's booth.

Klaus had now returned and stood at attention on the floor in front of his display. All three of the finalists were present, looking collectively like they were going to vomit. While the announcer spoke, working everyone into a frenzy of anticipation, Bâtarde made eyes at Wren, who did her best to return the favor. Inside, she too wanted to vomit.

Then, suddenly, she realized the winner had been announced. She turned her attention to the floor where Klaus Olafssen jumped up and down, wiping tears from his cheeks. A tiny, middle-aged woman, whom Wren assumed was his mother, Katrina Olafssen of aebleskiver fame, came running to the floor and threw herself into his torso, disappearing in his embrace. Another woman, a young, feminine blonde in a lime green dress also ran out on the floor to embrace him. The other two competitors crept away.

On his way to congratulate Klaus, Bâtarde paused at Wren's chair, putting a firm hand on her shoulder. "Wait for me," he commanded.

He seemed to have no doubt she would. Of course she would, but not for the reasons he imagined.

When he had finished his rounds of contestants, sponsors, organizers, donors and fans, he returned to Wren, putting an arm around her shoulder and walking her out of the room and down a wide hallway.

"Were you planning on going to the gala tonight?" he asked.

"Yes. I know someone in the company."

"Do you have a date?"

"Flying solo tonight."

Bâtarde stopped to push open the double doors to the outside, gazing meaningfully down at her. "You don't have to. I'd be honored if you'd accompany me."

"Thanks. I'd like that."

They both smiled as they emerged into the light of a low-dipping sun entering a bank of peach-colored clouds to the west. The moon, a full moon, had just made its appearance in the east, faintly visible through a lacy pattern of leafy tree branches. The midsummer moon, Wren noted, remembering Cassandra's prediction: *Thy fate will be sealed by the midsummer moon.*

They walked to a black sedan where a uniformed driver opened the rear door for them. Wren hesitated, imagining being in the backseat with this cad, but the stakes were high. It was worth it. She got into the car, deciding the best way to keep his mind off romance was to engage him in conversation.

"Do you have a favorite among your restaurants?" she asked as the car took off.

"Not really. Each has its own unique personality, but I suppose I favor Josephine a little. The firstborn, you know? Have you been there?"

"Yes. Very nice place." Wren thought it might be advantageous to get him talking about Eno if she could manage it. "I had your Dobos Torte there. Killer!"

He smiled gratefully. "Did you really like it?"

"Oh, yeah! I'll have it again next time."

He peered at her, his voice taking on a tinge of bitterness. "You didn't find it a little…dry?"

Wren felt anxious, as if he were looking right through her disguise at his enemy, but she decided it was just nerves getting to her.

"Dry? Not a bit! Why do you ask?"

He took a deep breath. "Oh, it's just this critic, this ridiculously pompous critic who's gotten completely out of control. He, or she, has forgotten the point of reviewing a restaurant."

"What is the point?" Wren asked, seriously interested in his answer.

"To promote the local economy by getting people out to eat, to celebrate fine dining. Panning my food won't serve that goal."

"You think a food critic should say only positive things?"

"Yes!"

"If every restaurant gets a first-rate review, then how do I choose where to eat? How do I know what to order? And, even worse, if a critic says great things about a bad restaurant, how can I trust anything he says? What's the value of his opinion, then?"

Bâtarde eyed her soberly.

Careful, Eno, she cautioned herself. *Get off your soapbox.*

"But, still," she said, "he or she must be an idiot to have found anything bad to say about that torte. It was chocolate perfection."

Bâtarde relaxed and smiled again. "Yes, a total idiot. He doesn't know a damned thing about Dobos torte and should be exposed for the charlatan he is and run out of the business. The problem is, this critic writes under a pseudonym and nobody knows his true identity."

"Interesting. So you can't defend yourself."

Bâtarde slapped the seat between them. "Exactly!" He lowered his voice in confidence. "But I've made this my mission for weeks now. I made a list of all the likely food writers. I've been plotting his movements, studying his style. I've been narrowing in, winnowing down the list bit by bit. I've followed him to Ashland. The list got considerably smaller once he came here. That was his mistake. A big fish in a small pond makes a big splash. I have a fair idea who it is now, but I need corroboration before I make my move."

"What exactly is your move going to be?" Wren asked fearfully.

Bâtarde clenched his right hand into a fist and pounded it into the palm of his left. "I'll destroy him...or her."

Wren flinched.

"First I'll expose him. Eno Threlkeld won't be able to go to any restaurant ever again with the protection of anonymity. And then I'll undermine his reputation. I'll dig into his past and credentials and education and family history and old lovers and find anything I can to use against him. When I'm done, Eno Threlkeld will be a joke, unfit to critique a pretzel stand on the street, let alone a five-star restaurant."

His focus was chilling, his plan broader than she had imagined. He was clearly obsessed with his revenge. She recalled the facts of his parentage, his mother's insanity, his father's bloody rampage driven by intense ambition and singularity of purpose, just like he was. Suddenly she thought he might be capable of murder after all. She shuddered involuntarily.

"Is it really that important?" she asked tentatively.

He narrowed his eyes at her. "It's only justice. With a few words, tossed off casually, coldly, as if it's nothing but a game of wits, a critic can destroy an honest, hard-earned reputation, a reputation that has taken a lifetime to cultivate, that has been nurtured like a tender seedling to grow, to thrive, to become strong enough to support itself. For a man like me, my reputation is my life, as central to who I am as another man's children are to him."

Wren wanted to defend herself, to insist that a critic performed a service that by definition had to include the good and the bad and that Eno Threlkeld was neither casual nor cold, but merely honest. She recalled many emails over the last several years from chefs and restaurant owners, objecting to her negative comments. Fortunately, they weren't all driven by the sort of monomaniacal impulses Bâtarde possessed. But they had all been disappointed and hurt. How to be a critic without hurting someone's feelings? Not possible. Still, he was blowing her one criticism completely out of proportion. Nobody else remembered it by now. Her words weren't that powerful. In reality, they did nothing at all to harm his reputation. All of his restaurants were still in business, still profitable, and still selling John Bâtarde's signature Hungarian Dobos Torte every day. If he were a reasonable man, he would see that and give up his quest to destroy her. But obviously he wasn't a reasonable man. He was a most unreasonable man. He had kidnapped the woman she loved, she reminded herself, and was plotting her murder.

"It's only a matter of minutes now," Bâtarde said, "before

I know the true identity of Eno Threlkeld." He looked triumphant.

"How will you find out?"

"I've found someone who can absolutely identify him, or her. Unfortunately, she's not cooperating. But not to worry. I've found a way to persuade her." He smiled distractedly.

"How?" Wren asked, trying not to let her dread show on her face. *O villain, villain, smiling, damned villain!*

Bâtarde looked at his watch. "I'm expecting a phone call at seven o'clock. I have to make sure I don't miss this." He took his phone from his briefcase.

When he got that call, she knew, it would be Raven giving her name, and her cover would be blown. There was nothing she could do. She still didn't know where he was holding Sophie. But she was beginning to worry that he couldn't be trusted to release her.

"You're going to give Threlkeld a scare, is that it?" she asked. "Make some idle threat to flush him out?"

Bâtarde looked up abruptly to face her. "Idle threat? I never make idle threats. If that call doesn't come in at precisely seven o'clock, Threlkeld will have blood on his hands tonight."

Wren let herself fall against the seat, now fervently hoping Raven would come through with the call.

"Why don't you move over here next to me," Bâtarde said softly, baring his teeth in a leering smile.

She bolted to attention, realizing this plan had its drawbacks. When it became clear to him that she wasn't moving, he slid closer to her, then put a hand on her thigh. She stiffened, holding back the impulse to claw through the ceiling. She pushed his hand away, pressing herself as hard as she could against the door on her side of the car. His disturbing grin persisted as he put one arm around her waist and pulled her up against him. She pushed against his chest with both arms as his mouth formed an exaggerated pucker. She was about to resort to violence when the sound of several cars honking captured their attention.

Bâtarde released her. "What's going on?" he asked the driver.

Wren noticed they weren't moving even though the light in

the intersection was green. They were behind two other cars that were also stopped.

"Looks like animals in the road," the driver replied just as the cars began to move.

As they took their turn through the intersection, Wren saw a line of goats exiting the crosswalk and gaining the sidewalk. There were six of them, variously colored, all does, looking unambiguously like the Tallulah Rose herd.

"Isn't that a sight?" Bâtarde remarked, hanging out the window to get a better look.

Wren was sure that was Rose in the lead, trotting along in the same direction they were headed, looking like she knew where she was going, like an animal on a mission. The car soon left the parade of goats far behind.

Bâtarde pulled his head back in and faced Wren. "Where were we?"

"Hey, look!" Wren pointed ahead, "We're nearly there!"

Indeed, their car was pulling into the circle at the entrance to Lithia Park.

Bâtarde looked at his phone again. "And it's now seven o'clock. We'll wait here a moment."

Wren held her breath, waiting for his phone to ring. As the seconds ticked by, she silently cursed her brother, knowing how easily he could be distracted. When the phone rang, it caused them both to start.

"Yes," Bâtarde answered, listening for a second. "You're sure?"

Wren sat on her side of the seat, her muscles so tense her legs began to hurt.

"I'll have to check this out before our deal is complete." He clicked off the call, then sat staring at the phone, looking perplexed.

"What?" Wren prompted. "What's the name?"

Bâtarde regarded her calmly. "I had a feeling all along it was a woman."

Wren gritted her teeth, waiting for him to say her name.

"But this one isn't on my short list." He put the phone away. "She wasn't even on my long list. In fact, I've never heard of her."

"Really?" Wren asked. "Who is it?"

He looked at her with his lips pressed together in contemplation, then said, "Annie Laurie."

"What!" Wren fell back against the car door. "Annie Laurie?"

Bâtarde nodded. "Do you know her?"

Wren stuttered, wondering why Raven would give a name from a Scottish folk song. "Uh, no, never heard of her," she lied.

With a renewed sense of purpose, Bâtarde exited the car, saying, "Wait for me here. I've got to go meet the truck bringing in Olafssen's display. Offloading is a tricky process. Once we get it on the cart, it'll be good to go."

Wren was stunned. She stepped out of the car and leaned against it as Bâtarde strode toward a delivery truck parked nearby. Why was Raven risking Sophie's life? What was the point of this trick?

"I'll kill him!" she muttered to herself.

CHAPTER THIRTY-THREE

...she is mine own;
And I as rich in having such a jewel
As twenty seas, if all their sand were pearl,
The water nectar, and the rocks pure gold.

—*The Two Gentlemen of Verona*, Act II, Scene 4

Sophie, Raven and Kyle arrived at Lithia Park amid a crowd of revelers and the distinctive chords of Elizabethan folk music. The costumes and makeup had taken longer to get into than they had anticipated, so the boys had been delayed, but Sophie had been able to make the phone call at seven o'clock as planned. She hoped it hadn't been a mistake to give Bâtarde a fake name. She had been trying to stall, to give Wren more time to find Poppy. After everything that had transpired between them, Sophie wasn't prepared to be the instrument that destroyed Wren's career, not even for the sake of their baby goat. But Sophie believed Poppy would be spared, either by Bâtarde himself or

244   Robbi McCoy

through the intervention of Wren. At least she fervently hoped so.

"This is so festive," Raven gushed, as they walked along a wooded path lit by variously colored hanging lanterns.

If Sophie had been less worried about Wren and Poppy, she would have been delighted with the evening. Both of her companions were charmingly arrayed, Raven as Titania and Kyle as Oberon in costumes of filmy green with petite wings on their backs, green tights, and crowns of gold. Kyle's costume left his chest bare and was accessorized with a sparkly green codpiece while Raven's was a more feminine variety with falsies.

They passed people in costume and others in street clothes. Most of the costumes were characters from *A Midsummer Night's Dream*: fairies, Athenians and tradesmen, or "mechanicals" as they're called in the play. There were also characters from the play within a play, *Pyramus and Thisbe*: a lion, a wall and a moon. One striking fellow wore a gold Athenian-style warrior helmet, a calf-length white robe trimmed in gold with a gold sash, leather sandals, and gold arm cuffs with a snake motif. The upper portion of his face was covered with the helmet visor. He stood tall and straight with a regal posture, his head inclined slightly upward. When he saw Raven and Oberon, he burst into an appreciative chorus of baritone laughter.

Shimmering cloth streamers and flower garlands had been woven through the shrubbery along the pathways. The park looked more than ever like an enchanted forest. They pushed on toward the music and the heart of this celebration, Sophie in the lead and Kyle and Raven skipping behind, holding hands.

The path finally opened up on an expansive grassy clearing where tiny flickering lights were strung through the surrounding trees, simulating fireflies or diminutive fairies. Nearby was a trio of musicians with medieval instruments, dressed in sixteenth-century costumes, playing a bright, merry tune. In the center of the clearing was a huge wooden contraption, brilliant red. As they neared it, Sophie saw it was the cupcake display, a gigantic flower, its plywood petals extending several feet in all directions. Arranged in neat rows atop the petals were hundreds of pastel-colored cupcakes. Suspended above those were small, swaying

Two On The Aisle   245

fairies, looking as if they were flying over the cakes. The indisputable focal point of the display was the enormous yellow stamen protruding from the center of the flower.

"Oh!" cried Raven, slapping his gloved hand to his chest. "Look at that!"

Through the crowd, Sophie recognized Klaus beside the display, towering over the others, and beside him was Dena, beaming, looking lovely and happy.

"Klaus won the bake-off!" Sophie cried, pointing.

They headed toward Klaus, who had changed out of his suit into a cream-colored sweater and brown pants. Sophie grabbed his arm to get his attention.

"Hi, Sophie!" He beamed. "I didn't know you were coming."

"Neither did I. You won!"

"Can you believe it?"

"Yes, I can," she assured him.

Dena took hold of his arm, smiling up at him.

Sophie took a closer look at the display. The huge scarlet flower sat upon a rectangular wooden cart with wheels. On the side of the cart was a sign that read *Cakes by Klaus*. Raven and Kyle stood in front of the display, looking up at the giant stamen with their mouths open in abject admiration. Katrina Olafssen was on the other side of the display, holding a tray of aebleskiver. She was dressed as usual in her long skirt and white blouse, her hair in the traditional braided bun.

Dena looked up at the stamen protruding over their heads and said, "Don't you think it's…stimulating?"

Sophie declined to answer. "There are a lot more people here than I expected," she said.

"Oh, yes," Klaus answered, "it's a big turnout."

"Is John Bâtarde here?"

Klaus nodded. "He came by a minute ago. He had the most gorgeous boy in tow." He pointed to the edge of the clearing. "There he is."

Sophie peered in the direction Klaus pointed and saw Bâtarde with a drink in hand talking to a woman in an Elizabethan dress. Next to him was a small young man who, from this distance, looked a lot like Raven Landry. Both of them were standing in front of a thick wall of rhododendrons.

"Excuse me," she said to Klaus and Dena before moving closer to Bâtarde, keeping to the shadows, until she could get a clearer look at his date, who looked more and more like Raven. He was dressed in a navy blue jacket and dress shirt, had a small goatee and similarly understated mustache.

As she stood on her toes peering over the shoulder of a man dressed in a purple velvet cape and blue leggings, someone tapped her on the shoulder. She gasped and spun around. It was Raven. Kyle stood beside him.

"Check this out," she said. "What do you make of that young man?"

Raven stared, squinted his glittery eyes, then looked astonished. Kyle looked equally perplexed.

"It's me," Raven said, unbelieving.

"It is you," Kyle agreed, staring again.

"What a handsome fellow," Raven announced, recovering his good humor. "What's he doing with that ugly old man?"

"That *bulky* old man," Kyle suggested.

Raven turned to Kyle, his mouth open.

"That's the guy who broke into our house," Kyle explained. "Looking for information about Eno."

"Him? That's the guy who caused me to accuse and misuse you, my poor darling?"

Kyle nodded solemnly. "I can't believe you'd think I could ever be interested in him."

"And that's the guy who stole Poppy," Sophie said.

"Fie! Fie!" Raven declared. "We should call him to account!"

Kyle was still staring at Raven's lookalike. "The resemblance is uncanny. Were you maybe triplets instead of twins?"

"I would know if I were triplets," Raven said, "if I had a brother. But I have to admit that if you dressed Wren up in an outfit like that and slicked back her hair and put a little mustache on her..."

All three of them stood silently watching Bâtarde's date for a moment, the same idea apparently entering all of their minds simultaneously.

"Oh, my God!" Raven breathed.

"What's she doing with him?" Sophie cried.

"She did say she was going to keep an eye on him," Kyle reminded them.

"Let's hope an eye is all she kept on him," Raven joked.

Sophie frowned at him. "I need to talk to her, to let her know I'm okay, but I don't want Bâtarde to see me."

"Maybe you should have worn a costume as I suggested," Raven said haughtily.

"Keep an eye on Bâtarde for me. I'll be back in a few minutes."

Sophie took a wide path around to the edge of the clearing, then slipped through a hedge and approached Wren's position from behind, hidden by the descent of darkness and the shrubbery. She knelt close to the ground and moved closer to Wren's legs, keeping an eye on Bâtarde, who spoke excitedly a few feet away, facing the woman he was talking to and unlikely to notice Sophie, as long as she could get Wren's attention quietly. She reached through the branches of a rhododendron and tugged gently at her pant leg. Wren shook her leg without looking around.

Bâtarde happened to turn just then and smile at Wren, sending Sophie's pulse into a panic, but he didn't notice her and returned to his conversation. She stood, intending to tap Wren on the shoulder, but Wren took a step forward, away from the bushes, so Sophie panicked and made an unplanned lunge for her, clamping one hand over her mouth and the other arm around her waist and dragging her in a single motion into the bushes where they both fell to the ground. Sophie held her hand tight over Wren's mouth as Wren fought against her until she could maneuver herself into a position where they were facing each other. Wren's eyes opened wide in surprise and she quit struggling. Sophie released her mouth, then put her finger to her own mouth and crawled further from the party with Wren following on all fours. They reached a paved path where both of them stood.

"Come here," Sophie instructed, taking hold of her hand.

She led Wren swiftly down the main path, then left the path

248   Robbi McCoy

and jumped a rocky creek. Wren followed as she continued up the bank to an old wooden gazebo, a place Sophie had been several times, an isolated, densely wooded area of the park she knew was infrequently visited, especially at night. The sound of music and laughter came to them faintly as they both fell onto a wide bench beside one another, breathing rapidly and laughing hysterically. The vertical posts of the structure supported well-established vines that were leafed out in full summer foliage, creating a private bower of lush growth all around them. Through the lattice above them the full moon shone vivid white through an opening in a cloudy sky, casting a romantic glow over their hideaway.

"You're safe!" Wren breathed, taking Sophie's face in her hands and kissing her, her little mustache tickling Sophie's upper lip.

"You look so butch!" Sophie pulled Wren roughly to her and kissed her again, more urgently, crazed with the desire she'd tried to resist for the last two weeks. She smothered Wren's mouth and neck and face with kisses. Wren too was breathing hard, groping Sophie's body with obvious need and possessing her mouth anxiously.

Sophie pushed Wren down on the bench, lying beside her, reaching between them to unbuckle her belt.

"Sophie," Wren whispered, "what if someone comes?"

"I don't care. I have to have you. I don't care about anything. I don't care that you're married or that your husband and brother are lovers or how any of this came about or what it means to us. All I care about is that I love you and I can't fight it anymore. I'll take whatever you can give me."

"But—" Wren moved to sit up.

Sophie touched a finger to her mouth. "Explain later." She covered Wren's mouth with her own, stopping her from further conversation, then slipped her hand under the waistband of Wren's trousers, into the warm, wet, waiting wonder of her womanhood.

CHAPTER THIRTY-FOUR

Here come the lovers, full of joy and mirth.

—*A Midsummer Night's Dream*, Act V, Scene 1

She's mine, mine, all mine! In her heart, Sophie rejoiced with uncharacteristic abandon. She felt like she could take a running start and lift off the ground like a plane. Now that Wren had explained the situation with Kyle, she knew there was no obstacle to their being together. Wren looked just as happy as she was. She couldn't stop smiling a cute, goofy smile, understanding finally why Sophie had been so aloof. Understanding, too, that they were both madly in love with one another, the most perfect situation two people could ever find themselves in on this planet, or, Sophie was certain, any other.

She didn't want to return to the party and she knew Wren didn't either, but there was still the problem of Poppy's kidnapping, so they reluctantly made their way back to the clearing where the crowd was still substantial. Sophie glanced about for Bâtarde as she and Wren walked hand in hand to where Raven and Kyle stood listening to the musicians.

"Where've you been?" Raven asked.

"Around," Wren said evasively. "Where's Bâtarde?"

"He's here somewhere."

"You were supposed to watch him," Sophie scolded.

"And you were supposed to be gone only a couple minutes. It's been over a half hour."

Sophie looked sheepish and evaded Raven's gaze.

"That's my suit you're wearing, isn't it?" Raven frowned at his sister. "Hey, where's your mustache and goatee?"

Wren reached up to feel her bare face as Sophie giggled. Raven and Kyle looked at one another meaningfully.

"You boys look fabulous, by the way," Wren said enthusiastically.

"Thank you!" Raven curtseyed low. When he lifted his head, he said, "Oh, look, there's Cleo."

He waved toward a statuesque woman with long, straight black hair with a prominent white streak along one side. She caught his eye and returned the wave, starting their way. She wore a black silky gown split up the left leg and a long purple cape. She had a gold tiara on her hair and carried what looked like a jewel-encrusted goblet large enough to hold a half a bottle of wine. On her forearms were metal cuffs and on her chest a heavy silver medallion. She presented a formidable image, a cross between Xena, Warrior Princess and the evil queen in Disney's *Snow White*.

"Who is she?" Sophie whispered.

"Raven's boss," Wren said. "Cleo Keggermeister."

"She's Hippolyta!" Raven announced as she stopped in front of them. "Queen of the Amazons."

As they were introduced, both Wren and Sophie mumbled a greeting and then simply gaped at the woman as she chatted with Raven. Before tonight, Sophie had known Cleo Keggermeister in name only, as the woman who had captured the heart of Ellie's father and had destroyed Cassandra's career. She was an attractive woman and must have been very beautiful in her youth. There was a hint of the exotic about her, the untamed beast.

Two On The Aisle   251

"Such a turnout!" Cleo gushed, sounding tipsy. "Best ever. The decorations, the music, everything's perfect!" She looked up at the sky. "Nearly perfect. I hope it doesn't rain. Are you boys having a good time?"

"Enchanting!" Raven proclaimed.

"How about that cupcake monstrosity? Isn't that wild?" Cleo cackled gleefully, then stopped mid-cackle. She was distracted by the man in the Athenian helmet and white robe standing by the wine booth. "Do any of you know who that is?"

Raven shook his head.

"My guess is Theseus," Kyle offered, "Duke of Athens."

"No, no, you idiot," Cleo said impatiently. "Obviously, he's dressed as Theseus. I mean, who is he behind the helmet? Nobody seems to know. I think I'll go talk to him and see if—" She let out a high-pitched cry of alarm, no longer looking at Theseus. Instead, she was glaring at something across the clearing.

They all followed her gaze to Cassandra, dressed as usual in her brown cape, pulling her dog Spot in the red wagon behind her, threading her way methodically through the crowd.

"What is that crazy woman doing here?" Cleo demanded. "Who let her in?"

"It is a public park," Raven pointed out. "And we did invite the whole town."

Cleo frowned with her entire face. She then took a defiant gulp of wine and stalked off. More than ever, she looked like the evil queen plotting her revenge on Snow White. When she had gone, Sophie, feeling protective of Cassandra, said, "Who does she think she is, the queen of Egypt?"

Wren shrugged and put a soothing arm around Sophie's waist.

A short person in a furry brown head with huge black eyes, long ears and long eyelashes stepped up to them. A donkey costume, Sophie realized. The donkey leaned on the arm of a tall, husky man wearing a cable-knit sweater and brown cords. A simple black mask covered his eyes and nose, Zorro-style, his only concession to a costume, leaving his wide, square chin and mouth exposed. No sooner had they arrived than Zorro spotted Katrina Olafssen and her tray of Danish pastries and was off in her direction.

"Raven, you're fabulous!" said the donkey. "Wanted to say hi, but had to wait for you-know-who to leave. Is this your boyfriend?"

"Tammy!" Raven called. "Great costume! Yes, this is Kyle. Tammy's our Dogberry, honey. And a stupendous one at that!"

Kyle bowed from the waist.

"You two are a riot!" Tammy laughed a muffled, hollow laugh.

"This is Wren," Raven said, linking his arm in hers. "You remember her? And her friend Sophie."

Tammy tilted up the donkey head to get a better look. "You look exactly like your brother in that getup!" She spun to the left, then to the right, peering out the snout of her costume. "This here's my husband." She spun around again, trying to locate him. "Where'd he go?"

"He's over there," Sophie said, pointing to where the big man was popping one of Katrina's aebleskivers in his mouth.

Tammy laughed again. "Of course, he's looking for food. As usual! I'll introduce you later. At least I got him off the damned boat for the evening. This is a red-letter day!"

As she stepped over to his side, Tammy's husband took a second aebleskiver. "I haven't had these in years!" he declared with obvious zeal.

"Take as many as you want," Katrina urged. "Ja! Big boy like you needs his Danish pastry like mama's milk. You're as big as my Klaus. Nice healthy boy."

He took three more, which fit easily in his palm. Tammy took one and shoved it through the donkey's snout almost up to her elbow, trying to reach her mouth. Even with the added height of the elongated head, she didn't come fully up to her husband's height. The two of them made a comical pair. To facilitate eating, Tammy removed her donkey head to reveal a round pink face with cheerful eyes.

"Aebleskiver, Sophie," Katrina offered, stepping toward her. "Klaus thought we could take advantage of the crowd to hook some new customers. He wants to sell these, you know, in his store."

"He told me," Sophie said, taking one. "I think it's a great idea. No jam?"

"I put it inside this time. This is my picnic version."

Wren grabbed an aebleskiver for herself before Katrina moved on with her tray, its contents rapidly disappearing. Sophie bit into the pastry and the gooey red jam inside oozed into her mouth.

Wren turned to her brother. "Annie Lauric?" she accused. "What were you thinking?"

Raven looked surprised at both her tone and question.

"Oh, that was me," Sophie explained. "I'm the one who called Bâtarde. I just didn't want to give you away."

Wren turned to Sophie and her expression softened. They both looked up as they felt the first raindrops. Sophie took Wren in her arms and held her close. There was so much she wanted to say now that she knew the truth. Starting with an apology.

Wren pulled Sophie closer and kissed her. Sophie felt herself getting lost in the soft luxury of Wren's mouth.

"What the hell!" said a nearby male voice.

Wren and Sophie both turned to discover John Bâtarde standing a few feet away, scowling at them. He stepped toward Wren, clenching his right hand into a fist.

"You think you can make a fool out of me?" he said, lunging toward her.

She leapt backward and held out her palm. "Stop! Even you wouldn't hit a woman, would you?" She pointed to her hairless face.

He stopped and stared, then his fist dissolved as he seemed to recognize her.

"You're Wren Landry!" he declared. "I knew you looked familiar."

Wren took hold of Sophie's hand. "Yeah, that's me. So what?"

"I knew it all along," Bâtarde sneered. "You and your goat farmer are in cahoots!" He pointed accusingly at Sophie. "That's why you were so determined to keep her secret. You're lovers! But the jig is up. Your reputation will be ruined. The name Eno Threlkeld will be worthless." Bâtarde threw both his arms

254   Robbi McCoy

into the air like a ringleader at a circus and made a booming pronouncement to the night. "Eno Threlkeld! You are exposed!"

Tammy's husband paused in the act of bringing the last of his three aebleskivers to his mouth and turned abruptly to face them.

"Are you speaking to me?" he asked.

Bâtarde frowned at the interruption, irritated. "Who are you?"

"I'm Eno Threlkeld. I thought I heard you say my name."

All five of them stared wordlessly at the man, who then removed his mask. Sophie, Wren and Raven gasped in unison.

Klaus? Sophie thought, but quickly realized this man who looked remarkably like Klaus Olafssen couldn't be Klaus. She peered more carefully at his broad, clean-shaven face, his light blue eyes, the reddish tint of his eyebrows. The resemblance was uncanny.

"Eno?" Wren ventured. "Is that you?"

"I am Eno Threlkeld," he repeated firmly. "Do I know you?"

"Oh, my God!" she blurted. "I'm Wren Landry. You remember me, don't you, Eno? From high school? And Raven? You must remember him?"

As Sophie looked at Raven in his Titania costume and Wren made up like a man, she tried to imagine this bewildering scene from someone else's point of view. Eno peered hard at Raven's face.

"Eno!" Raven cried, pulling both falsies out of his costume at once. "It's me!"

Eno's eyes lit up as he recognized them and an exuberant round of hugs ensued between the large man and the small twins, the girl masquerading as a boy and the boy masquerading as a girl. It was a strange but satisfying image. Still, Sophie was perplexed by how much Eno resembled Klaus, a fact that had not yet been explained.

The three old friends finally broke apart, revealing that Eno had tears in his eyes. His aebleskiver was now smashed into his sweater, its sticky red center smeared across his chest like he'd been stabbed in the heart. He didn't seem to notice.

"You're married to Dogberry here?" Raven asked.

"Yes. Happily married eight years." He pulled Tammy close and she laid her donkey head against him affectionately.

"What's going on here?" Bâtarde demanded.

Sophie realized they'd all forgotten about him.

"This is the real Eno Threlkeld," Wren announced.

"Yes, of course I'm the real Eno Threlkeld," Eno said. "Is there another?"

"Not anymore," Wren said with finality.

Sophie wondered what she meant by that.

Bâtarde stepped closer to Eno, looking angrily up at him. "So you're the jerk who insulted my Dobos torte?"

"Who is this guy?" Eno asked Raven.

"Eno," Raven answered, "do you remember how you used to protect me from all the bullies in high school?"

"Sure."

"For old time's sake, maybe you can do it one more time. This guy has been causing me and my sister so much grief. He's a true-blue bully and he needs to be taught a lesson."

Eno nodded slowly, then looked steadily and menacingly into Bâtarde's face while the Frenchman became visibly agitated. Eno reached for him and he ducked, then turned and darted away. Eno went after him.

"Don't kill him!" hollered Sophie. "We still need to find Poppy."

The four of them followed at a safe distance as Eno lumbered across the grass after Bâtarde, who ran faster than might have been expected, given his bulky physique. He used the crowd to his advantage, weaving through, popping in and out of view. But Eno caught up with him, trapping him in front of the Cakes by Klaus display as it began to rain in earnest. With his back to the giant hibiscus, Bâtarde faced Eno, hemmed in on either side by the crowd, which was now popping open umbrellas.

Eno made right for Bâtarde and didn't stop. Bâtarde screamed and closed his eyes as Eno grabbed him and lifted him off the ground, then flung him into the display with a mighty heave. He landed astride the erect golden stamen, and just for a split second he rode it before it snapped off and dropped him into the sea of pastel-colored frosting.

256   Robbi McCoy

After a shrill round of gasps and cries of surprise, the crowd and the musicians went silent. It was then that Sophie heard the familiar sound of a young goat bleating.

"Poppy!" she called, moving toward the sound, closer to the cupcake display where Bâtarde was thrashing amid the cakes, trying to get to his feet.

As soon as he was standing, his knees and hands smeared with frosting and bright red paint, the structure gave way under his weight and he went crashing through the red wooden petals and into the wheeled cart beneath. The cries of a goat were louder and more frantic now.

As Sophie dashed toward the cart where Bâtarde was banging around inside and hollering, Poppy climbed up through the new opening, apparently using him as a ladder, and jumped into the smashed cake and frosting, sliding through the mess trying to get a footing, smearing her belly through the wet paint. She seemed unusually clumsy and disoriented, but she finally made it to the edge of a long petal and jumped off to the grass below just as Sophie lunged for her and missed, crashing into the display. She pushed herself off the plywood petals, her hands and shirt dyed red from running paint. She looked around to see Poppy only a few feet away, clearly spooked. Her eyes flashed wildly at the crowd.

"Poppy!" Sophie called.

The little goat looked her way and fell into a barrage of panicked bleating. Sophie thought she heard bleating coming from the perimeter of the clearing and wondered if the trees were echoing Poppy's cries, but as both she and Poppy looked toward the sound, a small herd of goats came crashing through the bushes, running full-tilt toward Poppy, bleating emphatically and causing a chorus of surprised screams from the party guests. Rose was in the lead, heading right at Poppy, and when they met, they were both obviously overjoyed. They touched foreheads and Poppy started hopping about as if on four taut springs.

Sophie bounded toward them, but Rose took off across the open grass with Poppy and all the others in close pursuit. Sophie ran after them as they all crashed through the bushes on the far side of the clearing, vanishing from view, but still bleating furiously, leaving an audible trail for her to follow. She heard Wren call her name as she reached the edge of the clearing. She kept running, but waved a hand high over her head in acknowledgment, hoping Wren would wait for her, hoping they would somehow rescue a romantic night together from this crazy evening.

CHAPTER THIRTY-FIVE

Why, this is very midsummer madness.

—*Twelfth Night*, Act III, Scene 4

"Sophie!" called Wren, preparing to run after her into the woods in pursuit of the goats. But she was brought up short by the alarming appearance of Bâtarde walking toward her like a zombie from *The Night of the Living Dead*, his arms outstretched, his face and clothes besmirched with bold smears of lavender, yellow and pink frosting interspersed with red paint stains. His mouth was open, his eyes wild, his gait slow but directed. On his head, one of the little pink fairies from Klaus's display bobbed absurdly on its spring.

"You!" he accused, pointing an index finger as he neared her. "It was you all along!"

"Don't let him touch you," Raven warned, confusing Wren, who briefly assumed he was caught up in the whole zombie idea.

She cast him a questioning look.

"My clothes!" he cried, waving his fairy wand insistently. "That's my best jacket."

Understanding, she hopped back and prepared herself for a chase. But Bâtarde was intercepted by Eno, who lifted him up and slung him over his shoulder. As he carried him away, Bâtarde hung over Eno's back, shaking his fist at Wren.

"You'll never work in my town again!" he declared. "You're washed up! Your name is mud! You'll have nowhere to go but up!"

Bâtarde was still making threats as Eno carried him out of the clearing and down one of the paths toward the park entrance.

Wren heaved a sigh of relief, then looked around at what was left of the party. Most of the guests had left or were leaving. The cupcake display was still standing, but looking a mess with its busted stamen, smeared paint and layers of smashed cake and frosting. Sophie's sister Dena stood beside it, shaking her head. Cleo sat on the ground in front of it, her goblet still providing sustenance, though she had clearly had enough wine. She looked glum and dimwitted. Tammy had put her donkey head back on, an effective cover against the rain. She sat on a nearby tree stump, a fuzzy brown hand holding up her sad-looking head. Cassandra was nearby, clearly in her own world, standing off from the rest of them, looking up at the sky, her face lit by the moon, as her dog lapped up frosting. A light rain fell, making the flickering lights in the bushes glow and dance. The entire scene had gone eerily quiet.

"Where's Klaus?" Wren asked, realizing she hadn't seen him for a while.

"He and his mother went to get more aebleskiver," Kyle offered. "I hate to imagine his face when he sees this."

Eno appeared at the edge of the clearing, walking purposefully toward them.

"What'd you do with him?" Raven asked.

"Left him with a couple policemen on the street. They're taking him in on a cruelty to animals charge."

Dena suddenly came running over to Eno and threw her

260   Robbi McCoy

arms around his neck. "Oh, you poor thing!" she declared. Then she kissed him on the mouth, a lingering, fervent kiss. When she released him, he looked stunned.

"Oh, God!" Wren muttered. "She thinks he's Klaus."

Tammy jumped off her tree stump and grabbed hold of Dena's arm, spinning her around. Dena came face to face with the donkey head and screamed.

"What the hell are you doing kissing my husband?" Tammy demanded, throwing off her donkey head.

Dena backed away from Tammy, who lunged for her. Dena, who wore three-inch heels, tripped and fell backwards into the pile of soaked red plywood, picking up a good coat of paint on her skin and clothes. Tammy fell in on top of her, and the two of them began to wrestle, rolling over one another in the mess. Eno stopped the tussle by lifting his wife off Dena and setting her down behind him. Kyle reached in to help Dena to her feet. Dena was almost completely covered with red paint, her hair caked with frosting.

"That isn't Klaus," Kyle told her.

"It isn't?"

"No. It's a guy named Eno."

Tammy stood hugging her man possessively while Dena stumbled bewildered to a chair. Just then Cassandra took off running as best she could in her heavy garments, like a madwoman, pulling her wagon along behind her. It rattled noisily across the grass, Spot running after it and barking, as they headed straight toward Cleo where she sat in front of the ruined Cakes by Klaus display.

"What's she doing?" Raven gasped.

Wren understood the panic in his voice. Cleo, drunk and uncomprehending, was a sitting duck for the woman she had destroyed, who was rapidly closing the space between them.

Wren was about to go to Cleo's aid when the sound of a motorcycle engine drew her attention to the east. Simultaneously, the sound of bleating drew her attention to the west. Into the clearing ran the seven goats, moving at a good clip along a paved walkway. They were led by Maribelle with Rose and Poppy, her white parts stained pink, bringing up the rear. Sophie burst into view behind them, jogging, just as a motorcycle emerged on the other side of the clearing, traveling on the same paved path and heading for a head-on collision with the goats. It was Max, who looked their way and waved. Ellie rode on the back of the bike, her arms locked around Max's waist.

It was hard to know where to look, as there seemed to be impending disasters in every direction. Out of the corner of her eye, Wren saw Cassandra heave Cleo up from the ground and dump her in the Red Flyer wagon, then pull it away laboriously, its wheels straining under the load. Cleo clung to her goblet with both hands, trying unsuccessfully to prevent wine spillage.

"Max!" hollered Raven, pointing furiously toward the goats, "look out!"

Max looked ahead to see the animals only feet from her bike. She swerved abruptly off the path, barely avoiding a collision and sped directly at the cupcake display. Too late to effect another correction or stop the bike, Max collided with the display, flattening the plywood structure in a riotous crash that left the bike on its side and both Max and Ellie lying nearby on the ground. A few feet off to the side, Cleo lay limply in Cassandra's wagon, her legs hanging over the sides, a look of astonishment on her face as she must have realized how close she had come to being part of the disastrous heap in front of her.

Everyone ran to the wreck. Both Max and Ellie appeared uninjured. They leapt to their feet and reassured their friends. Sophie came up beside Wren, asking, "Are they okay?"

Wren nodded, noting Sophie's paint-stained shirt and sopping wet clothes. "What happened to you?"

"Maribelle. She butted me into the duck pond. They're all spooked. They just keep running away."

Though the goats were still circling around the perimeter of the clearing, they were now walking rather than galloping and seemed to be calmer. Niblets, who had broken away from the herd, trotted among the shell-shocked survivors of the night. She stopped in front of Cleo, lying sprawled in the little red wagon, and suddenly sprayed her with water from a hidden reserve in her mouth, then went running, laughing, back to join her mates.

262   Robbi McCoy

Cleo looked momentarily stunned, wiped her face with the back of her hand, then took another drink from her goblet.

"Poor Klaus," Sophie muttered, gazing at the pile of debris in front of them.

As if on cue, Klaus appeared at the edge of the clearing, heading rapidly toward his devastated creation, his mother scurrying behind him.

"Oh!" he cried. "Oh! What happened?"

Klaus looked from the calamity to the faces of those still at hand, such a sad and helpless expression on his boyish face. But his mother wasn't looking at the pile of red wood. She was staring in awe at Eno. She approached him, still staring like she was looking at the eighth wonder of the world.

"What's your name?" she asked, her voice shaky.

"Eno Threlkeld," he answered.

"Eno?" Katrina repeated. "That's a strange name."

"Yes, it is. My father said it was stitched on my clothes when he found me on the beach. I was just a baby, washed up to shore."

"Oh Gud!" Katrina gasped and put her hand to her chest. "He found you on the beach? Where? What beach?"

"Washington. Near North Bay. My father was a fisherman."

Katrina uttered a string of Danish words that Wren assumed were expletives.

Klaus was also staring at Eno, his mouth open in astonishment. Eno then saw Klaus and stared at him in a similar fashion. There was no doubt now, seeing them so close together, that these two were identical.

"My son!" cried Katrina, flinging herself into Eno's arms. "My long lost son Eric!"

"Eric?" Wren glanced at her brother, who shrugged.

"Eric?" Eno asked.

"Eric Niels Olafssen!" Katrina proclaimed. "My son! I sewed your initials on your clothes so I could tell you apart from your brother Klaus. E-N-O. Those were your initials, not your name!"

"My brother!" Klaus declared, joining the embrace with his mother.

The two big sandy-haired Danes completely hid Katrina between them, raining tears of joy down on her head.

"That's incredible," Wren observed, "that they should find each other like this."

Sophie turned to Wren and smiled. Wren reached for her.

"Don't touch her!" Raven commanded, pointing at Sophie's frosting and paint-covered clothes. Wren narrowed her eyes at him. He sighed. "Oh, what the hell!"

Sophie and Wren kissed one another, lost to the world until Wren felt something butting against her leg. She looked down to see pink and black Poppy. Sophie picked her up, clipping a leash on her collar. The rest of the goats were eating cupcakes from the ground, climbing over the collapsed planks of the centerpiece in a game resembling King of the Hill. They all seemed jubilant. Poppy licked Sophie's chin and bleated softly.

"Come home with me," Wren whispered. "The sooner we get you out of those wet clothes, the better."

Sophie nodded. "Gladly. But I have to get these animals home. I should also call my mother and tell her what's happened. She's worried sick."

"That won't be necessary," a woman's voice said behind them.

They turned to see Olivia and Dr. Connor approaching.

"Mom!" Sophie exclaimed.

"We've been tracking these critters for hours. Some folks in town told us they were here in the park. Looks like your celebration's run into some bad luck."

"You might say that," Wren said. "But I'd have to disagree."

Kyle and Raven stood nearby, leaning against one another fondly, watching the Olafssen reunion with contented smiles on their faces. Dena and Tammy stood apart, waiting for their men to return to them. Max and Ellie sat on a tree stump side by side, kissing one another tenderly. Cassandra pulled her wagon with Cleo still sprawled in it, and Cleo waved as she passed by like a queen in a fine coach, her tiara askew but still on her head. When the wagon came to a stop, Cassandra helped Cleo to her feet.

"You saved my life," Cleo declared, then wrapped her arms around Cassandra in a close, emphatic hug of gratitude. For the first time since Wren had first seen her three weeks ago, Cassandra smiled a genuine smile of undiluted happiness.

The rain stopped and the clouds parted to reveal the full moon above them, casting substantial light on the scene. Looking at the few who were left in the park, Wren saw a bedraggled group, most of them smeared with scarlet paint to some degree, like the last scene in a Shakespearean tragedy. But this was no tragedy. Just the opposite, in fact.

Olivia took Poppy from Sophie, cradling her in her arms and cooing at her. "You two go on. Warren and I can round up this lot. We've got the truck on the street right outside."

Olivia winked at Wren, then she and Dr. Connor went to round up the goats, clipping leads on all their collars while they continued their sugary feast.

Out of the corner of her eye, Wren saw the Duke of Athens striding toward the pile of rubble. He leapt atop the plywood, raising one arm above his head. In a deep, authoritative voice, he shouted, "Friends, lend me your ears!"

Everyone turned their attention to this commanding figure, his white robe glowing brilliantly in the moonlight.

"What remarkable events have here unfolded this midsummer night!" he declared. "And yet, the wonders of this occasion are not yet concluded."

No one spoke. Wren felt a shiver go up her spine. She instinctively took hold of Sophie's hand and gripped it tightly.

"Cassandra and Ellie," the duke continued, holding a hand out toward them both as he said their names.

Wren heard Ellie, who stood beside her, catch her breath.

"Your father, Anthony Marcus, took his leave from this place many years ago and wandered the globe like Odysseus. He was plagued by grief and love in equal measures, grief over the loss of his beautiful wife and the respect of his children. Love of those self-same children and love for a woman whose face was emblazoned in his mind like a firebrand." He held his hand out, palm up, toward Cleo, who stared up at him with her mouth open, transfixed. "A man cannot escape his fate." His voice had softened.

"My God," Ellie whispered.

The man standing before them removed his helmet, revealing a classically handsome, middle-aged face, a wide brow, deep-set, somber eyes, and a thick gray mustache. Wren was sure she glimpsed a resemblance between this Athenian and the young Anthony Marcus in the *Macbeth* poster at the theatre.

"I have returned," he announced, "to reclaim my family, my true love, and my place on the Ashland stage." He leapt off the platform and Cleo ran to him, flinging herself at him. He embraced her, kissed her, then held his free arm out for his daughters. "Will you forgive me, Ellie?" he asked.

Ellie and Cassandra both ran to him, and the four of them formed a huddle of tearful embraces.

Sophie and Wren turned to look at one another in amazement. Then they left the clearing, walking hand in hand on a curving path, the lights of the party dimming in the distance. Before leaving the park, they stopped and looked back at the flickering lights, looking not unlike forest sprites.

"This has been a magical night," Sophie observed.

"Oh," Wren said, leaning against her, "the magic has just begun!"

Sophie nodded. "'Lovers to bed; 'tis almost fairy time.'"

Raven and Kyle emerged from the shadows, running after them along the path, their filmy green wings flapping behind them.

"Wait for us!" called Raven. "We're going home too."

"And here come the fairies," Wren observed with a lighthearted laugh.

CHAPTER THIRTY-SIX

Our revels now are ended. These our actors,
As I foretold you, were all spirits, and
Are melted into air, into thin air...
We are such stuff
As dreams are made on; and our little life
Is rounded with a sleep.

—*The Tempest*, Act IV, Scene 1

Clustered around a table too small to fit four comfortably, Raven, Kyle, Wren and Sophie shared a piece of blackberry cobbler topped with vanilla ice cream at Pirandello's, a casual chic dinner restaurant in downtown Ashland. Every time Sophie glanced at Wren, they both broke into joyful smiles tinged with gratitude. Gratitude extended to one another and to the universe at large for bringing them together. Wren was suffused with happiness.

"If you were going to write about this dessert," Kyle asked, "what would you say?"

"I'd say," Wren began, knowing such a review would never be written. She smiled to herself. "Let's just say it's yummy and leave it at that."

Sophie looked fondly at Wren and took another bite, her expression revealing that she was thinking about the previous night, better in many ways than their first night together because neither of them had been holding back this time. Neither of them had been afraid of true feeling creeping into their bed. And true feeling definitely had crept in, adding love to their lovemaking. Wren put her hand over Sophie's where it lay on the table between them.

The wait staff seemed to be on heightened alert all of a sudden as they set a large table for five in a corner, adding a burgeoning vase of fresh freesias. None of the other tables had flowers, Wren noticed. When the waiter brought their check, she asked, "Who's that table for?"

"The famous food critic, Eno Threlkeld," the waiter gushed. "He has a reservation at seven. Very exciting!"

The waiter bared his teeth in a smile, then left.

"Indeed!" Wren said.

"God, this is so confusing," Sophie said. "That's the real Eno, right?"

Raven nodded. "Whose real name is apparently Eric."

Right on time, Eno's party arrived to the delight of the entire restaurant staff, who greeted him with an overflow of goodwill and led him to his roomy table. Eno wore a sport coat and tan slacks. On his arm was his wife Tammy. His mother, brother Klaus and Dena, wearing a lime green skirt and matching knit jacket, followed him in, all of them smiling and carrying themselves like royalty.

Raven waved at them and they all waved back as they took their chairs.

"What a surprise to run into him after all these years," Wren said.

"And what a surprise for him to find his mother and brother," Raven added. "All's well that ends well, I always say."

The four of them laughed.

"I think he's going to enjoy this meal," Wren suggested,

268   Robbi McCoy

watching a waiter pour Eno's bottled water into a goblet with a curl of lime zest. Their water, served in tumblers, had been tap water.

"An appetizer to start, sir," the waiter asked Eno. "On the house. The cold lobster ravioli with saffron cream is an excellent choice."

Wren sighed and turned back to her companions. "And that's why I didn't let them know who I was."

"How could you resist?" Kyle asked. "They're going to give that guy the best meal he's ever had."

"I hope he enjoys the attention while he can. As soon as Bâtarde's exposé hits the wire, the mystique of Eno Threlkeld will be over." Wren looked fondly at Sophie.

"You don't seem very upset," Kyle observed.

"The curtain comes down on every show eventually."

"But you could still write restaurant reviews, couldn't you?" Kyle asked. "You could find a different name. Annie Laurie, for instance. Or be yourself. Do it out in the open and get treated like that guy wherever you go." He indicated Eno with a nod of his head.

"You're right, Kyle. I could. And I may go back to it someday, but for now I feel like embarking on a new path."

"What path would that be?" Raven asked, licking his spoon.

"Tallulah Rose Creamery," Sophie said, "could use another hand now that Klaus is going seriously into the baking business."

"You're going to milk goats?" Raven asked, incredulous.

"And plant beets and carrots," Wren added. "Put down a few roots."

"What did I tell you?" Raven said. "Three weeks and they're moving in together. Women are just no good at casual sex."

Wren looked at Sophie and laughed. "What would you say, Sophie?"

"I'd say he's dead wrong. You were fantastic at it."

"I'd say the same about you. Mind-blowingly good at casual sex. And equally good at the more serious kind."

"I think we should celebrate," Kyle suggested. "Let's go over to the Stratford Inn and have a bottle of champagne."

"Good idea," Raven agreed. "I'm just going to say hey to Eno before we go." He skipped over to Eno's table.

"Meet you outside," Kyle said, scooting his chair back. "Got to use the little boy's room."

Sophie leaned her head against Wren's and wound their arms together. "They're right, you know. We were no good at casual sex."

"I know. Honestly, how would we even know that? We were in love before we ever kissed one another."

"Then spent a lot of time pretending we weren't."

Wren turned her head and kissed Sophie's mouth. "I love you, Sophie Ward."

"And I love you, Wren Landry."

Wren and Sophie went outside into the still-light evening. A half a block down the street, in front of Sprouts, stood Cleo, Max, Ellie, Ellie's father Anthony, and a beautiful young woman Wren didn't recognize. The young woman was dressed casually in a twill pantsuit. She hung upon Anthony's arm. No longer an Athenian, he wore a tan sports jacket and navy blue slacks and looked like an unremarkable family man in his fifties.

As they approached, the young woman on Anthony's arm looked in their direction and suddenly Wren knew she was looking at Cassandra. Wow! she thought, what a transformation! Cassandra's thick hair, previously so wild and unkempt, was pulled tight into a ponytail. She looked completely different and not the least bit scary.

"I'd forgotten how attractive Cassandra was," Sophie remarked.

The Marcus family stopped at the corner to wait for a light. Ellie waved toward them. Cassandra's face lit up at the sight of them. She let go of her father's arm and came running over.

"Hi," said Wren. "I guess you'll be going back on stage now, won't you? You and your father both. I'm looking forward to seeing you perform."

Cassandra suddenly transformed her face into the visage Wren had so dreaded during the past three weeks and held her arm out, pointing her index finger. "Beware the ides of March!" she hissed. Then she laughed in sheer delight and ran back to her family as they crossed the street.

"No, no!" Wren objected, stamping her foot. "Shit!"

"Oh, dear." Sophie reached out and put a comforting arm around her. "Try to forget that," she advised, "between now and March."

Her laughter was interrupted by a clattering, clanging metallic sound in the distance. As they stood on the sidewalk, the sound grew louder. Around the corner came a silver sedan trailing strings of empty cans all banging on the pavement.

Wren peered into the car, seeing a man and woman in the front seat. The car neared and moved slowly past them. On the back was a "Just Married" sign.

"Oh, my God!" yelled Sophie. She took off running toward the car.

Confused, Wren ran after her and caught up at the next stop sign where Sophie was at the passenger side window. As she arrived, Wren realized it was Olivia in the car.

"Mom!" Sophie called. "What are you doing?"

"We got married," Olivia replied, grinning ear to ear. "What does it look like?"

Dr. Connor sat behind the wheel wearing a blue suit and tie. His eyes twinkled joyfully.

"Just like that?" Sophie asked. "Without saying anything?"

"No time to plan a big to-do," Olivia explained. "Warren has to leave tomorrow for Zambia and I'm going with him."

"You're leaving? For how long?"

"Three months. Maybe longer if he signs up for another tour. Don't worry, Sophie. You'll be fine now that you've got your pretty little Wren here, won't you?" Olivia patted Wren's hand where it rested on the windowsill.

Wren nodded. "Congratulations, you two!"

"I'll see you at home," Olivia said. "You can make a toast to us and then I've got to pack."

The car moved off, clanging loudly, rounded a corner and disappeared from view. Wren and Sophie returned to the sidewalk.

Sophie looked stunned. Still staring at the empty street, she said, "I didn't see that coming."

"Really?" Wren hugged Sophie's arm close. "Everybody all paired up and happy? You didn't see that coming?"

Sophie smiled crookedly, then kissed Wren on the mouth as the clattering of the newlyweds' car receded into the distance.

Publications from
Bella Books, Inc.
Women. Books. Even Better Together.
P.O. Box 10543
Tallahassee, FL 32302
Phone: 800-729-4992
www.bellabooks.com

CALM BEFORE THE STORM by Peggy J. Herring. Colonel Marcel Robicheaux doesn't tell and so far no one official has asked, but the amorous pursuit by Jordan McGowen has her worried for both her career and her honor.
978-0-9677753-1-9

THE WILD ONE by Lyn Denison. Rachel Weston is busy keeping home and head together after the death of her husband. Her kids need her and what she doesn't need is the confusion that Quinn Farrelly creates in her body and heart.
978-0-9677753-4-0

LESSONS IN MURDER by Claire McNab. There's a corpse in the school with a neat hole in the head and a Black & Decker drill alongside. Which teacher should Inspector Carol Ashton suspect? Unfortunately, the alluring Sybil Quade is at the top of the list. First in this highly lauded series.
978-1-931513-65-4

WHEN AN ECHO RETURNS by Linda Kay Silva. The bayou where Echo Branson found her sanity has been swept clean by a hurricane—or at least they thought. Then an evil washed up by the storm comes looking for them all, one-by-one. Second in series.
978-1-59493-225-0

DEADLY INTERSECTIONS by Ann Roberts. Everyone is lying, including her own father and her girlfriend. Leaving matters to the professionals is supposed to be easier! Third in series with *PAID IN FULL* and *WHITE OFFERINGS*.
978-1-59493-224-3

SUBSTITUTE FOR LOVE by Karin Kallmaker. No substitutes, ever again! But then Holly's heart, body and soul are captured by Reyna... Reyna with no last name and a secret life that hides a terrible bargain, one written in family blood.
978-1-931513-62-3

MAKING UP FOR LOST TIME by Karin Kallmaker. Take one Next Home Network Star and add one Little White Lie to equal mayhem in little Mendocino and a recipe for sizzling romance. This lighthearted, steamy story is a feast for the senses in a kitchen that is way too hot.
978-1-931513-61-6

2ND FIDDLE by Kate Calloway. Cassidy James's first case left her with a broken heart. At least this new case is fighting the good fight, and she can throw all her passion and energy into it.
978-1-59493-200-7

HUNTING THE WITCH by Ellen Hart. The woman she loves — used to love — offers her help, and Jane Lawless finds it hard to say no. She needs TLC for recent injuries and who better than a doctor? But Julia's jittery demeanor awakens Jane's curiosity. And Jane has never been able to resist a mystery. #9 in series and Lammy-winner.
978-1-59493-206-9

FAÇADES by Alex Marcoux. Everything Anastasia ever wanted — she has it. Sidney is the woman who helped her get it. But keeping it will require a price — the unnamed passion that simmers between them.
978-1-59493-239-7

ELENA UNDONE by Nicole Conn. The risks. The passion. The devastating choices. The ultimate rewards. Nicole Conn rocked the lesbian cinema world with *Claire of the Moon* and has rocked it again with *Elena Undone*. This is the book that tells it all...
978-1-59493-254-0

WHISPERS IN THE WIND by Frankie J. Jones. It began as a camping trip, then a simple hike. Dixon Hayes and Elizabeth Colter uncover an intriguing cave on their hike, changing their world, perhaps irrevocably.
978-1-59493-037-9

WEDDING BELL BLUES by Julia Watts. She'll do anything to save what's left of her family. Anything. It didn't seem like a bad plan...at first. Hailed by readers as Lammy-winner Julia Watts' funniest novel.
978-1-59493-199-4

WILDFIRE by Lynn James. From the moment botanist Devon McKinney meets ranger Elaine Thomas the chemistry is undeniable. Sharing—and protecting—a mountain for the length of their short assignments leads to unexpected passion in this sizzling romance by newcomer Lynn James.
978-1-59493-191-8

LEAVING L.A. by Kate Christie. Eleanor Chapin is on the way to the rest of her life when Tessa Flanagan offers her a lucrative summer job caring for Tessa's daughter Laya. It's only temporary and everyone expects Eleanor to be leaving L.A...
978-1-59493-221-2

SOMETHING TO BELIEVE by Robbi McCoy. When Lauren and Cassie meet on a once-in-a-lifetime river journey through China their feelings are innocent...at first. Ten years later, nothing—and everything—has changed. From Golden Crown winner Robbi McCoy.
978-1-59493-214-4

DEVIL'S ROCK by Gerri Hill. Deputy Andrea Sullivan and Agent Cameron Ross vow to bring a killer to justice. The killer has other plans. Gerri Hill pens another intriguing blend of mystery and romance in this page-turning thriller.
978-1-59493-218-2

SHADOW POINT by Amy Briant. Madison McPeake has just been not-quite fired, told her brother is dead and discovered she has to pick up a five-year old niece she's never met. After she makes it to Shadow Point it seems like someone—or something—doesn't want her to leave. Romance sizzles in this ghost story from Amy Briant.
978-1-59493-216-8

JUKEBOX by Gina Daggett. Debutantes in love. With each other. Two young women chafe at the constraints of parents and society with a friendship that could be more, if they can break free. Gina Daggett is best known as "Lipstick" of the columnist duo Lipstick & Dipstick.
978-1-59493-212-0

BLIND BET by Tracey Richardson. The stakes are high when Ellen Turcotte and Courtney Langford meet at the blackjack tables. Lady Luck has been smiling on Courtney but Ellen is a wild card she may not be able to handle.
978-1-59493-211-3